PRAISE FOR JAN MORAN BOOKS & THE SUMMER BEACH SERIES

Coral Cottage: Now a *USA Today* Bestseller

"A compelling voice to follow." — *Booklist*

"Jan Moran is the new queen of the epic romance." — Rebecca Forster, *USA Today* Bestselling Author

"Jan rivals Danielle Steel at her romantic best." — Allegra Jordan, Author of *The End of Innocence*

"I love how the women in Jan's stories are always intelligent and strong. At the core of all her books is a strong, close-knit family." — *Betty's Reviews*

Praise for *The Chocolatier* and *The Winemakers*

"A delicious novel that makes you long for chocolate." – *Ciao Tutti*

"A wonderful, smoothly written novel. The love of chocolate drips from the page. Full of intrigue, love, secrets, and romance." – *Lekker Lezen*

"Readers will devour this page-turner as the mystery and passions spin out." – *Library Journal*

"Beautifully layered and utterly compelling." — Jane Porter, *New York Times* & *USA Today* Bestselling Author

JAN MORAN

Coral COTTAGE

THE CORAL COTTAGE AT SUMMER BEACH
BOOK ONE

Library of Congress Cataloging-in-Publication Data
Moran, Jan.
/ by Jan Moran
978-1-951314-13-2 (ebook)
978-1-951314-14-9 (softcover)
978-1-64778-001-2 (hardcover)
978-1-64778-002-9 (large print)
978-1-64778-003-6 (audiobook)

Cover design by Sleepy Fox Studio
Cover images copyright Deposit Photos

Sunny Palms Press
9663 Santa Monica Blvd STE 1158
Beverly Hills, CA, USA
www.JanMoran.com

For my all my beach-loving readers

Chapter 1

*S*ummer Beach, California

WITH ONLY A MIDNIGHT moon to light her way, Marina ducked under a wrought-iron archway covered in honeysuckle and wound her way along a pathway lined with tropical vegetation toward the old beach cottage. Breathing in the fresh sea air helped settle her tattered nerves.

When Marina reached the covered porch, she brushed sand from the high-heeled shoes she couldn't wait to kick off and rang the doorbell. While she waited, she glanced around. Next to her, a wooden swing creaked in the brisk wind that carried the scent of early spring. Beyond the house, moonlight illuminated the sleepy, beachside village that hugged the Pacific Ocean in Southern California.

No answer. She tapped on the beveled-glass window of the sun-bleached door and called out. "Ginger, it's me. Marina."

To one side of the wide front porch, pink bougainvillea bracts fluttered in the wind, petals scattering like confetti across the lawn. She brushed one from her silk blouse.

Marina rolled her aching shoulders. Her slim skirt felt restrictive, and she wished she'd taken time to change before fleeing the city. The drive from San Francisco had been arduous, not only because of the molasses-paced traffic through Los Angeles but also due to the wounds inflicted on her heart this morning.

Not to mention her professional reputation. Marina winced at the thought.

Marina ached to nestle into her grandmother's calming embrace—just as she and her sisters had always done—and lose herself in Ginger's spacious old kitchen. When Marina was younger, cooking with her grandmother usually soothed her teenage angst. Ginger would pour a glass of wine and tune in her old friend Julia Child's cooking show, insisting they cook along with Julia. Usually, they were successful, though sometimes they had a major flop. Through it all, Marina thrived in the glow of Ginger's unflappable approach to life.

Thinking back to those halcyon days, Marina wished she'd made a different choice and spent the last twenty years pursuing another career. Could she have made a living doing what she loved?

"Hello? Ginger, are you there?" Marina banged on the door again and then peered into a window. Inside the sprawling cottage splashed in a sunny shade of coral, comfortable, artsy furnishings were in their proper place, but there was no sign of Ginger.

Their proper places.

Marina's sisters knew their place in the world. And to the outsiders, so did Marina. Only on the inside did she often feel like she'd been forced into a fancy designer shoe two sizes too small.

Of the three sisters, Marina had always been the pragmatic, driven one who forged ahead and stayed the course—often to her detriment. Kai, the youngest, was the free-spirited dancer who was now on tour with a musical theater company.

Their middle sister, Brooke, was the homebody of the family with three rambunctious boys and a husband who was a captain in the fire department. She spent her days refereeing arguments and tending to her thriving vegetable garden.

Unfortunately, Marina's life had imploded in a spectacular fashion this morning on channel KSFB—a San Francisco Bay area television station—where she'd been delivering morning news for almost two decades. Only this time, Marina had been part of the story.

She'd arrived on set before dawn as she always did, ready to deliver the morning news to the early risers of San Francisco. As she passed Babe Barstow, who covered entertainment and local news, the younger woman had a strange, smug expression on her face, but Marina had become accustomed to that.

Even though Marina knew Babe was angling for Marina's job, when the cameras were rolling, they were professional and friendly. At fifteen years younger than Marina, Babe still had a lot to learn. For starters, why did she insist on using her cutesy nickname when she wanted to be taken seriously as a news anchor?

While Marina was reviewing her notes, Babe was covering the lighter news. "Lulu Godiva, whose recent song, *Love Me in the Afternoon*, hit the top of the charts, recently revealed the story behind the tune, saying a San Francisco man inspired it." Babe paused dramatically. "And it's none other than our local architect to the stars, Grady Ashworth, who designed Lulu's getaway in Napa Valley. The singer spilled the story when questioned about her dazzling engagement ring this weekend."

Babe swung back to Marina with a smirk of satisfaction. "What do you think about that, Marina?"

As Babe delivered the *coup de grace*, the camera shifted back to Marina.

"Well, I don't think Grady...could mean that..." Marina

blurted out a mishmash of intelligible words, adding, "This isn't a gossip show, Babe, and I don't think our viewers are interested in who Grady Ashworth is dating."

"You're missing the point," Babe said coolly. "Lulu Godiva is a gorgeous, successful star. Lucky Grady, right?"

Frantically, Marina tried to blink away the hot, angry tears welling in her eyes. She waved the camera away, though the operator kept rolling, seemingly oblivious to her distress. Her skin felt hot and prickly, and her face was probably turning bright red. She swiveled her chair back with force to finish the news, trying to conceal a quick brush of tears, but somehow her heel snagged on a cord and jerked her from her chair. A cry escaped her lips.

"Back to you, Marina, for the rest of the morning's news," Babe said. "Marina?"

While Marina was gripping the desk to haul herself up, the floor director was barking orders and insults through her earpiece.

By then, Babe was smoothly taking over. "While Marina is out of commission, let's go on to other entertainment news."

When they cut to commercial, their boss burst out. "What just happened?" Hal demanded. "Moore, you—of all people —know better than to fall apart on the air."

"Babe set me up," Marina said, though she knew that was a thin excuse. "She could have come to me any time before the show with that information to prepare me."

"You're a pro, Moore," Hal shot back. "Or you *were*. The fact is, ratings are down, and it's time we had a fresh face."

Marina gaped at him, slowly comprehending what he was saying. "It won't happen again," she said, reining in her anger. She'd always had the support of her old boss, but when the station was acquired three years ago, Hal Reilly, son of the billionaire media conglomerate owner, was brought in.

Hal was in his late twenties and dangerously hip. His father had charged him with changing the format from news to anything that drove ratings. That meant more controversy and charged opinions on the air.

Marina wasn't comfortable with this approach—or with Hal. She'd managed to ignore his disgusting double entendre remarks and dodge his wandering hands, but she wasn't so sure about Babe.

A knowing look passed between Hal and Babe.

With an exasperated huff, Hal slid a hand over his shaved head and removed his designer glasses. "Look, Moore, I hate to do this to you, but—"

Marina knew Hal was relishing this. She quickly cut in. "I'm giving my official notice." Marina wasn't going to plead for her job in front of Babe and the entire crew. "I'll gather my belongings and leave."

And bang, just like that, at forty-five she'd lost her job and fiancé in less than five minutes. *Probably some sort of record,* she thought ruefully. She'd call her agent tomorrow, but for now, all she wanted to do was sleep and forget today had ever happened.

As for Grady, maybe he'd done her a favor. She'd waited years to date until her children were older, although the first time she'd dipped her toe into that choppy sea of dating, a shark had bitten. She didn't need a man who would choose a twenty-something pop star over her. Still, she was hurt and humiliated. Not to mention unemployed.

If only she hadn't let Hal and Babe get to her.

Marina blew wisps of hair from her face. At least she felt a measure of relief here at the beach. *Away from that hectic world.* Here, she could hide out and recuperate. But only for a short while, because her children's college tuition wasn't cheap. Heather and Ethan were in their first year of college on the east coast. This past year, Marina had gone from having bois- terous twins underfoot to sudden silence. And Grady had seized on her loneliness.

No answer. Marina turned the doorknob of her grandmother's beach cottage. *Locked.*

Car lights flashed on the street. Could that be her grandmother? Or a neighbor who lived on this stretch of sand?

The car passed the cottage and turned.

Marina paced the front porch before flopping onto the swing. Despair crashed over her like a furious high tide. If Ginger was here, she'd crush her in a hug and tell her how Grady wasn't good enough. Marina knew that now, but it didn't lessen her pain.

Blinking back useless tears of self-pity, Marina sprang from the swing, eager to get inside. Perhaps Ginger had left a window open.

As Marina circled the house, trying every door and window, she considered her options. Brooke lived an hour south of San Diego, near the Mexican border. It was far too late to wake her. Besides, with a house full of teenagers, Marina would be sleeping on the couch and listening to silly adolescent jokes.

Though she loved her nephews, that was not what she needed right now.

Shivering against the cool ocean breeze, Marina tugged at her old bedroom window until she heard a pop. "Whoa, ouchy mama!" she cried out in pain, reverting to the creative cuss words she'd used when the kids were young that had somehow stuck.

The window didn't budge, but one of her artificial red nails had snapped off, taking part of her natural nail with it. She held up her throbbing forefinger, assessing the damage. "That's it. You're all coming off." One more vestige of her former life she could get rid of for a while. She shook her hand. "Yowzer roo," she muttered through clenched teeth.

At the studio, Babe had once heard her, arched a finely tattooed eyebrow, and walked away, shaking her head as if Marina were an old dinosaur.

"Where are you, Ginger?" Marina peeked in another window. When she had fled the disaster of her life in San Francisco this morning, it hadn't occurred to her that Ginger might not be here. Besides, her grandmother was often a night owl, a habit honed from her time spent in Europe with her husband Bertrand Delavie, a career diplomat.

The fashionable people often dined until after midnight, dear child.

That memory earned a fleeting smile, despite her pulsating injury.

Marina marched toward the front porch. *Get creative*, Ginger would always say. She could sleep on the porch until Ginger returned, but that could be days if her grandmother had gone on a trip. Or she could find a motel or inn.

As she ducked under a set of low-hanging wind chimes she hadn't recalled, her spiky high heel caught between two pavers and snapped, jerking her ankle at an awkward angle. Flailing and cursing under her breath again, she regained her balance, though her ankle protested.

"These are going, too," she muttered in disgust. She tore off her shoes—two-hundred dollars on sale at Nordstrom down the drain. For that price, she could've bought several pairs of comfortable walking shoes or great massages—which would have made her feel so much better.

She was tired of nosebleed heel heights, though that was the style expected of her at work. Hal had called her stylish kitten-heels and flats *old-lady shoes* and asked if she was getting ready for retirement.

The nerve of that brat. Women didn't need to all look like Babe-the-Barbie. Son of a billionaire or not, Marina had told Hal precisely what she thought of him on the way out the door this morning.

Marina hobbled along the side of the house toward the swing to nurse her injuries.

How many times had she sat on that swing, kicking sand from her bare feet and listening to her grandmother? No one could tell a story like Ginger, so nicknamed because of her ginger-colored hair at birth, which she still kept stylishly tinted. But Marina preferred to think it was because of her grandmother's spicy personality.

Ginger's stories, even the ones that were supposedly true, were forever morphing in her nimble mind. Some might think it was because Ginger was nearly eighty now, but no, Marina had been listening to stories that shifted like the tides for as long as she could remember.

Ginger seemed to have lived as many lives as a cat. Maybe Ginger did that to entertain them, sort of like Pippi Long-stocking. When called out on details that didn't jibe with an earlier version of the story, Ginger would simply arch an eyebrow with a Mona Lisa smile and say, "That's how I remember it today."

Now, every time Marina put pressure on her foot, sharp pains ripped through her ankle. *Only a few more steps.*

As she turned the corner, a powerful flashlight cut through the darkness, blinding her.

A man's voice rang out. "Who's there?"

Marina screamed and stumbled back, her ankle collapsing on her. Waving her arms in slow motion, she crashed to the ground. *Pepper spray,* she thought frantically, but it was safely tucked in her purse. *In the car.* Would she become a lead story —*if it bleeds, it leads*—like the ones she had delivered for years? The self-defense training Ginger had insisted all the girls take kicked in. She couldn't run, but she could kick.

"Ma'am, I am not going to hurt you," came a firm, reassuring voice. "I'm Chief Clarkson of the Summer Beach Police Department. Are you hurt?"

Shielding her eyes, Marina gazed up at the towering, barrel-chested man who loomed above her. With cropped, curly black hair and clad in a Hawaiian shirt and Bermuda shorts, he looked like a Marine on vacation. "How do I know that?" she demanded. "Why aren't you in uniform? And what are *you* doing creeping around my grandmother's house?"

He swung the flashlight toward his car, illuminating a door emblazoned with *Summer Beach Police Department.* "Here in Summer Beach, we look after residents' homes. Now, what's your name, ma'am?"

"I'm Marina Moore. Ginger Delavie's granddaughter from San Francisco. She's not home, or she's not answering. I'm worried about her."

"You must be the anchor lady from the big news show." Chief Clarkson broke into a grin and extended his hand to help her up. "Well, why didn't you say so?"

She'd forgotten how small Summer Beach was. The locals knew each other and looked after their own. Marina knew some of them, too, from childhood summers she spent here. But that was a long time ago.

Gripping Chief Clarkson's broad hand, Marina tried to stand. "Ouch," she cried out, hopping on one foot. "I think I sprained my ankle."

While supporting her at a respectful distance, the chief said, "You needn't worry about Miss Ginger. She's gone for a few days. Took a cruise to Catalina and Ensenada. Was she expecting you?"

"No, I just decided to drive down."

Marina had tried to call along the way, but her cell phone had died, and Grady—she winced at the memory—had taken her car charger several weeks ago. She usually took BART—the San Francisco rail system—to work, and she'd forgotten to replace the charger. As she thought about it, she realized Grady had been a taker all along—who'd hidden behind a veneer of romance.

Ethan hadn't liked him from the beginning. Marina thought her son was overly protective, but now she understood he'd seen through Grady. Ethan had gone golfing with Grady once—her son was a consistent scratch golfer—and he'd come back incensed that Grady had cheated at golf.

Marina gestured toward the house. "Wish I had a key to the cottage." She did—in San Francisco. But since she'd driven straight from the television studio, she hadn't thought to get it. In her anguished mind, she'd thought Ginger would be here.

"Can't help you there," Chief Clarkson said. "Do you have a place to stay tonight?"

"I'll find a motel," she said. "Do you know of any nearby?"

"We have a couple of inns here in town," the chief replied. "There's a big wedding party at one, but you might try the Seabreeze Inn down the road."

"Do you have an address?"

The chief grinned. "Hard to miss. It's the largest structure on the beach. You might remember it. Although, as I understand, it was usually closed back then."

A memory clicked in Marina's mind. "You mean, the haunted mansion on the beach?"

"I don't think it's very haunted anymore." His deep baritone laugh rumbled in his chest.

"That's not a joke," Marina said, shivering. "Even a little haunted is disturbing."

"You'll be fine there. Two women, who are very much alive, run it now." The chief glanced at her car and added, "You can follow me there."

She started to say something snarky about his making sure she was actually going there and not staying behind to rob Ginger's house, but she held back her comment. This wasn't the big city. Life was different here in Summer Beach. Even celebrities, such as the popular singer Carol Reston who had an estate on the ridgetop, could stroll around without being bothered.

"That would be nice, thanks," Marina said. She tested her

foot again, but as soon as she put pressure on it, pain shot through her ankle. Reluctantly, she asked, "Could you help me to the car?" She wasn't accustomed to relying on people—especially strangers.

"You should have that ankle looked at tomorrow," Chief Clarkson said, frowning at the swelling. "The sisters who run the Seabreeze Inn—Ivy and Shelly—can probably arrange a doctor for you tomorrow." He jerked his chin toward her small vehicle. "Hope that car is an automatic. I'm afraid your clutch foot is out of commission."

"It is." Marina managed a polite chuckle. She'd carted kids and gear to matches around the bay area in an SUV, but after they left for college, she'd downsized to a turquoise Mini Cooper convertible. She could squeeze into the smallest parking space in the city and drop the top on sunny days. Besides, it was fun. Heather had been trying to get her to affix eyelashes over the headlights. *When it's yours, you can do that,* she'd told her.

The police chief helped Marina to her car, and she followed him a short distance to the inn. He waved her around to the rear of the grand old house and got out. Marina stayed in her car and rolled down her window. Overhead, palm trees rustled in the wind.

The chief pressed a yellow doorbell button that had a cheerful, painted bumblebee above it. A hand-painted sign read, *Give us a buzz after hours.*

Instantly, a light flicked on above them in what Marina imagined was a bedroom. A couple of minutes later, an attractive woman with shoulder-length brown hair opened the door. They had probably woken her. "Hi, Chief. What's going on?"

Leaning over the steering wheel, Marina stared at the woman. She seemed vaguely familiar.

Chief Clarkson jerked a finger over his shoulder. "We've got a local's granddaughter who needs a room. Ginger Delavie is away on a cruise. And this one has a bad ankle."

"We have room in the back on the downstairs level," came the reply. The woman motioned past an enormous pool with statues and columns that looked like it belonged at the Hearst Castle.

Marina leaned out the window and waved a credit card. "I'll take it." She was mentally and physically exhausted. Right now, she could sleep anywhere.

Chief Clarkson helped Marina from her vehicle, supporting her as she half-hopped, half-walked through tropical gardens to the room. Lush pink bougainvillea, fragrant pikake blossoms, and glossy green ferns made her feel like she was in a Hawaiian resort.

This was the respite she needed.

The woman hurried ahead and unlocked the door. Turning around, she gave Marina a sympathetic smile.

"I'm Ivy Bay. If there's anything you need, let me know." She fished a card from her pocket. "This is my cell number so you can text or call. In the morning, let me know when you'd like breakfast, and we'll bring it out to you. And I'll bring some ice for that ankle. You might want to elevate it, too."

"Good idea," Marina said. "I'm so grateful that you opened for me." *Ivy Bay. Her name seemed so familiar.*

"Do you have any bags I can bring in for you?" Ivy asked.

Marina groaned. "I took off from San Francisco with nothing but my purse because I knew I had things at my grandmother's house."

Ginger always had well-stocked guest rooms for Marina and her sisters. Sundresses, swimsuits, flip-flops, and hats. That was all she needed in Summer Beach. Marina figured she could buy anything else.

After Chief Clarkson left and Ivy had dropped off a bag of ice, Marina peeled off her clothes and hobbled into the bathroom to ice her ankle. Keeping her foot elevated, she took a long soak in the tub with a lavender sachet she'd found in an amenity basket. Closing her eyes, she listened to the soothing roar of the ocean.

After Marina got out of the tub, she slipped on a soft terry-cloth robe she found in the closet, and then she snuggled under the down-filled duvet. Picking up the remote, she flicked on the television to a late-night show she enjoyed but hardly ever had a chance to watch. She was feeling marginally better now.

However, that progress was short-lived.

The show host was performing his opening monologue. "And now, today's most embarrassing moment goes to a news anchor in San Francisco who found out her boyfriend had just gotten engaged to Lulu Godiva—on the morning news. You're going to love her reaction."

Marina watched in horror as the host played the news clip, which ended with her falling out of her chair.

"Whoops, there she goes, folks!" The host and the television audience burst out laughing. "Not winning any awards for grace under pressure, is she?"

Listening to their derisive howls, Marina felt like she was going to be physically ill. She'd had enough emotional battering for one day. Clicking off the television, she pulled a pillow over her head.

How was she ever going to live this down and reclaim her life?

Chapter 2

*T*he next morning, Marina had just dressed in her wrinkled outfit from yesterday when she heard a tap on the door. When she opened the door, she found a pink canvas beach bag with a note attached.

For Marina. From Ivy, Shelly, and Poppy at the Seabreeze Inn. Call us for breakfast delivery or join us in the dining room.

A freshly laundered, cornflower-blue cotton sundress, matching flip flops, and a white sun visor peeked from the bag. And leaning next to the doorway was a pair of crutches.

"How thoughtful," Marina said, pressing her hand against her heart. This kindness went a long way toward restoring her faith in humanity after the dreadful events of yesterday.

Immediately, she removed her city clothes, grateful to have a fresh change of clothing. She pulled her shoulder-length hair into a ponytail. Sitting on the edge of the bed, she slid her feet into the flip-flops, pondering her next move. *Literally.* Her ankle was swollen and tender to the touch. And it was a lovely shade of purple.

She mused over her choices. She could cloister herself in her room and cry until her grandmother returned. Or she could drag herself to the beach and hide under a sun visor and dark sunglasses.

Finally, she could brave the new world order and present her newly single, damaged self to other guests in the dining room.

Option A sounded pretty appealing. She kicked off the flip-flops and flopped back onto the bed, where a dull, throbbing headache greeted her.

Marina groaned. She knew what that meant. As a morning news anchor, she'd become addicted to coffee. Not just any coffee, but dark, blast-awake brews that snapped her to attention. Without it, withdrawal headaches set in fairly quickly. That was the last thing she needed now.

Throttling herself into action, she stretched for the wayward flip-flops, hopped across the floor, and opened the door again. Testing the crutches, she positioned them under her arms and swung herself forward in an awkward movement. Fortunately, the last person who'd used these was as short as she was.

Above her, a dog barked, a door slammed, and footsteps clomped down the stairs.

A male voice called out. "Need some help?"

"I need a new ankle." She raised her swollen foot.

A man about her age with a thick head of messy morning hair and a wrinkled T-shirt came into view. "Ouch. Sprained or broken?"

"How would I know? I'm not a doctor." This guy was a little too happy at this hour of the morning. She winced. Her headache had just passed from the dull phase to the pounding stage. She'd slept later than usual, and now she really needed that jolt of java.

He stared at her in amusement, his blue eyes a little too bright for the morning. "You got me there. Need a hand with anything?"

"Nope. I got this." She couldn't quite place his accent,

which was an odd combination of a soft drawl and clipped words as if he'd lived in different areas. An urban-rural combination, she decided, what some would call *citified*. Working in broadcast news, she noticed these subtle things. Gritting her teeth, she set off again.

"The name's Jack," he said. "Heard you arrive last night and saw the police. Were you in an accident?"

Did emotional wreckage count? Measuring the distance ahead, she grimaced. "Okay, Jack. Would you open that door for me?" *And please stop chattering.*

She navigated the ramp to the house, thankful for the access.

Standing with the door open and a grin that reached eyes too blue to be trusted, Jack looked at her that way people have when they're trying to place you. Morning news viewers often recognized her, but when she was off the screen and in casual clothes, it was more difficult for them to place her. "You seem awfully familiar. Have you spent much time in New York or Chicago?"

"Nope. San Francisco."

Jack shook his head. "That's not it."

"I can't imagine." With misery, it registered with Marina that he might have also seen that television clip on the late show. She maneuvered through the door.

"It will come to me," he said, following her inside. "Where do you want to go?"

Why on earth did he care? "I need coffee."

"The dining room is this way. Or you could go to Java Beach, that's where all the locals hang out."

"Not likely this morning, Jack," she said, indicating her swollen ankle. "But *you* should go."

"Might do that," he said with the same unflappable smile.

Jack sauntered through the wide hall, and Marina swung along behind him. She turned her attention to the stately old beach house, admiring the high ceilings and vintage chandeliers.

Her ankle was throbbing, and she knew her arms and shoulder would also be sore after this. She'd once sustained an excruciating sprain in high school in Claremont, a small university town on the outskirts of sprawling Los Angeles. She'd been on the gymnastics team, and she'd come down hard after losing her balance on the beam.

"Here you are." Jack paused at the entry to a grand dining room. "And good luck with that injury. Hope to see you around."

In the wainscoted dining room that included a vintage beach mural in fresh shades of blue and turquoise, the woman Marina had met last night waved to her and hurried toward her. *Ivy Bay.* Why did that name seem so familiar? She was about the same height as Marina, with bright green eyes. And she looked—*happy*. Marina glanced around. Everyone seemed in good spirits. Crestfallen, she realized she was the only one who wasn't, even though she certainly had good reason.

"Good morning," Ivy said pleasantly. "Glad you joined us for breakfast, but we could have brought a tray to you."

"I needed to get out," Marina said. "And thank you for your care package. You're Ivy, right?"

"That's right." She pulled out a chair for Marina. "My sister Shelly and I run the inn, along with our niece, Poppy. Shelly is in charge of yoga classes and the grounds, while I'm on indoor duty, art classes, and morning beach walks."

"Count me out of all activities for now," Marina said, easing into a marine-blue, slipcovered chair.

"I'll put those by the chair for you," Ivy said, taking the crutches. "Right here, so you can still reach them. Would you like some coffee?"

"You're an angel. I'd love that." Glancing around her surroundings, Marina noted more details—a habit from her years in journalism. Vintage crystal chandeliers, a richly veined marble fireplace, wooden parquet floors, and fine European antiques. Contemporary paintings of the ocean and beach graced the walls.

When Ivy returned, Marina asked, "Are any of these your paintings?"

"The seascapes are mine, and I've hung a few others around the house." Ivy slid a tray onto the table. "I brought blueberry and cranberry muffins, yogurt, and strawberries. I can make eggs any way you want, and we have steel-cut oatmeal, too."

"These muffins look delicious." Marina sipped her coveted coffee, and then she broke off a piece of the cranberry muffin. *Heavenly.* The muffin burst with fruit, and it was topped with cinnamon crumbles, dusted with sparkling sugar crystals, and baked to perfection. Someone knew what they were doing in the kitchen. Yesterday, she had stopped only once on the way for greasy fast food, which tasted of rancid oil, so she hadn't finished it. Now, she was starving.

"We get our baked goods from Java Beach," Ivy said. "Mitch has the best coffee and bakery in Summer Beach."

"Sounds like a popular place." That's where Jack was going. Marina cupped her hands around the generous mug and sipped her coffee. Glancing down at her dress, she said, "I'll buy some clothes in town and return this outfit to you."

"It's yours if you want it," Ivy said. "People leave all sorts of things here—including crutches. Some of our international guests buy new clothes on vacation, and since they have luggage weight limits, they leave what they no longer want here. We collect clothing for a shelter in San Diego."

"I appreciate it," Marina said. "And this is such a beautiful old home. When I was younger, we used to call this the haunted mansion, but I don't know if that was true or we were just trying to scare ourselves. I'm curious if you have ever seen any."

"Not really." Ivy laughed a little, though her eyes darted to one side.

Uh-huh. Definitely haunted. Marina had interviewed enough people to know how to read body language.

Behind her, a slender woman in yoga clothes with a messy top knot paused. "Did someone see another ghost?" she asked.

"Absolutely not," Ivy said, slicing the air with a hand. "Marina, this is my trouble-making sister, Shelly."

"If it's any consolation, it's a friendly ghost," Shelly said, making a face at Ivy. "I think it's the former owner checking in. My sister refuses to acknowledge that Amelia Erickson is still in residence here at her beloved Las Brisas del Mar. We changed the name, but I don't think Amelia minds."

When Ivy rolled her eyes in a good-natured manner, Marina immediately picked up on the sisterly bond.

Glancing at the crutches and Marina's ankle, Shelly's face softened with empathy. "You must be the one who came in late last night. Have you had anyone look at your injury?"

Marina shook her head. "I should probably go to an urgent care facility."

"We know a doctor who can drop by to look at it," Shelly said. "He's tended to other guests. We can call and see if he's available this morning."

Marina agreed. She studied the two women, who both seemed friendly and at ease. Marina wondered if living in Summer Beach had that effect on everyone.

"I'll put in a call for Dr. Russ," Shelly said, excusing herself.

Idly, Marina wondered what it would be like to have a business at the beach like this. Not that she could afford that with the twins' college tuition. Even though Marina had earned a good salary, the cost of living in San Francisco and taking care of those she loved always stretched her budget. She figured she had about six months of savings to see her through, so she'd have to call her agent immediately.

Marina remembered other calls she had to make. "I left without a cell phone charger. Silly, I know. I'll have to buy one right away, but do you have one I can use to charge my phone now?"

"We have a box of extra chargers. Poppy can take care of that for you." Ivy waved to a lanky young woman with long blond hair, who crossed to the table. Ivy introduced her and added, "Would you find a charger that will work with her phone?"

"Sure," Poppy said. "Mind if I take it?"

"Not at all, thanks."

After Poppy left, Ivy leaned forward with interest. "You said you remember this house. Are you from Summer Beach? You look so familiar."

Marina smiled despite a fleeting thought about the late-night show. "My grandmother, Ginger Delavie, lives here. My sisters and I used to spend our summer vacations at her beach cottage."

Marina hesitated, recalling that last blissful summer vacation at Ginger's cottage, when she had practically lived on the beach, and her parents were still as much in love as they'd been in high school.

Before the accident.

During her first year at college, Marina's plans came to an abrupt halt when a freak traffic accident claimed the lives of her youthful parents. Ginger moved in to look after the younger sisters and encouraged Marina to return to school. Marina studied during the day and worked evenings in a cafe, where she met Stan. After they married, Ginger returned to Summer Beach with Brooke and Kai. Marina and Brooke were only two years apart, but Kai had been the surprise. At seven years younger than Brooke, she had always been the carefree sprite of the family. Their parents had so loved the water that it inspired all their names.

"Did you ever surf?" Ivy asked, resting her chin in her hand.

"As often as I could." Marina snapped her fingers. "Of course. We surfed together one summer, didn't we?"

"And you made the most incredible s'mores over the fire." Ivy laughed and patted her plump middle section. "I looked a lot different then."

"You had blond hair, right?" As Ivy chuckled and nodded, Marina took another gulp of coffee. "Back then, I think we were all spritzing on Sun In to get blond streaks and slathering on the tanning oil." That was her last carefree summer before college. "It's so good to see you again. Have you lived here all these years?"

"Oh, no. I left to go to school in Boston and stayed. After my husband passed away, I returned." A wistful smile crossed Ivy's face. "After he died, I discovered that he'd just emptied our retirement to buy this place. It was complicated, though, and the old grand dame needed a lot of work."

"Looks like you've done a lot here."

"My family helped me a lot. Shelly moved in from New York, and our brothers helped us renovate. We converted the house to an inn and managed to make a go of it last year. The house has had quite a history, too."

"I'm sorry about your husband," Marina said, touching Ivy's hand. Even eighteen years later, she still missed Stan and her parents. If not for Ginger, she and her sisters would have been adrift.

"I appreciate that," Ivy said. "He died suddenly, and I don't know what I would have done without Shelly and Poppy. I never dreamed I would return to Summer Beach, but I'm so glad I did. Are you married?"

"Not now. I was widowed when I was pregnant, but my twins are in college now." She didn't mention Grady; she'd wasted enough time on him. As much as that stung, she was more worried about her finances and finding another job. *Time to move on,* Ginger would say.

"I also have two daughters," Ivy said. "We'll have to continue this talk later. We have so much in common."

"I'd like that. I remember we had such fun that summer." Marina tried the yogurt, which was also delicious. "Do you remember lounging around the beach bonfire, listening to a surfer guy play the guitar?"

"Do I ever." Ivy chuckled. "That surfer is now the mayor. Bennett Dylan. A wildfire swept across the ridgetop last year, and several locals moved in while their homes were being rebuilt. Bennett is living in the old chauffeur's apartment above the garage."

"No kidding?" Marina shook her head. "Guess we all grew up."

"And what do you do now?" Ivy asked.

"I've been a news anchor on a station in San Francisco." Marina hesitated. "I'm in the process of finding another position right now. Until then, I thought I'd check in on my grandmother."

Ivy smiled. "Ginger is a sweetheart. And very interesting."

"That she is," Marina said, wondering if she could reach her on board the ship. Not that this was an emergency. If Marina put the situation in perspective, it was merely an inconvenience—on her part, not her grandmother's. Why should she disturb Ginger? Still, it would be nice to know when Ginger was returning.

Ginger traveled often. She was fiercely independent and frequently left on holidays or work assignments on short notice. Even at her age, she was still in demand. Marina knew little about what her grandmother did, other than Ginger was a skilled statistician.

Just numbers, darling. Nothing as glamorous as what you do. No one is ever interested in what I do at cocktail parties.

Maybe that's why Ginger loved to tell stories. Yet, Ginger

was brilliant in math. She loved finding and explaining patterns, and she'd helped them all with their homework. *If a kid from a farm in Oklahoma can be good in math, so can you.* Marina had learned fractions at the age of five by helping Ginger bake cookies—she was that good.

"Would you like a refill on that coffee?" Ivy asked.

"I'd love one," Marina replied. As she finished her breakfast, the two women caught up. Marina was fascinated with Ivy's story of the valuable artifacts found concealed in the basement and throughout the house. Marina loved listening to people, which was one reason she'd made a good reporter—a job she enjoyed more than being a news anchor, but she'd needed the salary increase for the twins.

As they spoke and laughed over shared memories, Marina touched Ivy's arm. "I'm so glad we've reconnected. It's nice to find a friend here." She saw kindness and strength in Ivy's eyes.

"I think we're going to be very good friends again," Ivy said, smiling. "You're going to like living here."

"I wish I could, but I have to find another job soon."

"Maybe you'll find something to do here. Lots of people telecommute or run businesses from home these days."

That was something Marina hadn't considered, and it was intriguing.

A little while later, Poppy appeared holding Marina's phone, her eyebrows arched in concern. "I found a charger that you can keep, but while I was helping another guest, a lot of messages poured through. It's been dinging all the way here." She handed Marina the phone and charger.

Marina sucked in a breath. She saw Heather's number on the screen, as well as messages from Ethan and Brooke and Kai. Marina's heart quickened. What on earth had happened? "I have to return these calls right away. Is there a place here…?" She glanced around.

"In the library," Poppy said. "It's private. Here, I'll help you."

Marina struggled to her feet and awkwardly made her way to the library. Ivy rushed behind with a glass of water for her, and Poppy plugged in the charger and the phone.

"Let us know if you need anything," Ivy said, giving Marina a quick hug. She and Poppy closed the door.

What could have happened? Marina pressed a hand to her heart and called her daughter first. Heather answered on the first ring.

"Mom, where are you?" Heather's words tumbled out. "I've been trying to reach you since yesterday. Aunt Brooke called the police, and the landlord let them into the apartment. You weren't there, and I've been so worried, and—"

"Calm down. I'm in Summer Beach. I came down to see Ginger. I'm sorry to worry you, but I didn't have a charger for my phone. What's wrong?"

Heather paused. "So…you haven't been on social media?"

"No, why? Should I check?" Marina shuddered, wondering if the news clip had gone viral.

Heather cried out, "No, Mom, don't. Please, just don't. It's awful."

Chapter 3

*A*lone in the library, Marina stared at the screen on her phone with a sinking heart. Her daughter's voice floated to her, imploring her not to look.

She had to. And when she did, her self-esteem took a direct blow, leaving her gasping for air.

Marina stared at an awkward moving image. After working hard for years to attain her professional status, she had been reduced to a meme, a silly video clip that played the worst blunder of her career over and over. She watched herself break into tears and flail at the desk. Below that, the ridicule was coming in fast.

Oops, she's out of a job—forever! So, honey, was he worth it? Ha, ha, ha! Typical bubble-headed news anchor—not a brain in her head! What an idiot!

And worse. Much, much worse.

Marina squeezed her eyes against the hateful comments.

"Mom, are you still there?"

She sighed and lifted the phone. "I'm here."

"You looked, didn't you?"

"I did." Marina hesitated, hating to tell her daughter

about the late-night show, but needing to shield her from being blindsided by it. She quickly told her.

"That's horrible, and I'm so angry," Heather cried. "It's all Grady's fault. Ethan and I never liked him."

"I know, sweetheart." At the time, Marina had thought her children were jealous after having had their mother to themselves all these years.

"You weren't on the air this morning," Heather said softly.

"I turned in my notice. It was either that or wait ten seconds to be fired. Guess I should call Brooke, huh?"

"And Kai. I called her, too. And every friend of yours that I could reach. Oh, Mom, now I know how it feels when you can't reach me. I'm so sorry I've worried you in the past. I really thought something had happened to you, that you might have had an accident..."

"Don't worry about me, sweetie," Marina said. She'd never heard such concern in Heather's voice, and she felt bad for worrying her. "I'm going to stay here for a couple of weeks and sort out my life. I've booked into a pretty bed-and-break-fast called the Seabreeze Inn until Ginger returns." She hesi-tated. "I should speak to Ethan, too. Is he around?" The twins shared an apartment near the Duke campus in Durham, North Carolina.

"He's taking an exam right now, but you can call him later."

"How's Ethan doing in school?" Marina asked, worried about her son's progress. Ethan had struggled with dyslexia throughout school. However, he had a natural talent for sports, and he'd received a golf scholarship, which helped. Heather had followed her brother to Duke to help him with his academics.

"Ethan is improving," Heather said, sounding upbeat. "It's tough for him, but he'll be okay. His golf game is on fire, so he's happy about that."

"Thanks for helping him," Marina said. However, she

suspected that Ethan was struggling more than either of her children wanted to admit. She worried about Ethan. He was smart, but he simply needed more time to complete his studies, which frustrated him.

After calling her sisters and reassuring them, Marina dialed her agent's number. "Hi Gwen, it's Marina."

"Hi, Marina. Figured I'd hear from you soon."

"Well, it looks like I'm finally available," Marina said airily, trying to diminish the severity of the situation.

"About that," Gwen said, sounding uncomfortable. " I think you need to take some time off."

"I am, but I'll be ready to go back to work in two or three weeks."

Gwen sighed. "Have you been online? Watched television at all?"

"I have, and while those videos are unfortunate, I have a long career that speaks for itself."

"In a few months, when this mess dies down, I might be able to place you in a smaller market."

Marina pressed her lips together in a grim line. That would mean moving out of San Francisco. "How much smaller?"

"A lot. Look, given the recent events and your age—"

"I'm at the top of my game, and I look good for my age," Marina shot back. She certainly did everything she could to keep herself camera-ready. Her male co-host could develop a little belly, but not her. And if her hair or dress weren't to viewers' liking, they'd hear complaints. Never mind the writing, interviews, soundbites, camera presence, and other things required of her. "I'm more than a news reader. You know I've always excelled at my job. This snafu was a one-off event that any guy would be forgiven in ten minutes."

"You've known there would come a time," Gwen said gently.

Marina grew quiet. "As it did for you." Her agent had once been a top news anchor.

"Once this fiasco passes, maybe you could do special interviews. Softer news, celebrity interviews. You could still be a big fish in a smaller market. Of course, you'd have to move."

"There's nothing in San Francisco?"

"I've already checked," Gwen said. "I knew you'd be calling. Take some time off. Six months, a year."

"I can't afford to. My twins just started college."

"I'm sorry, Marina. Believe me, if I could create a position for you, I would. Tough break." She paused. "If it's any consolation, Babe was reprimanded, too. Though she's still there."

Marina clenched her jaw. "You'll let me know if anything pops up?"

"Of course. Try something else for a few months. You could write a book, lecture at a college, or tutor."

None of that would pay anywhere close to what she had been making. After Marina hung up, she sat in the stillness of the old mahogany-paneled library. Leather-bound books stared silently down at her.

As she had so many times since Heather and Ethan had been born, she thought about Stan and wondered what he would advise. He'd been her best friend from childhood. That was a lot like her parents, who'd known each other in school. Only she and Stan had waited to have children, unlike her parents, who married and started their family right after high school.

When Marina returned to college after the accident, Stan had been her rock. They'd married right after graduation, eager to start their lives. He entered an officer's training program in the Marines, and they moved around the country as he was stationed at different bases. Marina always found work in restaurants, favoring quaint little cafes. And then just as they'd decided to start a family, Stan was deployed to Afghanistan.

A month after Stan left, Marina discovered she was pregnant. Marina was delighted. She had told him what she suspected, and he was thrilled. *Get a test and make sure, sweetheart. Can't wait to hear the news.* The day her test results were confirmed she could hardly wait to tell him.

Instead, two uniformed officers knocked on her door. She could still hear their words: *The Commandant of the Marine Corps has entrusted me to express his deep regret...*

As she thought about Stan—and his sense of honor and duty—she was even more ashamed of her relationship with Grady. How could she have been so gullible as to fall for someone like that?

Never again.

Marina pushed herself up onto her crutches. As devastating as the events of the past two days had been, she would not buckle—not this time, not any time.

That afternoon, Dr. Russell Stein had stopped by and recommended icing, elevation, and compression. Now, with her ankle wrapped, Marina decided to make the best of the situation and sit by the pool, deserted on this midweek day.

Ivy helped Marina outside and found a spot for her under a marine-blue umbrella on a chaise lounge.

"What spectacular architecture," Marina said, gazing up at the old grand dame of a house surrounded by tall palm trees as stately as sentinels on guard. She wondered what this place was like in its heyday in the 1920s and 1930s, although it was still an elegant old home.

"Julia Morgan designed it," Ivy said. "She was the first licensed female architect in California, and she also designed the Hearst Castle for William Randolph Hearst, the newspaper magnate. This house belonged to the Ericksons of San Francisco. It was their summer home."

"What a great location on the beach for you," Marina

said. Wide stone steps from the veranda and terraces led right to the sand. Statues stood around a pool decorated with marble and serpentine tiles. "Although I can't imagine what the electricity bill runs."

"That's why we run it as an inn," Ivy said. "Still, the ocean breezes keep the house fairly cool for most of the year."

Marina put a cushion under her leg to elevate her ankle. "I'm impressed with how you handled the situation after your husband died. How did you know what to do?"

"We didn't," Ivy said, perching on a chair next to her. "Shelly and I had our share of challenges, but we also had a lot of fun getting the business underway. And I love getting up every day. It's not like work at all; it's just what I love to do."

Marina grew quiet, listening. She could hardly imagine feeling that way about work.

Shelly came out of the kitchen carrying a tray with a tall drink on it. "Here at the inn, we have a delicious concoction called a Sea Breeze. Grapefruit juice and cranberry juice and a splash of lime."

"Is that virgin or fully loaded?" Ivy asked. "Meaning vodka."

"Optional by request," Shelly said.

Marina took a sip. "It's perfect as it is. So refreshing."

"Call us if you need anything," Ivy said before she and Shelly left.

As Marina sipped on the cool juice cocktail, she tried to call Ginger, but the call went straight to voice mail. She left a message, trying to sound upbeat. *Thought I'd surprise you.*

"Well, you look comfortable," Jack said, strolling past her chaise lounge.

"You couldn't give me a break?" Marina waved at her ankle, which was propped up on cushions and covered with an ice pack.

"Since you brought it up, did you find out if it's a break or a sprain?"

"Mild sprain, the doctor says, although it sure hurt. Evidently, I have youthful ligaments." She made a face and tugged the straw sunhat Ivy had given her lower over her sunglasses.

"Well, that's a relief." Jack grinned and stripped off his T-shirt.

"What are you doing?"

A shadow of a smile crossed Jack's face. "Going for a swim. Don't get any ideas."

Marina rolled her eyes. Behind her dark sunglasses, she caught a glimpse of his muscular back before looking away. *Not too bad*, she thought, grudgingly. Seconds later, he splashed into the pool and began swimming.

Folding her arms, Marina watched him plow through the water. Here she was, trapped with a boy-man with no means of a rapid escape. At least he was underwater. Marina eased back on the chaise lounge.

At once, her phone rang.

"Darling Marina, I just heard your message," Ginger said over the phone. "I'm so glad you've come for a visit. How long can you stay?"

"Oh, a couple of weeks or so." Marina tried to sound nonchalant.

"Is anything wrong?"

She couldn't fool Ginger. "It's a long story, but I quit my job."

"I see. Well, I'll be home tomorrow. I'm glad you're at the Seabreeze Inn. I'll see you tomorrow afternoon."

After she hung up the call, Marina leaned back and closed her eyes, trying to doze off under the soft sway of palm trees, their rustling fronds lulling her into a relaxed state she hadn't known in a long time. In the distance, she could hear a dog barking. It sounded like it was coming from somewhere on the property.

She was almost asleep when she felt droplets of water land on her face and sunglasses. "Hey," she cried.

"Oh, sorry," Jack said. He slung a towel over his shoulders and brushed his wet hair back. "Are you in town for long?"

"Not really," she said, trying to be noncommittal.

"I just realized I don't know your name."

She sighed. "I'm Marina. And what brings you to Summer Beach?"

"I'm working on a story."

"Hmm. Journalist or a novelist?"

He looked impressed. "Investigative reporter by trade, now on a sabbatical. Tossing around some book ideas."

"About what?"

"I'd rather not say."

Marina eased her sunglasses down and glared over the top of them at him. "It's not like I'm going to steal your idea."

"I'm not implying that you would." He held her gaze for a moment longer than was necessary, and then, grinning, he stood up. "I'll see you around."

Marina watched him go. Something about Jack irritated her. Maybe he was too much like Grady. Sure of himself and his attractiveness.

She certainly didn't need that anymore.

The next afternoon, Marina said goodbye to Ivy and Shelly. She put the convertible top down on the Mini Cooper to bask in the sunshine. After she turned onto the lane, she passed a handcrafted, driftwood sign rendered in coral paint to match the house: *The Coral Cottage.* Her daughter Heather had made this for Ginger. Marina recalled painting a similar sign when she was a teenager.

This house was steeped in memories. The cottage has always been there for her, just like Ginger.

In the daylight, Marina could see the cottage better. The sprawling, stucco house had a terracotta-tiled roof and a broad beach view. To one side was a wildlife preservation habitat, and on the other, the property opened up to the village of Summer Beach. The cottage was mere steps from the beach and a short walk or bike ride to town.

After parking her car, Marina got out and plucked her crutches from the back seat. She was becoming fairly adept with them. Dr. Russ didn't think she'd need crutches for more than a week at the most. Unless she took another tumble, which she assured him was unlikely. She swung herself along the path and onto the wide front porch that caught the ocean breezes.

Palm trees arched around the house, swaying in today's light breeze. Pink bougainvillea bracts fluttered, and petals had scattered like confetti across the lawn during the night.

The door burst open. A tall, ginger-haired woman wrapped her arms around Marina. "Why, you poor dear. You didn't mention this new development. What happened?"

"Revenge of the stiletto."

"Gave them up years ago for the same reason. Do come in, I just arrived." Ginger was tall and angular, in contrast with Marina's petite frame.

Marina had clearly taken after a different side of the family. "You went on a cruise?"

"A short one with old friends," Ginger said with a wave of her hand. "No one you'd know. Come in, and I'll make a pot of Earl Grey tea just as they do at Claridge's in London. That's where Bertrand and I used to entertain the Prince, you know. The hotel is practically an annex to Buckingham Palace."

"I thought it was the Duke."

"Both of them, my dear. Along with a bevy of barons for good measure."

Laughing, Marina followed her grandmother into the kitchen. She eased down on a chair by a red Formica table with chrome legs. The large kitchen dated to the early 1960s. On one side sat a hulking, fire-engine-red O'Keefe & Merritt stove with two ovens and six burners, which was quite advanced for its day. Marina had learned to cook and bake here under Ginger's tutelage.

Marina glanced around the open kitchen and the adjoining dining area and den, where Ginger kept a desk and computer. The beach cottage had been a wedding present from Ginger's husband many years ago. He had been a diplomat, and they'd traveled the world, though they'd always returned to Summer Beach.

The eclectic décor was a mixture of mid-century beach modern with accents from Ginger's travels around the world. A Murano glass paperweight and a Greek letter opener sat on an antique hand-carved desk she'd shipped from Bali. The white slipcovers that protected the sofa and chairs were a sign of her grandmother's spring cleaning preparations for summer. Ginger's loafers tapped on the Saltillo tile floor as she bustled around, preparing tea.

On the dining room table, a cut-crystal vase held tall stalks of blazing, orange-and-blue bird-of-paradise, probably cut from the garden.

Ginger wore a white blouse with the cuffs turned back and a pair of slim blue jeans. Her posture was still erect, and she moved with the energy of someone half her age. Whenever she had to reveal her age at the doctor's office or when buying a bottle of wine—*isn't it obvious I'm old enough to drink?*—people were generally surprised. She attributed her good health to having great genes, walking on the beach, swimming in the ocean, and tending her organic vegetable garden. And the occasional glass or two of wine. *Vital for stress management*, she'd say.

After boiling cold water and letting the tea steep for just the right amount of time, Ginger placed a teapot and two porcelain cups on the table and sat down. She poured tea with a steady hand. "Now, start from the beginning and tell me what happened."

Marina groaned. "It all started with Babe Barstow." She told her grandmother how she'd quit her job, fled San Francisco, and twisted her ankle in the dark.

"No, dear, it all started with Hal, his father, and Grady. Put the blame where it should be. You were a casualty of the system. Babe capitalized on it by seizing that knowledge for her gain. And it worked. For now, anyway."

"You mean, I should have been stronger," Marina said.

"It's rarely that simple." Ginger rested a finger on her temple. "What else is bothering you?"

Stalling, Marina sipped her tea and stared at the fresh basil growing in a colorful Mexican Talavera pot on the window sill. Ginger always sensed what was beneath the surface.

"After Grady proposed, we talked about opening a restaurant together in Napa and traveling the world. The thought of leaving my job and beginning a new phase was enticing."

Ginger arched an eyebrow. "Perhaps more so than the actual man."

"I'm ashamed to admit that to anyone but you," Marina said. She hadn't even admitted that to herself. "In my profession, I have a responsibility to deliver news impartially, but I'm tired of the constant stream of human suffering. Every day seems worse than the last."

"When you lose your purpose, you lose your joy," Ginger said, topping off Marina's tea. "You're burned out. That is the root problem of your situation."

Marina gazed at the ocean through the window. "It's not that I couldn't handle the job. My heart was no longer in it. I often wonder how my life would have been if I'd taken a different path. But I can't now, not with the twins in college. That was my state of mind the other day when Babe caught me off guard."

Ginger leveled her gaze at Marina. "So, try something

new. At least you won't have to deal with a problematic man anymore. For that alone, you deserve a break."

"I'll have to. My agent advised me to take at least six months off. Even then, I'll have to move to a smaller market."

"You do what you have to," Ginger said. "Might as well stay here and save your money. And I could use the company."

Marina glanced at a little cottage behind the main house. "Has anyone rented the little cottage?"

"Haven't advertised it yet," Ginger replied. "I usually don't. Somehow, the right people seem to find it every summer."

"Last year you had a film composer. Have you heard anything from her?"

Ginger nodded with pride. "She landed a gig scoring an important new film. That little cottage is magical, I tell you. Everyone who stays there has good fortune."

Marina smiled at her grandmother's conviction. "Then maybe I should move in there." She chuckled at herself.

"Stay in your old room," Ginger said, patting her hand. "I love having you nearby."

"Guess it's time to reinvent my life." She'd had to do that when Stan died. Though she loved working in the cafe, the pay wasn't enough. Ginger had helped, but Marina didn't want to rely on her. When a customer at the restaurant referred her to the television station manager, she'd gone on the interview. After starting as a receptionist, she'd worked her way up.

"That's the spirit," Ginger said. "Never give up. Glad you decided to stay in Summer Beach."

"For a little while." Marina smiled. It was useless to argue with Ginger.

Marina wasn't sure what she was going to do in Summer Beach, but one thing was certain. She had to decide what to do with the second half of her life.

Chapter 4

*J*ust after daybreak, Jack walked along the water's edge, tossing a stick for Scout, who charged through the surf to retrieve it. The yellow Labrador retriever leapt with glee and then returned, dropping the stick like a gold-plated prize in Jack's outstretched hand.

"There's a good boy." Jack rubbed the dog's neck before rearing back and throwing the stick again. Scout waited, barely containing his enthusiasm until Jack gave the signal. "Fetch it up."

The beach was nearly deserted at this time of the morning, giving Jack the solitude he needed to think. Yesterday, he had received a call that he'd never expected.

Still reeling from the news, he was unsure of whether to believe the veracity of this situation. He'd left a message for a friend from college who practiced law in Los Angeles to get his opinion. Waiting was the worst.

Jack turned around. Behind him, a lone figure jogged from the inn. Bennett Dylan, the mayor of Summer Beach, lived in an apartment above the garages at the Seabreeze Inn. Over coffee one morning, Bennett told him a fire had damaged many of the homes on the ridge, his among them. As he ran toward Jack, Bennett raised his hand in greeting.

Jack tapped the brim of his cap in answer. He hadn't seen the woman on the crutches for a couple of days, and he'd found himself roaming around the property in hopes of running into her again. He'd thought about knocking on her door but decided that would be borderline creepy. Jack glanced back at the Seabreeze Inn.

Soon, Ivy would be leading a beach walk for guests. It hadn't taken Jack long to figure out that Ivy and Bennett were dating. They shared little smiles and were quick to help each other. He'd learned from other guests that Bennett and Ivy were both widowed, but besides that, they just seemed to fit together. Watching them made him long for someone special in his life.

One of Ivy's daughters also lived at the inn, along with her sister Shelly and their niece, Poppy. Jack enjoyed the family atmosphere at the inn and missed having a family of his own. Chasing stories, he'd moved too often to form a lasting relationship.

On the plus side, when he ventured into dangerous situations, he didn't have to worry about family as his colleagues did. He sighed. He was just Jack Ventana, solitary guy. And then he'd received that phone call from Los Angeles that he'd never imagined.

"Join me for a run?" Bennett called out.

"Another day," Jack said. He couldn't keep up with Bennett's pace. They were about the same age, but Bennett clearly had more endurance. Jack had also quit smoking two months ago on doctor's orders.

Slowing to scratch Scout's neck, Bennett grinned. "Going to hold you to that, you know."

"I'm working up to it." Jack's dad had started smoking during the war, so he'd grown up around the habit. And when he'd apprenticed at a Dallas newspaper, his mentor had been a chain smoker. During his first traumatic story, he caved. Smoking helped him manage his stress. But now, at forty-six, it was time for him to get healthy. He imagined himself running with Scout on the beach soon.

"Start small," Bennett said. "And listen to your knees." Scout rolled at Bennett's feet, begging for more attention.

"Give me a few weeks." Jack had joined Ivy's beach walking group one day and Shelly's yoga class the next. While his fellow guests were interesting, he needed solitude to figure out his life.

"Breakfast afterward?" Bennett asked, squinting into the morning sun. He scratched Scout's stomach. "I'm buying at Java Beach."

"Then I'll see you there."

Bennett grinned and turned around, picking up speed on the sand as he jogged off.

"Stay," Jack said, picking up the stick that Scout had abandoned.

Tilting his head, Scout whined after Bennett.

"Traitor." Jack tossed the stick again. "Fetch it up, boy." With a leap, Scout took off.

This is the life, Jack thought. Scout loved splashing in the surf and daring the waves. He had an awkward gait, but his enthusiasm made up for it.

Could this be a place to call home? Gazing through the dissipating morning mist, Jack might as well be a million miles from New York. Or Dallas, where the spreading metropolis had swallowed the small farm he'd called home as a child.

For two decades, Jack had been writing for newspapers, first in Dallas, and then in Chicago and New York, always one step ahead of lay-offs in the contracting newspaper industry. He broke stories that changed history, earned a Pulitzer Prize, and reported on increasingly explosive situations.

But inside was an emptiness that grew every day. Moving around, he'd never developed roots. Everywhere he went, he asked himself if he could live there. The answer was usually no.

Yet, after covering a story in Los Angeles a few months ago, he'd rented a car and cruised south to clear his mind. A couple of hours later, he felt compelled to exit the highway and found himself in a quiet little community hugging the coast.

As soon as he'd arrived in Summer Beach, he'd felt at home. He imagined himself with a house on the ridge looking out to sea, writing books in the morning, and running on the beach in the afternoon. He had money he'd saved to take a sabbatical and a file of ideas for books he'd been jotting down for a decade.

His boss had agreed to six months. Jack packed a bag, checked out of his latest iBnB room, and bought a restored VW van. Inspired by the author, John Steinbeck, Jack drove across the country to Los Angeles, searching for the heartbeat of America along the way.

Jack whistled for Scout. Now he had the dog, too. He almost named the overgrown pup Charley, after Steinbeck's standard poodle.

Scout bounded back to him, dropping the stick at Jack's feet and wagging his tail for another pitch.

"Last time, buddy." Jack heaved the stick again. He'd parked his van at the house of friends near the Griffith Observatory in Los Angeles. One day, he had walked past rescue volunteers in the parking lot of a grocery store.

Adopt a Pet Today, a sign read. Two young women watched over several dogs. One gangly, yellow Labrador retriever looked like it needed a hug as much as Jack did.

"That's a quiet one," the college-aged women said as the dog perked its ears toward Jack. "Oh, my gosh. You're the first person he's paid any attention to all day." She watched in amazement while Jack played with him.

"What's your name?" She snapped a form onto a clipboard.

"Jack Ventana."

The woman nodded knowingly. "Actor, right?"

"No. Why?" Jack scratched the dog behind the ears until a back foot began thumping.

"That's such an actor name."

"I'm a writer." The dog's lips were curling up, and Jack could swear the pup was grinning at him.

"Same thing." She shrugged. "He has a little limp from being hit by a car, and he's generally a little skittish. Probably from the way he was treated." She smiled at the two of them. "I think that dog is going home with you. Must get lonely working from home all day. Where do you live?"

Jack hesitated. "Summer Beach." He'd been planning to go there anyway and figured he'd find a place when he rolled into town. With a van he could sleep in if he had to, he seldom bothered with reservations.

"Your dog is going to love it there. I went to an art show there last summer at a place called the Seabreeze Inn. You must know the place." She thrust the clipboard toward him. "Fill this out, and the two of you will be running on the beach by the weekend."

"My dog, huh?" It wasn't such a bad idea. He'd been a little lonely on his drive from New York. Jack thumbed through the application. "This is eight pages long."

The woman shrugged. "I don't make the rules."

He started to give the application back, but the dog whimpered as if pleading with him to fill it out. "Okay, okay," he said.

After decamping to a coffee shop in the shopping center to fill out the application, Jack kept glancing at the dog, who refused to engage with anyone else. The overgrown puppy sat and stared at him. He seemed to be willing Jack to return.

At one point, Jack was tempted to crumple up the application. Beyond the usual questions, they also wanted to know where he worked, how many hours he was away from home every day, and what his socialization plans were for the dog.

"Beers on the beach," he said to himself, chuckling, although he didn't write that. Soon, only one questioned remained unanswered. *Address?*

"Hmm." He tapped his phone and searched for the Seabreeze Inn. There is was. Right on the beach with rooms available. *And pet friendly.* "Good enough." He jotted down the address.

As soon as he stepped out of the coffee shop, the dog leapt up and barked.

Jack handed the application to the woman.

"We'll check it out and let you know."

"How long is this going to take?" Jack asked. The dog wagged his tail so hard his entire body shook with anticipation of being freed.

"We'll expedite it," the woman said with an understanding smile.

Jack ruffled the dog's fur. "Got to find a new name for you, bud. Charley's taken, but you look like a champion—champion of the underdogs. How's Atticus?" The dog shook its head. "Nah, you look more like a Scout."

"That's a cute name," the woman said. "Scout." She wrote it down on the application.

Barely two hours later, his phone rang.

"Scout is ready for you," the woman said. "Your employer is so cool. Wow, a pet park on-site, annual retreats with dogs, *and* weekly doggie massages. That is truly amazing."

"Uh, yeah." Jack rubbed his chin. "Who'd you talk to, by the way?"

"Hank. Said he was your boss."

"Right," Jack said. Hank was a fellow reporter who had always been a prankster. "I'll be right over."

Now, as Jack walked the beach with Scout, he realized he'd

committed to a lot more than a dog; he'd committed to a new way of life. Dogs had to be fed and walked regularly. Scout needed chew toys and toilet breaks. And most of all, the pup wanted to play.

Jack hadn't been this grounded in years. Although it felt strange, he was growing used to having a companion. He whistled again for Scout, and the two of them started back to the inn.

After showering and slipping on a T-shirt and jeans, Jack combed back his thick brown hair. This summer, he didn't even need to get a haircut unless he wanted to. He slid his feet into flip-flops. Scout was curled next to the bed. When the dog heard the jingle of the room key, he jerked his head up.

"Yeah, yeah, come on."

As Jack left his room, he saw the morning beach brigade stretching behind Ivy. Idly, he wondered again where his neighbor had gone. Not that she'd be out walking on crutches, but he hadn't seen her around. Her toy car was gone, too. He could just imagine her spinning around in that little turquoise Mini Cooper. Even though she seemed stubborn and opinionated, he'd liked her spirit. She didn't play the victim, though she could have. She'd probably taken off.

He sighed. Another missed opportunity.

"Come on, boy," Jack said. He snapped on a leash and started for Java Beach.

When Jack walked into the local coffee shop, Bennett was already there. He'd showered and changed into a casual shirt and khakis, which Jack figured was standard issue for mayors of small beach towns.

Bennett was talking to a younger guy with spiky blond hair. *Surfer*, Jack pegged him. He waited, taking in the details of the crowded restaurant's tiki theme. Authentic, old fishnets filled with starfish, conch shells, and buoys hung from the ceiling. Vintage Polynesian travel posters lined the walls, and reggae music played above the friendly din. A door to the beach stood open, letting in the ocean breeze with the briny scent of kelp and fish that he loved. Sun-bleached chairs, tables, and chaise lounges lined the patio to the sand.

His kind of place. Jack could see himself writing here.

Scout's tail slapped Jack's legs. "Hey, you like it, too, huh?" He tugged gently on the leash. "Sit, boy." Scout tucked his hind legs under him and looked up expectantly, so Jack slipped him a small dog biscuit from his pocket. Scout was smart, and he was taking well to training.

"Hi, Jack," Bennett said, clasping his hand. "Have you met Mitch?"

"Not officially," Jack said, shaking Mitch's hand. "Best coffee I've had in Summer Beach, though."

"Are you passing through or staying a while?" Mitch asked.

Jack pushed a hand through his hair. "I've got five months left on a sabbatical to write a book. Then we'll see."

"Cool." Mitch shook his head. "Going to be hard to leave after that."

"That depends," Jack said. "Hey, do you guys know of a place I can rent that takes dogs? Scout needs more space, and Ivy said my room is booked. She said I could relocate to an attic room, but that's not going to work with Scout. He got a whiff of a Chihuahua and went crazy. "

"That must have been Pixie," Mitch said, chuckling. "She belongs to Gilda, one of the locals on the second floor. If you find anything missing, it's a good bet that Pixie is behind it."

"A kleptomaniac Chihuahua?" Jack grinned. "Sounds like there's a good story there." But not the type he usually wrote.

Mitch smiled and shook his head. "You have no idea what kind of stories Summer Beach holds."

"There's one place that might work," Bennett said, snapping his fingers. "Ginger Delavie has a house on the beach and rents out a guest cottage on her property in the summer. I don't think she would mind you having a dog. The last guest had a little terrier."

"Ginger's cool," Mitch added. "Smart lady. An older woman, but still sharp as they come."

"Sounds good," Jack said. *Ginger Delavie.* Oddly enough, her name seemed familiar. Maybe he had come across her while researching another story. He'd written hundreds in the course of his career, so it was possible.

"I'll call her to see if it's available," Bennett said.

Jack was starving. He glanced up at a menu written on a chalkboard. "What's in the California omelet?"

"A crowd favorite," Mitch said. " Has avocados, tomatoes, chives, charred corn, and gruyere and white cheddar cheeses. That's the fancy bit. Want it with bacon?"

Scout whimpered at the mention of bacon. Jack had already spoiled him.

"Sounds good. Better put some on the side for my pal here." From what Jack had seen, the menu changed every day. "How are the croissants?"

"Great," Mitch said. "Made them this morning."

"You made them?" Jack asked, surprised.

"Not too hard once you learn how." Mitch chuckled.

"I'm a harsh critic," Jack said. "I spent a lot of time in Paris." He'd also done a stint as a foreign correspondent.

"Dude, I think you'll be surprised," Mitch said, grinning.

"If it's as good as the coffee, I'm in." Jack reached down to scratch Scout behind the ears.

"And we'll bring water and a treat for the pup," Mitch added.

After ordering, Jack sat outside where Scout could watch the seagulls swooping overhead and people setting up for the day on the beach. Bennett placed his call.

A couple of minutes later, Bennett clicked off the phone. "Ginger said she'd be happy to talk with you if you'd like to come by this morning."

"I hope it's not too early." It was just eight o'clock, and this was a beach town.

Bennett waved a hand. "I often see her out early on the beach. And she wouldn't have offered if she didn't mean it."

They talked while they waited for their food, and Jack told him about his sabbatical. "This will be the first time I've had a chance to focus on writing outside of my job."

"So, what are you writing? If you can talk about it."

Jack shook his head. "Funny enough, I don't know yet. I have so many ideas, but I need time to sort through them and decide."

"Do you write every day or wait for inspiration to strike?"

"In my line of work, if I waited for inspiration, I'd starve." Jack had done relatively well for himself, mostly because he hadn't had time to spend the money he earned. He traveled light. No wife, no house in the suburbs, no private school loans.

Mitch called out their order.

"I'll get it," Bennett said.

Scout looked up as if to ask where his meal was. "It's coming, boy," Jack said. Scout had flopped onto Jack's feet.

As Jack watched the waves rolling in, he thought about the woman he'd met at the inn again. *Marina.* They'd only exchanged a few words, but something about her intrigued him.

Not that he'd ever see her again. He'd learned that when you met a woman at a hotel, you were both just passing through.

"Just as well," he said under his breath. He had a lot of work to do.

Chapter 5

*V*oices outside her bedroom window woke Marina. She glanced at a wind-up alarm clock on the nightstand. *Almost ten o'clock.* She'd turned off her earlier alarm, needing the extra sleep. Ginger had allowed her a pity party last night, saying *Go ahead, get it out* as she'd refilled her wine glass. Stretching under the white cotton-covered, down-filled duvet, she looked around the room that she'd first stayed in as a child.

Her old collection of white seashells filled large glass pickle jars. A few faded sundresses hung in an antique burl wood armoire, and flip-flops filled a basket by the door. Around the perimeter of the room ran a border that Ginger had painted with a coded message that always made Marina smile.

She rolled out of the old iron bed, testing her weight on her sprained ankle, which seemed better this morning. Her head throbbed a little from the wine. Or was it from Ginger's Coral Cottage Coolers that they'd had first? She hobbled across the wooden floor and pushed blue canvas drapes aside to let in the morning sun. Outside, she saw an old VW van, but no sign of Ginger or anyone else. Maybe they were around the back. She lifted the wooden sash to let in the morning breeze.

Marina stretched in the sunshine like a plant denied of warmth. At least she'd had a good dinner last night. Ginger had grilled salmon and vegetables with brown rice, which was healthy enough, though Marina had second helpings of everything, along with sourdough bread slathered with butter. And then there was the chocolate mousse with whipped cream and Mayan chocolate shavings. Not to mention copious amounts of wine.

With her small frame, she'd always had to watch what she ate. It didn't help that the camera seemed to add weight to her face. Last night, she'd felt such relief that she could actually eat whatever she wanted. And she was going to do it again tonight.

Because she'd been hungry for almost two decades.

On the weekends in San Francisco, Marina would visit one of the farmers markets that sprouted among the neighborhoods. Or she might visit the market at the Ferry Building, always in search of fresh produce and handcrafted specialties. She loved tinkering with recipes and creating new dishes. Seeing pleasure on the faces of her children and friends was her greatest reward.

Now, she decided she'd earned the right to sport love handles if she wanted. If she found work in a smaller market, perhaps expectations would be lower. That would be welcome. Even if her agent Gwen could find work for her in six months or a year, did she still want her old career?

And yet, what else would she do? She'd loved working in cafes years ago, when she and Stan were young and they were moving around for his career, despite her degree in communications. She'd always laughed and argued with Stan that food was a form of cross-cultural communication.

While she was at her happiest in the kitchen puttering around and making food, that didn't pay the bills. She wrestled with this thought for a while. Ginger's words floated to mind. *Problems don't solve themselves.*

Using her crutches, Marina swept through the old house she loved so much. To Ginger, spring cleaning was a sacred ritual. Out came the white canvas slipcovers, which were cleaned and pulled over the mid-century modern furniture that had been in the cottage for years. Ginger had started the tradition to guard against wet, sandy swimsuits when the girls arrived for the summer.

Aquamarine seashell pillows brightened the white canvas slipcovers, and colorful Mexican Talavera pottery flanked the fireplace where they'd sat and talked last night. Anthuriums and peace lilies silently cleansed the air, their red and white spikes on guard against indoor pollution.

The house was quiet. Marina put on a pot of coffee, and as she waited for it to brew, she glanced out the kitchen window.

A large, gangly dog was digging with fervor in Ginger's newly planted garden.

Grabbing a crutch, Marina half-hopped out the kitchen door, waving her arms. "Hey, you! Get out of there!"

The yellow Labrador retriever looked up with a quizzical expression. Seedlings were broken and smashed into the ground, while others had been dug up in a frenzy and cast from the garden, withering unmoored in the sun.

"Go on, get out!"

The overgrown puppy rolled over, leapt up, and now, covered with dirt, raced toward her. The dog latched onto the base of the crutch, playfully mouthing it before Marina waved it away.

"Stop it, wrong, down, sit," Marina called out, hoping he knew one of those commands.

Instantly, the dog sat—on her feet.

"Eeew, wet dog," she said, sliding her feet back. Its fur was matted with sand and Ginger's organic compost; the dog had probably been gallivanting on the beach before taking on the garden.

"Where is your parent?" She gazed toward the beach. No one seemed to be looking for a dog, but she had to find its owner.

And here she was wearing tiny sleep shorts and a shrunken cotton tank top emblazoned with the word *Dream!* In sparkly pink sequins that her sister Kai had probably left here. Reaching inside the back door, she grabbed a pair of flip-flops.

"Come on, you. Maybe you belong to someone out there."

The dog looked at her, panting, its mouth open in what looked like a grin.

"With that silly look, you have to be a boy." She bent down. "Yep. I called it. Okay, let's go. Come, or heel. Are you smart enough to know those?" She patted her thigh as she started walking, and the dog followed her toward the beach. Trudging along with a crutch on the sand wasn't easy.

Seeing people on the beach, she called out. "Anyone lose a dog?"

A few heads turned her way, but no one claimed the dog. She turned around, and a moment later, the dog bounded toward the water and leapt in.

"At least he'll be a little cleaner," she muttered.

That state was short-lived because right after he shook himself, he dropped and rolled in the sand again.

"You're a mess. Let's go. Come, heel!"

The dog fell in beside her again.

"Thank goodness someone trained you. Wish they'd trained you to respect gardens." Marina limped back to the cottage. She thought she recalled seeing a leash in a kitchen drawer. Ginger used to have a border collie, and she still had a few leads.

At the back door, Marina said, "Sit. Stay." She wedged herself inside and shut the door. After trying a few drawers, she found one. Just as she pulled out the leash, the back door opened.

Thinking it was Ginger, Marina turned. "Did you see the—no!"

The dog had somehow opened the door and was streaking through the kitchen. Marina tackled him, but he squirmed free and headed toward the living room, his toenails clattering on the wooden floor.

"Stop!" she screamed, but it was too late. He jumped onto the couch and curled up as if staking his claim and daring her to do something about it. His tongue flopped to one side, and he grinned at her again.

"Down, off," she said sternly, snapping her fingers and pointing to the floor.

He eased his head down between his front paws and looked up at her with doleful eyes. "No, you don't." She hobbled toward him and reached for the scruff behind his neck, trying to pull him off the couch.

But he wasn't budging. Losing her balance, Marina fell onto him. Wet sand and fur slicked onto her skimpy top and chest. She spit fur from her mouth.

"This is ridiculous."

The dog nuzzled her with his head and licked her cheek.

"Stop it. I don't fall for kisses anymore." She folded her arms and looked at him. The dog weighed almost as much as she did and was undoubtedly more muscular, so brute force wasn't going to work.

Marina limped to her bedroom and grabbed her phone. *Surely Summer Beach has an animal control department.* She hopped back to the living room to keep an eye on the critter. Now that she was a mess, too, there was only one place to sit without getting another slipcover dirty.

Beside the dog.

"Sorry to send you to doggie jail, but we've got to find

your owner." She tapped her phone, searching for a number to dial.

Just then, the front door swung open, and Ginger's eyes widened. "What on earth is going on here?"

Behind her was the cheeky guy from the inn. *Jack.* "Hey Scout, come." He glared at her. "What have you done to my dog?"

The dog leapt off the couch and raced toward Jack. "Sit," he said, and Scout flopped onto Jack's feet.

"What have *I* done?" She pointed toward the garden. "Your dog decimated my grandmother's newly planted garden."

Ginger rolled her eyes. "Oh, dear. Well, we can plant again. I'd only just started, so it's not that bad."

Marina returned Jack's glare and gestured with her phone. "You can't let your dog roam free. I was just about to call animal control."

"He wasn't loose." Jack stared at her defensively. "He was in the guest cottage."

Folding her arms, Marina shot back. "Why was he in there?"

"Because Mr. Ventana has rented the guest cottage," Ginger said. "We walked to the bank so he could draw cash out of the ATM."

"Please, call me Jack, ma'am."

Her grandmother smiled and pressed a hand against her chest. "And you may call me Ginger." She turned back to Marina. "Now, Marina, I know you love dogs, but you shouldn't have let the dog in here. You'll have to wash that slipcover again."

Marina stood up, wincing as she did. That ankle wasn't quite as healed as she'd thought. Pointing at Scout, she said, "That dog opens doors. I was looking for a leash when he opened the door and galloped past me toward the sofa."

"Looks like you were playing with Scout." Barely

suppressing a smile, he motioned to her clothes. "Nice outfit, by the way."

"Oh, shut up," Marina said, pulling up the neckline she realized was gaping. She felt her blood pressure rising.

"Marina, that's no way to speak to our guest." Ginger sniffed. "Why don't you take a bath, and I'll prepare lunch for us?"

"He's staying?" Marina shot a look back at Jack.

"Of course. He's moving in today."

"We just talked about this," Marina said. "You didn't think to ask me?"

Ginger leveled a gaze at Marina. "You might want to think about what you just said." To Jack, she added pointedly, "Forgive my granddaughter's manners. She just lost her job."

"That must be tough," Jack said. And then he said to Marina, "I thought I'd recognized you from somewhere."

Marina wished she could disappear. He'd seen the late-night show or the meme. Maybe both.

He clipped a leash onto Scout's collar and took him outside.

Through the window, Marina saw Scout sit by the swing, and Jack returned. She groaned and hobbled toward the kitchen. All this, and Marina still hadn't gotten the morning coffee she so desperately needed. She poured a cup, but then found it difficult to navigate smoothly with the crutch.

Seeing her issue, Jack said, "I'll carry that for you. Where are you going?"

"Back to bed." She whipped her hair around and swung toward the bedroom. "Since you've already unleashed a beast in our midst, you might as well make yourself useful."

Jack followed her to her bedroom and placed her mug on the nightstand.

"Thanks," she muttered. If she wasn't hungover, in desperate need of caffeine, and reeking of *Eau de Wet Dog*, she might laugh at the absurdity of this situation.

"And will there be anything else?" Jack asked as he executed a quick bow.

"Doubtful." She tossed her crutch aside.

And then it struck her. Jack had the same cheesy grin as his dog. "Please shut the door behind you."

After he'd gone, she gulped her coffee and peeled off her smelly clothes. She managed a bath and then wrapped on a robe and climbed back in bed to finish her lukewarm coffee.

She could hear Ginger laughing and talking in the kitchen and Jack egging her on with questions. And then it dawned on her.

Jack was flirting with Ginger.

Narrowing her eyes, Marina wondered what Jack's angle was. She'd heard plenty of cases of much younger men who latched onto older women. Usually, it ended badly. Occasionally, the remnants of the relationship ended up on the morning news with one party shot or strangled or poisoned.

Marina shuddered. *Could Ginger be in danger?* Maybe she was overly cautious, but she would definitely conduct an internet search on him.

Though her stomach was calling for breakfast, Marina closed her eyes, willing Jack to leave so she could return to the kitchen.

Just then, her phone buzzed, and she answered it. "Hello, Kai, how's theater life?" After talking to Heather, she'd sent her younger sister a text to say that she was okay and in Summer Beach. She'd also been trading messages with her other sister, Brooke, who always seemed busy with her family.

"Hey, you. Glad to hear your voice." Kai's melodic voice bubbled over the connection.

"Sorry I worried you the other day."

"Just glad you're okay," Kai said. "Did Ginger tell you what happened?"

Marina sat up in bed and clutched her phone. "What's wrong?"

Kai's sweet, high-pitched voice floated over the phone. "The last theater the musical was booked into had a fire, so it's closed for remodeling. That means I'm officially free for the entire summer. I'm coming for a couple of weeks."

"When?" Marina sat up and tucked her legs under her. Except for holidays, she and Kai hadn't been able to spend much time together since they were children.

"I'm almost there." Kai's voice squeaked with excitement. "I got a ride-share from the airport, and I'll be there soon. We're going to have so much fun this summer."

Marina could have picked Kai up at the airport, but Kai was as independent as Ginger. Still, her spirits lifted. Kai had always been the entertainer of the family. By the age of three, she was belting out children's tunes, singing at the top of her little lungs in her toddler car seat as their parents sang along with gusto. By seven, she knew every Disney song, and at twelve, she had moved on to Broadway show tunes. Kai's natural exuberance had manifested itself in song and dance all her life.

Marina went into the room next to hers and opened the windows to air the room.

Voices floated from outside.

"Well, hello handsome," Kai said in a flirty voice. "Are you a friend of Ginger's?"

Marina peeked out. Kai had arrived in a blaze of glitter with a stack of leopard-print luggage. Jack was outside with Scout.

Jack hooked a thumb into the belt loop of his jeans. "I just leased the guest cottage for the summer."

Kai stuck out her hand. "I'm Kai, Ginger's granddaughter."

Shaking Kai's hand, Jack grinned like his oversized puppy dog. "Jack Ventana."

The front door slammed, and Ginger strode out, her arms open wide to Kai. "Hello, darling. I see you've met my new summer tenant. Jack is writing a book." She embraced her granddaughter and kissed her on the cheek.

Inside, Marina rolled her eyes. And Kai was here all summer. Marina sensed trouble. She stepped in front of the window and called out, "Kai, your old room is ready."

"I'll be right in." Kai glanced at her luggage and turned to Jack. "Would you be a dear and—"

"I'll get them." Jack grinned. "I know the way."

After Jack brought in Kai's stuffed suitcases and left, Marina joined Kai in her room. Lounging on a white chenille bedspread, she watched her sister unpack.

Dancing in the musical theatre production kept Kai in great shape. She was the tallest of the three sisters and had taken after Ginger. Kai's strawberry blond hair waved down her back, and her green eyes often sparkled with mischief.

Marina adored her lively younger sister, but she often wondered if Kai was truly happy or simply perpetually busy.

After unzipping a large suitcase, Kai lifted a handful of fancy cocktail dresses on hangars, transferring them straight to the closet. They were more big-city glitz than lazy SoCal beach.

"You pack like a pro," Marina said, admiring her sister's organizational deftness.

Kai paused with a hand on her hip. "As much as we travel, you learn to pack and unpack in record time." She tossed two zippered, mesh pouches that held lingerie into drawers. In another suitcase, an envelope-style pouch held jeans and T-shirts. High-heels, flats, and a cosmetic case emerged from the smallest case. She beat even Ginger for efficiency.

At last, Kai brushed her hands. "All done in less than five minutes. Have you been to town yet?"

"Not with this ankle. Don't you want to change? Glitter and gold might be a little much for beachwear."

"Oh, right," Kai said, kicking off her high-heels and

quickly changing into a soft, buttercup-yellow sundress that accented her hair.

"Heard you flirting with Jack," Marina said. "Hello, handsome."

"Actually, I was talking to the dog." Kai grinned. "Jealous?"

"Jack might be good-looking, but he's hardly my type," Marina said.

"He's way too old for me." Kai brightened. "But more your age, right?"

"Ouch. You, too?"

Kai laughed. "I didn't mean it to sound like that. But after the Grady debacle, you've earned some fun this summer."

"Absolutely not with that specimen of man," Marina said, slicing her hands through the air. "Besides, I have to find another job."

"You don't sound excited about that." Kai hung up her traveling clothes and turned to Marina, drawing her finely arched brows together. "Don't you think it's interesting that Brooke is the only one of us who is happily married?"

"You forget that I once was."

"I know," Kai said, sitting beside Marina and taking her hand. "But that was so long ago."

"Eighteen years." Marina blinked. *And it still seems like yesterday.* Every time she looked at her children, she saw her husband in them. Heather's quick smile and misty, blue-gray eyes were reflections of Stan, while Ethan was a near replica —even down to his golf swing. It was uncanny how Ethan's movements echoed Stan's, as if such muscle memory was in the DNA. Stan was everything she'd ever wanted in a man; he was kind and even-tempered with a zany sense of humor.

"That Grady guy was never good enough for you," Kai said. "Was he at least fun?"

"He was different, that's for sure. He professed his undying devotion from the first date. Now I know not to trust insta-love." Marina twisted her lips to one side. "I was really too old to fall for that."

"Out of practice." Kai leaned her head on Marina's shoulder. "Would you think I was crazy if I told you I'm dealing with a similar issue?"

"You're seeing someone?"

Fidgeting with her hair, Kai said, "It happened so fast. We've been seeing each other barely a month, and he's already proposed."

"And what did you say?"

Kai got up and opened her purse. She withdrew a ring box and opened it. A large emerald flanked with diamonds caught the sunlight. "What should I say?"

"Wow, that's quite a statement," Marina said. "But you're not wearing it. That says a lot."

Kai tucked it away. "I'm not sure."

"What's the rush?" Marina asked.

Kai shook her head. "It's complicated. I'll tell you later. Come on, let's see what Ginger is up to."

Chapter 6

*J*ack looked up and saw Mitch walking across the patio of Java Beach. He pushed his notebook away. While his intentions of writing were good, he'd had too much on his mind to brainstorm ideas, and all he'd been doing was sketching little cartoon figures of seagulls for his nieces and nephews in Texas.

Jack needed to talk to someone who knew more than he did about this unusual situation.

"Here you are—today's California fusion omelet with a toasted onion bagel," Mitch said, placing a hot dish in front of Jack. His tie-dyed T-shirt was a bright spot on a cloudy morning.

"Great, thanks." Jack could have cooked in his little kitchen in the guest cottage, but he liked walking here and enjoyed hearing conversations. That made him feel less alone. Checking out the generous portion, he said, "If this is breakfast, what's for dinner?"

"Java Beach closes after lunch," Mitch said. "In the beginning, it was just me, and I could only work so many hours a day and still have time to enjoy living here. I have a boat and take visitors in the afternoon a few times a week."

"Sounds like you keep busy."

"Not as busy as usual today." Mitch frowned, and Jack detected a sense of concern on his new friend's face.

"Any particular reason for that?"

Mitch jerked a thumb toward the South. "The next community over let in some big box stores and chain restaurants that are advertising cheap deals and stealing our tourist traffic. Some of the locals, too. Today is Endless Breakfast day."

"I don't see how anyone could want any more than this," Jack said, motioning to his omelet.

"I know, but it's affecting a lot of local restaurants here. Shops, too. Some might not be able to weather the loss of business."

"That's tough." Instantly, Jack felt terrible. He'd planned to go to one of those big stores to replace Ginger's garden. Reaching down, Jack slipped Scout a slice of crispy bacon. "Say, is there a local garden center in town?"

"You bet. The Hidden Garden is about three blocks down on the left. Tell Leilani and Roy that I sent you."

"Think they have vegetable plants?"

"The best. That's where I get mine." Mitch nodded toward a raised planter bursting with healthy herbs and young vegetable plants. "What do you want to grow?"

Jack raked a hand through his messy morning hair. "Probably tomatoes, peppers, and the usual. I promised Ginger I'd replace her garden. Scout made a mess of it." At the mention of his name, Scout raised his head. "Yeah, I'm talking about you, champ. Who knew this dog knew how to operate doorknobs?" He had to make sure he locked his doors now.

Mitch winced. "Off to a rough start?"

"Ginger is great, but her granddaughter is in constant attack mode," Jack said, shaking his head. "I'm sure she's angry about losing her job, and I'm afraid I haven't helped matters. Do you know Marina?"

"Not really. Kai comes around in the summer between her touring schedule, but I've only seen her with Ginger. I think Ivy knows Marina from way back." Mitch glanced over his shoulder at a woman with royal blue hair and a rhinestone visor calling for him. "I've got to check on Darla, but let me know if you need anything else."

Jack dug into his omelet, which was as light and flavorful as any he'd ever had. Today, it was filled with green onions, orange tomatoes, and pink salmon. Topping the fluffy eggs were creamy avocados and a garnish of orange tobiko, a caviar or roe that often accompanied his favorite sushi. He wasn't going to go hungry in Summer Beach.

Jack had just finished his breakfast when his phone rang. "Jack here."

"Hi, my name is Imani Jones. Seems we have a mutual friend in LA"

It was the attorney his friend had recommended. "Thanks for getting in touch," Jack said. "Any chance I could meet you at your office today? It won't take long, but I could use some good advice."

She hesitated. "What's the problem?"

"It's kind of sensitive," Jack said, lowering his voice. "Can we talk in person?"

"Okay, but just so you know, I don't practice much anymore," Imani replied. "I left that rat race in the city. But you're welcome to stop by Blossoms, my flower stand in the village. Happy to chat in between customers and point you in the right direction."

"That would be great. Where is Blossoms?"

"Where are you now?"

"At Java Beach."

"Tell Mitch hello for me. When you leave, walk past a hardware store called Nailed It and turn toward the beach. You can't miss it."

"And how will I know you?" He realized too late that was a silly question.

"You haven't been in Summer Beach very long, have you?"

"No, ma'am."

"Look for a woman with long black hair and a sun hat."

"I'll be the guy with a yellow Labrador."

She laughed. "So I've heard."

After clicking off the phone, Jack left Java Beach with Scout trotting beside him on a leash. He'd never faced a situation like this before, though he wasn't one to shirk his responsibilities. This, however, represented an enormous obligation that would change his life. As he walked to Blossoms, a cascade of emotions swept through him.

Imani was correct. The flower stand wasn't hard to find. The scent of roses, lilies, and tuberose filled the air. Peonies and sunflowers spread their cheerful petals under the morning sun. At the center of it all, a woman in a plum-colored, batik-print dress with long sisterlocks and a broad-brimmed sun hat tended to customers.

Jack waited until she finished wrapping up a bouquet of yellow roses for a young woman. "Are you Imani?"

"You must be Jack," she replied, shaking his hand. "Welcome to Summer Beach. Are you staying long?"

He told her about his sabbatical. "That could change, though, depending on this situation." He might have to return to Los Angeles.

"The situation is what, exactly?"

Jack glanced around. It wasn't that he was ashamed, but he wasn't ready to make an announcement. Eating at Java Beach, he'd already figured out that Summer Beach had a lively gossip network.

"I received a call from a woman I'd known a decade ago. We were both covering a story in a dangerous venue." He paused, remembering the standoff between the FBI and a heavily armed, pseudo-religious cult. Fortunately, the children were released early. In the end, no one was hurt, but tensions were insanely high. "Now, she's not well. She has some final wishes that involve me."

"And just what are these wishes?"

Jack hardly knew how to explain this. "After her death, she would like for me to raise her son." He waited, searching her face. If Imani had a reaction, she didn't let it show. He'd bet she was great at poker.

Imani cleared her throat. "This might sound callous, but are you sure she's that close to death, or is this a ploy to gain financial support?"

Jack hadn't thought about that, but Vanessa had always been a straight-forward reporter, searching for the truth. "I think it's for real. Unfortunately for her."

"What age is the child?"

"He's ten years old."

"Have you met him?"

"Not yet."

Imani was quiet for a few moments. "And why do you think a woman would give up her child to someone she hasn't seen in years and barely knew then?"

Jack ran his knuckles across the bristle on his chin. "She thinks that I might be the child's father."

"Ah. Now we're getting somewhere." She gave him a sympathetic smile. "Is this the first time you've ever heard of this boy?"

Jack nodded. "I had no idea he existed. When I asked why she didn't tell me, she said her family would've disapproved. Vanessa never saw the point in contacting me." He shook his head. "I truly wish she had. That is, if she knows for sure."

"And do you think she's telling the truth now? I hear you're an accomplished writer. Pulitzer Prize and all. You've got to have a little tucked away."

"A little," he agreed. "But I don't think money has

anything to do with it. Vanessa said she has an independent income. She's been battling a rare disorder. I'm not sure how much time she has left, but it's not long, and she doesn't have anyone to take care of her son. She said she wants him to know his father."

Jack swallowed hard. He couldn't imagine facing such a predicament alone, and his heart went out to Vanessa and her son. "Leonardo is his name. She calls him Leo."

Imani gazed intently at him as if she were trying to look into his soul and judge the veracity of his words. "First, you'll want to establish paternity. And then, you—and the court—will do what's in the best interest for the child."

Jack nodded numbly. Beside him, Scout whimpered as if he felt Jack's pain. "As in a DNA test?"

"That's one way," Imani said. "You can also sign a voluntary declaration of paternity. At that point, you'll have the legal rights and responsibilities that go along with being a parent. That means visitation and physical custody rights, as well as the financial responsibilities that accompany those rights."

Jack breathed out. "So, if I do that, then no test is required?"

"Wouldn't you want to know for sure?"

"That's a valid question, but I'm not sure I want to know." The way he saw it, a little boy was about to be alone in the world, and Vanessa had reached out to him. She believed he could do the job. Did he want to complicate the issue with a test?

"Excuse me," Imani said as a man asked to pay for a bouquet of lilies.

Jack stepped aside, rocking on his heels as he thought. On the other hand, perhaps Vanessa had more faith in him than was warranted. What if he wasn't up to the task? Undoubtedly, more suitable people existed to take care of a little boy.

Yet, if he knew he was the father, Jack worried that he

might get caught up in the notion of fatherhood—which he knew little about—and neglect doing what was truly best for the boy.

Investigating stories often took him to far-flung locals on a moment's notice—he'd never been a house-and-picket-fence kind of guy. If he didn't return to his nomadic existence, what else could he do? Writing a book had been a dream for a six-month sabbatical, not the rest of his life. If he had offspring to support, he couldn't take some *Travels with Charley* kind of journey in his VW van with Scout. Not without some semblance of income.

He'd been wrestling with this dilemma for days. When he'd mentioned he was going to Summer Beach, Vanessa had said that there was a hospice facility there. She longed to be close to the ocean in a more tranquil place than Los Angeles. What if she came here?

A wave of guilt washed over him. Hiding out by the beach and writing a book now seemed so trivial compared to what Vanessa was facing.

When Imani turned back to him, Jack realized he was taking up a lot of her time. "Looks like you have more customers," he said, blinking back emotion welling inside him.

"I'll be right with you," Imani called out to a couple dressed in beach attire. She turned back to Jack. "A little boy's life may hinge on you and your decision. I'd like to talk with you more about this."

"I'd like that," he said, relieved to have a confidante. He'd have to get back to Vanessa soon.

"I'll call you later," Imani said before turning to help her customers.

Jack strolled through the village toward the garden nursery, checking out the local shops. He passed Antique Times, Rosa's fish taco stand, several boutiques, and First Summer Beach Bank, where Ginger had taken him.

A few minutes later, Jack saw a wooden sign that read, *The*

Hidden Garden. Ducking his head to pass under a rose-covered archway, he stepped inside the shady oasis. Baskets of purple petunias, pots of mauve hydrangeas, and buckets of crimson bougainvillea looked extremely healthy. Everything was well-tended. The tranquility of the space washed over him, and he welcomed it.

"Hi, looking for something in particular?"

"Vegetables." Jack turned to face a man about his age who looked sturdy and friendly. "What a great place. Mitch from Java Beach sent me. Are you Roy?"

"Guilty," the man replied. "What can I help you with today?"

"This big fella demolished a fresh-planted garden," Jack said, rubbing Scout's neck. "And I have to replace it."

"Do you know what type of plantings you need?"

"I saw the remains of tomatoes, sweet peppers, cucumbers. Probably a few other things, too. Maybe you know Ginger Delavie." Since this was a small town and many people knew each other, he thought he'd start there.

"Sure, my wife usually helps her. Hang on." Roy waved to a woman with dark, braided hair adorned with the snowy white pikake flowers that reminded him of his visit to Hawaii last year, covering the still active volcano.

"Leilani, do you recall what Ginger bought for her garden?"

She approached them with a sunny smile. "Sure, why?"

Jack rubbed Scout's neck. "My sidekick here destroyed it. I need to replace the plants."

Leilani put her hands on her hips and cast a stern look at Scout. "You're not going to do that again, are you?"

"We're working on that." Jack frowned at Scout. "He's still learning the rules."

Leilani laughed. "Marigolds dissuade a lot of dogs, as well as other critters and harmful insects, too. The flowers are pretty, but their smell is a deterrent to them. We should include some of those in your order. You can also take other steps, such as planting thorny roses or installing fencing. While you look around, I'll go inside and see if I can find Ginger's order."

Roy nodded toward his wife. "She'll find it. Most organized person I know. Are you on vacation, or do you live here?"

"I've rented Ginger's little cottage by the sea," Jack replied. "It's a sweet spot to get some writing done." He still couldn't place where he knew Ginger's name from, but he had a lot of old notes to sort through.

"That it is," Roy said, hooking a thumb into his jeans. "Where do you call home?"

"Most recently, New York."

"Great baseball there, huh?"

Jack chuckled. "Depends on which team you're rooting for."

They talked a little about the latest sports news, and then Leilani returned waving a receipt like a trophy. "Got it right here. Several varieties of tomatoes, cucumbers, sweet peppers, chives, and onions, among other things. Do you want them all?"

"Sure, and something special, too," Jack said, shifting on his feet. "As an apology."

"Ginger was looking at more of our potted red anthuriums, which are great indoors." Leilani gestured toward a lush green plant with waxy red blooms. "That might be a good *mea culpa* gift."

"I'll take them," Jack said, relieved that Leilani knew what to replace. "And whatever else you think would thrive here. Lettuce and strawberries would probably do well in this climate, right?"

"Sure, Leilani will help you," Roy said. "I'm making deliveries this afternoon, so I can drop everything off for you."

"Great. I want to plant these as soon as possible."

"Jack's from New York City," Roy said, raising his brow.

Leilani exchanged a look with her husband. "Jack, have you ever planted a garden before?"

"Yeah, though it's been a while," Jack replied. "I think I'll need a few of those tomato cages, too."

"We'd better send instructions," she said, striding toward a row of plants.

"Don't worry," Roy said. "Ginger can give you some good tips, too."

Chuckling, Jack thought about how hard he'd worked to eliminate his Texas accent when he worked in Chicago and New York. He found it funny how people used to view him as a country bumpkin, and now they only saw him as a guy from the big city.

Jack returned to his cottage, where he sat down and penned a letter to Vanessa. He could have emailed or texted, but putting his words down by hand on paper gave him a chance to pause and think to better articulate his thoughts. He was almost finished when he saw Roy arrive at the front of the property. He turned the paper over and placed his pen on top of it.

After making sure Scout had ample food and water, Jack locked the door to keep the scoundrel inside and went to meet Roy. While he was helping Roy carry plants to the garden, Marina emerged from the house. She had a pair of oven mitts tucked under one arm and a splotch of flour on her blue chambray sundress. A savory smell wafted through the open kitchen window.

"No crutches today?" he said, trying to be friendly.

She lifted a shoulder and let it drop. "The ankle is a lot better."

"That's good," he said.

"Going to plant all those?" Marina asked.

"You bet," Jack replied. It would keep his hands busy, which was one of the most difficult challenges of quitting smoking. He seemed to be forever reaching for a pack of cigarettes, which he knew better than to keep around.

Roy gave Jack several sheets of planting instructions that Leilani had printed for him. Jack thanked him, folded the papers, and slid them into the back pocket of his jeans. He picked up a pair of large anthurium plants. "These are for Ginger," he said to Marina. "They should go indoors."

"That was nice of you. I'll take them." Marina gave him a funny look, cradled the plants in her arms, and went inside.

"Good luck," Roy said. "Call us if you need anything else."

"Will do," Jack said, sauntering toward the garden. After squatting down, he smoothed the dirt with his hands, enjoying the feel of fresh-tilled earth between his fingers. He dug a pocket knife from his jeans and flipped it open. It wasn't perfect, but it would do. He began poking holes about a hands-breadth apart.

Jack was working on the second row when a shadow fell across him. He looked up, shielding his eyes from the sun.

Marina stood over him with her hands on her hips. "You can't be serious," she said.

Chapter 7

"*T*he tomato plants will be far too close together," Marina said, pointing toward the offending plants.

Clearly, Jack had never planted a garden before. Although Marina hadn't gardened in years—she lived in a vintage apartment in San Francisco with a view of the bay—she'd often helped Ginger plant vegetables when she was young. Jack didn't even have gardening tools. He was using a pocket knife, for heaven's sake.

"That's for the cilantro," Jack said, pointing at the first row.

"Those aren't cilantro." The tomato plants were sitting by the holes he'd made. She was sure he didn't have a clue about what he was doing. Jack covered up a hole he'd made in between two others. "There we go. How's that?"

"Just don't do anything else, please." This guy was going to waste a second batch of plants if she didn't step in and do something. "Give me a minute, and I'll help you. I have to take some bread from the oven."

"Okay, I'll get the plants ready," Jack said, pulling a plant from its container.

"Go easy on that poor plant," Marina said, exasperated.

She saw a slight grin curve his mouth. That little movement reminded her of Kai, who often called Marina out for bossiness. She threw up her hands. "Come inside and wait for me. I made fresh lemonade. You can have some if you want."

"Sounds good." Jack snapped the pocket knife closed and stood up, brushing his hands on his jeans.

Marina hurried inside, anxious about her bread. Jack followed and sat down at the kitchen table. She could feel his eyes on her, but with two loaves in danger of burning, she didn't welcome the distraction. "I'll thank you to stop staring at me," she said as she pulled a loaf pan from the oven.

"Sorry to disappoint, but I had my eyes on the bread. What kind did you make?"

There she went again. *Assuming a fact not in evidence*, as Ginger would say. "That one is rosemary, and this one is a chocolate cinnamon-swirl," Marina said, reaching for a second loaf in the oven. She could feel her cheeks burning. Surely not from anything but the not oven.

"Sounds like babka. Do you bake often?"

"Not as much as I'd like," she said. "But now, I've got time. Helps me think."

"About what a jerk your new neighbor is?" Jack spread his hands. "I'm really not, you know. I can bring letters of reference from several very accomplished women."

Marina sighed. "As you might have seen, I'm not in a good place right now." She usually didn't take out her feelings on others, but she had a lot on her mind. Maybe she hadn't given Jack a fair assessment.

"Aw, those stupid videos and memes die out eventually."

So he had seen them. Marina's cheeks grew hotter.

Jack glanced around the kitchen. "Looks like a pretty good place to work out whatever you need to. What a great stove that is."

"It's vintage," she said. "You know, my sisters and I are lucky to have Ginger." Marina removed her oven mitts and opened the refrigerator. After taking out the pitcher of lemonade she had made with the fruit from Ginger's tree, she poured two tall glasses and handed one to Jack. "Our parents are gone, so she's all we have. Just in case you have ideas about dating a rich older woman."

Jack's eyes widened with surprise. "Excuse me? Your grandmother is very nice, but I assure you that thought never crossed my mind." He shook his head, drawing his dark eyebrows together. "But I'm sorry about your parents. That sounds like a tough break."

Embarrassed about her assumption, Marina focused on fishing a lemon seed from her glass. "I still miss my parents every day. And what about your folks? Where did you grow up?"

"Texas, although I haven't lived there since I left school. My parents are no longer living, though I have a more responsible sister in Dallas."

"And how did you decide to take time off to write a book?" Being that free to take time off was intriguing.

"I know a couple of editors at publishing houses, and they've both expressed interest in looking at what I produce."

Marina leaned against the counter, recalling their brief conversation by the pool. "Can you share what you're writing, or is that still off-limits?"

"At the moment, I'm sorting through ideas," Jack said. "I find ordinary people engaged in extraordinary pursuits fascinating. Sometimes those people are our neighbors or family members. Like the teacher who lived beneath her means, traded in stocks, and left a fortune earmarked for scholarships to her alma mater after her death. No one knew anything about her investing activities."

As he went on, sparks of excitement filled Jack's eyes. "I've been researching civil rights leaders, Mother Theresa, Doctors Without Borders...there's no shortage of inspiring stories about regular people who take on extraordinary tasks—and end up changing lives through their dedication to a cause. Amid darkness, I turn a spotlight on hope, of the triumph of the human spirit for good and man's search for meaning."

"Oh, well then." Astonished, Marina stared at Jack. He had more depth to him than she had imagined. Was this the same man who'd given her a cheesy grin at the inn when they met? It dawned on her that she might have misjudged him. Grady's insensitivity had so blinded her that she, in turn, had also been insensitive. What was that saying about anger begetting anger?

Jack drained the last of his lemonade. "Shall we finish what I started in the garden?"

"Maybe we could have it done by the time Ginger returns," Marina said, picking up a gardening basket that she'd once given Ginger from a shelf by the back porch. "She took Kai with her to speak to a group of high school students. My grandmother connects students to mentors in the community. Many kids are college-bound, but others are floundering. Ginger believes the community needs to be there for these kids."

"That's noble," Jack said. He stared at the basket of gardening tools. "Is that what you're going to use?"

"Of course. Why?" Inside was a floral-printed spade and gardening gloves that still looked like new. Marina pulled on the gloves.

"No reason. It's…cute." He put his glass in the sink and went outside.

Marina turned off the oven and then followed Jack toward the garden. One of her favorite things to do in San Francisco had been to go to the farmers market in the plaza by the Ferry Building. She loved that area of San Francisco on the ocean with the bay view. Surrounded by the freshest produce with the most tantalizing aromas and flavors was a little slice of heaven.

Marina recalled that Summer Beach had once had a

farmers market. She wondered if it was still in operation and made a mental note to ask Ginger.

Ahead of her, Jack was already arranging the plants.

"Ginger planted the tomatoes over there last year," Marina said, pointing to a spot she recalled from the past summer. "We should put them there again."

"It's better to rotate crops," Jack said, shaking his head.

"How's that?" He pointed to another place. "I also had some tomato cages delivered. I didn't know if Ginger had any, but these babies are going to grow up fast. This early variety is about five to six weeks to harvest."

Marina stared at Jack. "I didn't think you'd ever planted anything before."

Jack leaned back on his haunches and rested his hands on his thighs. "Well, it's been a while. But my folks had a farm, and I helped out."

She laughed at herself. "I assumed you were a neophyte."

Jack could have gloated, but he merely shrugged off her comment. "Everyone has to eat. I can help Ginger tend the garden this summer." He paused and looked at Marina. "That is, if it's okay. I think a lot when I'm working in a garden."

"I'm sure Ginger will welcome that. My gardening skills are a little rusty."

"They'll come back." Jack continued working. "Scout made a mess of this. I can manage if you need to do something else."

"That's okay. I've missed digging in the dirt." She gathered the full skirt of her blue chambray dress and knelt on the grass across from him. Marina no longer found Jack as irritating as when she'd first arrived.

She watched him work with a deftness that seemed second nature to him. Sharing the gardening tools, they spoke little while they worked. Together, they finished the job quickly.

Marina rose, her back aching from the exertion of reaching and bending. "Thank you for putting Ginger's garden back together. And the marigolds are pretty. You've been very considerate."

"The owners of The Hidden Garden told me dogs aren't keen on the scent of marigolds," Jack said. "I'm also working with Scout on impulse control to keep him out of the garden. If that doesn't work, I can rig up a fence that can be removed later."

"Ginger will appreciate that."

"It's the least I can do."

Marina gazed at the way the sunlight shone on his wavy brown hair and lit his blue eyes. Though he seemed easygoing, his eyes had an intensity and intelligence that probably missed little. Surprisingly, she'd enjoyed his companionship today. "Think you could handle a couple of slices of warm bread?"

"I'll do my best."

While Jack checked on Scout, Marina sliced the rosemary and chocolate cinnamon swirl breads. The flavor profiles were different, but she wanted to try both. She arranged the bread on a tray with a pitcher of iced water.

The front door slammed, and Marina looked up to see that Ginger and Kai had returned. "Something smells delicious," Ginger called out.

"In the kitchen," Marina replied. Her grandmother and sister joined her. Kai was humming a Broadway show tune. "Is that 'Aquarius?'"

Kai belted out a few lines from the rock musical.

Ginger laughed. "It's from *Hair*. I remember that first performance at the Biltmore Theater in 1968. It ran for months before it moved to Broadway."

Kai's lips parted. "Wasn't that the one, um, without costumes?"

"Only briefly at the end of the first act," Ginger said, dismissing the comments with a toss of her head. "And it was very dimly lit; one could hardly even see. You should know your theater history, Kai. I thought I taught you better than that."

Marina and Kai traded looks. Somehow, Ginger had often been at the center of cultural happenings. But then, she had taken them to the off-Broadway opening night of *Hamilton* in New York, so why should they be surprised?

Ginger motioned toward the garden. "Who replanted the garden? It looks even better than the first attempt."

"Jack did it," Marina said. "And he brought you two beautiful anthurium plants." She gestured toward the dining room where she'd placed them on the table.

"Wasn't that classy?" A smile flitted across Ginger's face.

"Oh, no, you don't." Marina knew exactly what her grandmother was thinking. She'd have to talk with her later. *No more men.* Quickly, she changed the subject. "Would you two like some bread? It's fresh from the oven."

Kai didn't wait. She picked up a slice of the cinnamon bread and bit into it. "This is divine. Oh, my gosh, you could sell this."

"You think so?" Marina turned to her grandmother. "Say, is that farmers market still going in town?"

"It is," Ginger replied. "I can put you in touch with the organizer."

Marina rested her hands on her hips. "Might be a way to keep busy and bring in a little cash while I figure out my life." Still, she needed more income than what a few loaves of bread would bring. College tuition and room-and-board for the twins wasn't cheap.

"Testing the market?" Jack had stepped inside while they were talking.

Marina noticed he had changed his shirt and ran a comb through his hair.

"Isn't that what people do before they go into business?" Marina scooped a slice of rosemary bread onto a small plate and handed it to Jack, who devoured it in a few bites.

Kai's eyes lit. "You're seriously thinking of going into business? I think that's great."

"Mmm, she sure could," Jack said. "This rivals the bread at Java Beach."

"It should," Ginger said. "Who do you think taught Mitch how to bake? By the way, thank you for replanting the garden."

"I'll be sure to keep Scout away from it," he said.

Marina twisted her lips to one side. "I hope you didn't share my bread recipes with Mitch."

"They weren't yours to begin with, now were they?" Ginger said. "But no, I didn't. When Mitch arrived in Summer Beach, he was hardly more than a kid. Selling coffee on the beach and barely getting by. But he had a way with customers, and they loved his coffee. Bennett noticed and called me to help him with the numbers portion of his business plan."

Marina smiled. Ginger often did things like that without talking about it. "And the baking part of this story?"

Ginger went on. "Bennett funded him, and Mitch was a hard worker. In between figuring out his income and expenses, we baked. Croissants, bagels, muffins, cookies. Mitch was an eager student and a quick study."

"No wonder I love having breakfast there," Kai said. "I always thought it tasted homemade."

Jack leaned against the counter, clearly intrigued. "And how did you learn to bake like that?"

"It was in the '60s in Cambridge," Ginger said with a faraway look in her eyes. "Bertrand and I met the Childs, and Julia taught me how to make the most marvelous croissants, among other culinary delights. I'm sure you know Julia and Paul lived in France for years. Those were the days, indeed."

"Let me get this straight…" Jack leaned forward, now seemingly captivated. "You studied under Julia Child?"

"I wouldn't call it studying, *per se*," Ginger said. "We were simply having the grandest of times. Julia was such fun in the kitchen, as well as incredibly accomplished. Bertrand and I always brought the wine and never skimped. One simply didn't, with Julia. Her husband Paul was superb at blending cocktails. We created the Coral Cottage Cooler for brunch one day. Champagne or prosecco with fresh-squeezed blood orange juice, strawberries, and mint. Marvelously refreshing."

Marina laughed. "Our grandmother always surprises us. Just wait; the stories will get even better. Especially if you open a bottle of wine."

"Preferably the best," Kai intoned. She broke off another piece of rosemary bread.

Ginger shrugged. "Everyone is good at something."

With another bite, Kai finished off the slice. Licking crumbs from her finger, she added, "Ginger is a math genius, too. She taught us all to recognize patterns and such. We were always way ahead in class."

"And what did you do with that talent?" Jack asked Ginger.

Marina studied Jack, picking up on his interview training. Ginger seemed happy to talk to Jack about herself, but for how long? She leaned in, listening.

"Oh, I've been a statistician for years," Ginger replied with a vague gesture. "Excuse me, I just remembered I have a call to return."

"That's the end of the interview today," Marina said as she submerged the bread pans in hot, soapy water.

"Your grandmother seems like a woman ahead of her time," Jack said, staring after Ginger.

"Our grandfather was a career diplomat, so Ginger lived and worked all over the world with him," Marina said. "But she seldom talks about it." Marina might have worked her way up in the broadcast news business by interviewing people, but her grandmother still eluded her.

"She must have some amazing stories," Jack said. "I'd like to talk with her more."

"The best place to get her talking is on the beach," Kai offered. "But you have to rise early to keep up with her."

After Jack returned to the guest cottage, Marina and Kai sat on the swing on the front porch, looking out over the beach and beyond. Shorebirds skittered across the sand in an endless quest for sustenance.

Kai had poured two glasses of chilled prosecco. She touched her glass to Marina's. "To your new life ahead."

"New beginnings, indeed," Marina said. "So, tell me about Mr. Giant Emerald." She clasped a knee and leaned back against the swing.

Kai let out a long breath. "His name is Dmitri."

"How romantic." Marina sipped her wine. "Especially judging from the size of that ring. Is he?"

"Plenty," Kai said, smiling shyly. "Dmitri has called several times a day since I left. He's one of the show's producers, and he invests in other theater productions as well. Even from the beginning, I thought this could be the real deal. True love."

Marina knew that dreamy look in Kai's eyes all too well. Kai had always been in love with love. Maybe that was part of her natural creative bent. Still, a lifetime commitment demanded more. "And are you sure about that yet?"

Kai sipped her wine. "That's a firm maybe."

"Sounds like you have a lot in common, at least." Marina was trying to be supportive, even though she knew it took more to make a marriage.

"We're good together, but this relationship has gone pretty fast. I mean, that's what I want, but..." Kai's voice trailed off.

"Can't you slow down and get to know each other better?" Yet, the first time Marina had met Stan, she had known he was the one. When you met the right one, you just knew. The problem was that the contenders dulled your judgment.

"I suppose I can." Kai gazed out at the ocean. "I've always

pictured myself having children. And at my age, I should get on with it."

Marina heard Kai's voice catch. "Is there a problem?"

"When we were at the season wrap party, everyone was congratulating us on our engagement. One of the actors was teasing us and asking how many children we'd have. It was a little corny, but we'd all had champagne and were having a good time. Dmitri has been married before, and he has three grown children. Still, I hoped we'd have at least one child together. When I said so, he replied that he was done having children."

"You've only been dating a month," Marina said. "He might change his mind."

"No, he's *done* done. As in, he had a vasectomy. I asked Dmitri when he was going to tell me that." Kai sighed. "He was insulted and asked me if I valued him more as a human being or as a baby-maker. I mean, that's usually a woman's argument, so what could I say? I brought up adoption, but he told me he doesn't want to raise any more children. Now I have to choose whether I want to marry Dmitri or try to meet someone else to have a child. It's not like there's a line around the block, either."

"I see," Marina replied softly. She couldn't imagine why any man wouldn't want to marry her beautiful sister, but she also knew that Kai's outgoing personality could be intimidating. Reaching out, she took Kai's hand. "I'm sorry you have to deal with this."

Kai brushed tears from her cheeks. "I'm pretty sure I love Dmitri, but I want to be a mother, too. Touring with the theater troupe has been a dream, but I want more. I want a family like you and Brooke. Why can't I ever get this right?"

Marina wanted to offer encouragement and paint a pretty picture for her sister, but they were too old for fairy tales. The truth was more important now. "Life doesn't always serve up exactly what we want, but it does serve up what we need to make us stronger and more resilient. In that, you have to trust."

Kai was quiet for a moment. "You mean, like our parents, and Stan?"

Marina touched her glass and nodded. "We've had our share of heartbreak. After Stan died, the thought of having one baby, let alone two, was overwhelming. But now I'm so grateful for my children. And you've been a wonderful aunt to Heather and Ethan. Sending them tickets to your performances and helping them learn to play the piano—they treasure those experiences."

"I will always embrace the family I have," Kai said. "But I still want to make a home of my own somewhere." She lifted her chin to the ocean breeze. "I know what I want."

"Then, as Ginger always says, go after it with unwavering fervor."

They leaned against one another, each offering solace to the other against the vicissitudes of life. Marina stroked Kai's hair. *Because that's what sisters do.*

That evening, after making dinner with Ginger and Kai and sharing a game of dominoes, Marina made her way back to her bedroom. As she was getting ready for bed, her phone chirped with a message from Gwen, her agent.

Urgent! I'm at a dinner party, can't talk, please call me first thing in the morning.

Marina slid under the soft duvet, wondering what Gwen might have to share. Part of her hoped that it was a job offer, while another part of her wondered if this entire turn of events was a signal from the universe that she needed to make a change in her life.

Just as she had advised Kai. *With unwavering fervor.*

Before Marina went to sleep, she resolved to find out. She wasn't a kid anymore, and if she planned to live life on her terms, she had to start now.

Chapter 8

*M*arina walked along the water's edge after sunrise, carrying her flip-flops and squishing the cool sand beneath her toes. White gulls with broad wingspans and pink legs soared overhead. Terns with carnelian bills dove into the sea, fishing for breakfast, while shorebirds skittered around her pecking at the sand. All around her, the sounds of nature—birdsong and rushing waves—helped calm her nerves. She clutched her phone, waiting for Gwen to answer.

"Marina, I'm so glad you called," Gwen said.

"I hope you have good news," Marina said, taking the positive track.

Gwen hesitated. "I'm sorry. I'm afraid it's not, but you need to know. Your old boss was at the dinner party I was attending."

Bracing herself, Marina asked Gwen to go on.

"Hal is blaming the downturn in ratings on your departure," Gwen said. "He gave Babe a try, but she couldn't tone down the cuteness and giggles enough to deliver the news. But before you start gloating, he's blaming you for breaking your employment contract. Hal is asserting that your action caused the sharp decline in ratings, resulting in damages. " She paused. "Marina, I thought he'd fired you. That was the word I'd originally gotten from him. Which is it?"

Marina's heart sank. "I beat him to it by a few seconds." *Damages.* Immediately, she realized what this meant. "He's planning to sue me, isn't he?"

"I'm afraid so," Gwen replied. "Hal was drowning in martinis and said more than he should have. I wouldn't expect a reference from him."

A cold wave rushed around Marina's calves, nearly knocking her off balance. "I suppose this is going to make my job search more difficult."

Gwen agreed. "Hal is telling everyone that you're difficult to work with. That's code for *don't hire her*. But I promise to do my best for you. I'm also referring this to my contract attorney to review."

While Gwen tried to reassure her, Marina could hear the doubt in her voice. With her former life crashing around her, it was even more evident to Marina that she had to take control and figure out an alternate path. But what?

Marina thanked Gwen and hung up. Facing the ocean, she gulped in sea air to clear her mind. Once she'd regained her composure, she turned around. On her way out of the house this morning, Ginger had mentioned that the farmers market would be in the village today. Marina could pick up fresh fruits and vegetables and see if there might be a fit for some of her homemade breads and cookies.

As Marina turned toward the village, she saw Ivy walking in the same direction and called out to her. Ivy hurried toward her.

"It's so good to see you. How's the ankle?" Ivy asked, hugging her.

"Much better," Marina replied. "The doc said it was a mild sprain, so as long as I don't overdo it, I should be okay now." She lifted the long coral skirt she wore, revealing the compression sock she was wearing. "I'm heading to the farmers market. Would you like to come along?"

"That's where I'm going, too," Ivy said. "We can walk slowly."

The two women fell into step together and began to chat about the old times in Summer Beach. That helped Marina take her mind off her conversation with Gwen.

As they neared the vendor tables laden with fresh lettuce, oranges, strawberries, tomatoes, and avocados, Marina felt her spirits lift. She loved the energy she felt here. But could she live here and make a go of it? She turned to Ivy. "Are you glad you returned to Summer Beach?"

Ivy smiled. "This time last year, my life was in utter turmoil. When I arrived here with Shelly, we faced a lot of challenges, but most of the bumps have been smoothed out now. Frankly, I wouldn't live anywhere else."

"Was it hard starting over by yourself?" Marina asked.

"Yes, but it helped to have Shelly and Poppy here," Ivy said. "What one of us couldn't figure out, another one could."

As they threaded their way through the vendor stands selecting produce, Marina considered this. "My sister Kai is spending a couple of weeks here. Last night, we had one of the best talks we've had in years. We're both at crossroads in life." Marina stopped to buy a basket of beautiful ripe strawberries, and the woman gave them some raspberries to sample.

"Mmm, I'll take a basket of these, too. And those blueberries." Marina was thinking about making berry tarts. The woman filled a bag for her.

"If you could do anything, do you know what you'd do?" Ivy asked.

Marina waved a hand around her. "I'd surround myself with great food and people having a good time. Like this." She paid for the berries, and they walked on.

"Does that mean you're thinking of changing careers?" Ivy asked.

"Maybe." An idea was taking shape in Marina's mind. She could take a stall here and build her clientele. "I'd like to test some recipes first. I used to work at cafes, but I'm a little rusty. At one, years ago, I began waiting tables and took over the kitchen when the cook quit and the owner was eight months pregnant."

"Guests are always asking for restaurant recommendations," Ivy said, nodding thoughtfully. "If you open a cafe, I can help by sending customers."

Marina's mind was whirring. When she stayed at the inn, she'd hobbled over one night and enjoyed a meet-up in the music room with other guests. "Would you mind if I contributed some hors d'oeuvres to your afternoon tea-and-wine events at the inn?"

"Guests would love that," Ivy said. "Though I would insist on paying you."

Marina started to assure Ivy that she didn't have to, but given her financial predicament, any income would be welcome. Besides, she'd have food costs. She'd already paid tuition for Heather and Ethan, but by September, she'd have another year to pay for.

"I'd appreciate that," Marina said.

Ivy smiled at her. "That's what friends are for. We support each other."

For the first time in years, excitement over a project raced through Marina. Opening a cafe would require a sizable financial commitment, which was worrisome.

"There's a lot to do first," Marina said. "Besides testing dishes and creating a menu, I'd have to find a location, get the proper permits, and figure out how I'm going to make money."

"Hi, ladies," Bennett said, approaching them.

"And here's the man who can point you in the right direction." Ivy smiled as Bennett leaned down and kissed her on the cheek. "Mr. Mayor, where would you advise a woman who is thinking of opening a cafe start?"

Bennett's face brightened. "Summer Beach could use another good restaurant. Have you ever operated one before?"

"No, but I worked in restaurants when I was younger," Marina said. "And Ginger taught me a lot about cooking."

Bennett grinned. "I heard she was good friends with Julia Child."

"That's Ginger for you." Marina thought about the cost and risk of opening a restaurant with no proof of concept. "The initial outlay and overhead of a cafe would be risky, but we have a patio at the Coral Cottage. Is there any law against me throwing some dinner parties there? Sort of a pop-up cafe in the evenings for paid guests."

Marina could just imagine sharing great food and good wine with guests and strolling on the beach afterward. Ginger could even regale them with her stories. However, if the parties were successful, she would need to expand the patio. It was only large enough for one table right now, and it was a little dark.

Bennett smoothed a hand over his chin in thought. "The state has new legislation concerning microenterprise home kitchen operations, along with temporary food service pop-ups. You'd have to apply for permits and follow guidelines, but this bill is intended to help people earn their way and entertain others. As long as there's no pushback from neighbors." Bennett and Ivy exchanged a look.

"Has that been a problem here in the past?" Marina asked.

"I won't gossip about my neighbors in public," Ivy said. "But it's something you should be prepared to address."

"Come over to City Hall, and we'll get you started," Bennett said.

"I will," Marina said, feeling more hopeful and empowered than she had in a long time. What had started as a terrible day with her call to Gwen was now brightening considerably.

Out of the corner of her eyes, she saw Ivy squeeze Bennett's hand in silent appreciation. The two of them seemed so much in love. And Marina? She had to deal with a creep like Grady.

Yet strangely, she could almost thank him for forcing a change in her life.

Almost.

"I've got a meeting at City Hall, but it's nice seeing you again," Bennett said to Marina. "And if you need any taste testers, you know where to find me."

Ivy winked at her, and Marina just smiled. She was glad to have rekindled their friendship.

As Marina and Ivy continued their shopping, Ivy introduced her to several people along the way. "This is Jen, who runs the hardware store, Nailed It. And Arthur, who knows all about antiques. You can find him at Antique Times, and his wife Nan works with Bennett at City Hall."

"So glad to meet you," Marina said, happily noting names and faces.

They waved at Imani, who also lived at the Seabreeze Inn while her house was being rebuilt after the Ridgetop fire. She introduced them to her son Jamir, a tall, lanky young man in the premed program at the University of California in San Diego.

Gilda was there with Pixie, the nervous Chihuahua. Marina had met the magazine writer at the Seabreeze Inn. Her ridgetop home restoration was also in progress and nearing completion.

As they were walking away, Marina spied Jack at Imani's flower stand. The two of them seemed to be having a serious conversation. Marina wondered what was going on—not that it was any of her business.

Ivy stopped to chat with more friends who had once lived at the Seabreeze Inn. "This is Celia and Tyler. They sponsor the music program in the schools."

"So nice to meet you," Celia said, swinging a cascade of straight, dark hair over her shoulder. "We all adore Ginger here. If you like to sail, we'd love to have you both out on the boat sometime. And be sure to stop by our craft at the upcoming Open House at the Marina. It's a fundraiser with a lot of food and decorations. We're serving my grandmother's secret Chinese recipes."

"I'd really like that," Marina said.

Tyler clasped his wife's hand. "Ivy, we have some friends who'd like to take one of your sunset suites for a few weeks this summer."

"You go ahead and talk," Marina said. "Ginger suggested I find a woman named Cookie before I leave."

Ivy stood on her tiptoes to see over the crowd. "There she is. The woman in the white apron."

Marina made her way toward the woman, who was the organizer of the farmers market.

"Hello, I'm Marina Moore, one of Ginger Delavie's granddaughters."

"They call me Cookie," the woman said, thrusting out a hand. "You probably don't remember me, but I watched you and your sisters grow up here. I had the bakery on Main Street for years."

"Oh yes," Marina said, remembering how Ginger used to take them to the bakery for soft, oatmeal-raisin and black-and-white cookies. Cookie had the same round, cheerful face she recalled. "Are you still running the bakery?"

"I'm retired, except for running the farmers market," Cookie replied. "Unfortunately, the bakery closed. An L.A. couple who bought the business thought they could be out-of-town operators." She shook her head. "They deposited one of their wild young kids there, and he gave away the shop. Wasn't long before it closed, but the town gained another ice cream parlor in its place."

"That's sad when it happens," Marina said. "I have an idea to start a cafe, but I'd like to build up my clientele in the community first. If I can start here, selling some of my baked items, preserves, and desserts, I can get to know people."

Cookie nodded thoughtfully. "Smart way to go about it. Are you using Ginger's famous recipes?"

"Quite a few, but some of my own, too." Marina couldn't wait to start brushing up on her skills and testing new ideas for dishes.

Having lived in San Francisco, she'd dined at many fine restaurants in the city and surrounding communities. She was a big fan of Alice Waters and her restaurant Chez Panisse in Berkeley, particularly her farm-to-table concept. To her, the seasonal vegetables were works of art. Simple, fresh, and flavorful. Except for a few vacation cooking classes Marina had taken at Rancho La Puerta spa in Mexico and a vineyard in France, she wasn't a trained chef or even a fancy cook. Still, she knew good food.

Summer Beach needed a place like that.

She needed that.

Cookie eyed her. "Don't go spending all your money at once on leasing and decorating a space." Frowning, she brushed her hands on her apron. "I run a community table you can join. An incubator of sorts. You're welcome to take a corner and see if you get interest." Her face softened. "Heard you had a rough time up in San Francisco. Bunch of bullies."

"That's over now." Marina blinked in dismay. Her meme had made its way even to the locals of Summer Beach. Despite this embarrassment and Hal's threats, she had to forge ahead. "I appreciate the spot. I'll get ready right away."

"Tuesdays and Fridays," Cookie said. "You'll meet everyone in town there."

Marina picked out a beautiful, leafy head of romaine

lettuce and added it to her bag. She bought a jar of local honey from another vendor. Soon, she'd be one of them.

Looking forward to that lifted her spirits.

As she made her way back to Ivy, she took a short cut behind the stands. Away from the crowd, Jack and Imani were in a deep discussion that looked private. She wasn't eavesdropping, but she overheard Imani asking a question. "Can you make arrangements for the young boy right away?"

Jack heaved a great sigh. "As my son, I'll have to."

A child. Marina wondered what was going on. Maybe Jack had been married before—or perhaps he still was.

Yet, Jack's personal life was of no concern to her. He was Ginger's summer renter, not hers.

Still, the conversation disturbed Marina. Why wouldn't Jack want to look after his child?

Chapter 9

*E*arly that morning, Jack left Scout in the cottage with plenty of food and water for the day. He'd asked Kai to let him out once or twice, and she assured him she'd take Scout to the beach for a run. With that arrangement made, Jack made the two-hour drive north to Los Angeles. On arrival, he parked in front of a near, two-story home in Santa Monica, an urban beachside community on the western edge of Los Angeles County.

Peering up at a pole that held several *No Parking* signs for various days of the week, hours, and overnight, Jack calculated that he was safe for two hours of parking. Doubling checking the address with the numbers tacked above the porch, he verified the house.

Vanessa's house.

A tall banana plant arched its waxy green leaves over the sunny yellow stucco house, and bright red geraniums spilled from a railing on the front porch. A young girl and boy on skateboards whizzed past on the quiet street, and as they did, the boy turned and grinned at him, flashing a peace sign. The pair stopped, flipped up their boards, and raced into the house next door. A *For Sale* sign was on the front lawn.

Drawing a deep breath, Jack paused to collect his thoughts.

If what Vanessa had told him was true, he was about to meet his son for the first time. Jack stroked his smooth chin. He'd shaved his stubble and put on his best jeans for the occasion, but he wondered if he should've dressed up more to show respect.

His gut churned with anxiety. He'd never felt so lost in facing a situation. At times like this, he wished he could call his mom or dad to ask for their advice, but they'd passed away a few years ago. More than ever, he appreciated what they had done for him as a child. Perhaps he'd call his sister in Texas later, but he could just imagine what she'd have to say. He'd call once he figured out what was going on.

Imani, whom he'd retained as counsel, had cautioned him to try not to lead with his heart, but to assess the situation first. Although that was part of his professional training, he wasn't sure he could do that.

"I can come with you," Imani told him when they'd met at the farmers market.

"No, I owe Vanessa the respect of meeting with her. As old friends and colleagues." *And intimate friends.* During that hazardous assignment, some reporters, including the two of them, had been caught in a crossfire of bullets. One reporter had been critically injured and airlifted to a hospital. After that, everyone was on edge. Crazy things happened in tense situations, and he and Vanessa had sought out each other for comfort. No one knew if that day would be their last.

"Ask her for the name of her attorney," Imani had advised. "If she's as organized as you recall, and she's thought this through to the point of contacting you, then she is probably getting her affairs in order. If she doesn't have a lawyer, that's a red flag."

Jack had held Vanessa in high esteem as a fellow reporter. He'd tried to call her several times, thinking that they might pursue a relationship. When she'd finally returned his call, she told him that what they'd had was over.

He'd followed her byline for a couple of years. Several times, he had commented on a story she'd written. Vanessa had been cordial, but she gave no indication that she wanted anything other than a professional relationship with him.

Now, the movement of a curtain in the window caught his eye. Reflexively, Jack reached for a cigarette in his breast pocket before he remembered he wasn't smoking anymore. If ever he needed a few puffs, now was that time. Instead, he gripped the steering wheel and drew another breath. In a matter of moments, his life would change. Jack got out of the car.

The front door cracked opened before he got to it. He barely recognized the thin woman who peered out.

"Jack." Vanessa smiled and held the door open.

She wore a vivid orange and yellow scarf around her head, its fringes falling over one shoulder. Gone was the luxuriant mane of shiny black hair he remembered, but he recognized the dark eyes that shone with intelligence and compassion.

"Vanessa." Jack stepped onto the porch, trying not to let his shock register on his face. "I'm glad you called."

Laughing softly, she said, "I've changed a lot, haven't I?"

His heart breaking for her, Jack shook his head. "You're as beautiful as you've always been."

She lifted a corner of her mouth. "Now I know you're lying, but thanks for the memory. Come in."

"Vanessa, I'm so sorry that you're sick." Feeling awkward, Jack went to hug her, but she stopped him with a touch of her fingertips to his chest.

"My immunity is quite low," she said, taking a step back. "Thanks for understanding."

"Oh, sure," Jack said, feeling like an idiot. "Are you feeling okay?" As soon as the words were out of his mouth, he wished he could take them back. "I'm sorry, I said the wrong thing, didn't I?"

Vanessa shook her head. "It's all right. This is tough on everyone." She paused. "In case you're wondering, what I have is a rare illness. It's termed an orphan disorder, which means it's so rare it's hardly worth studying, except for those who like oddities." She managed a wry smile. "I'm being facetious. I have wonderful physicians, nurses, and medical providers of every type. However, they're not magicians."

Jack had to ask. "Are you in much pain?"

"Only when the meds wear off," Vanessa replied. "And don't worry, I'm not contagious. My condition was exacerbated by years of smoking, so I fervently hope you stopped."

"Uh, yeah, I did." A cold sweat broke over him. *Why did this have to happen to her?* He wished he could trade places with her. Even though no one survived planet Earth, to go this way didn't seem fair to her or her son.

Jack stepped inside, glancing around a spacious living room furnished in bright, cheerful colors. Vanessa's taste was impeccable. A woven serape in red, blue, and green covered a cornflower-blue sofa. In a light-filled corner, a collection of ferns and orchids filled pottery painted in vivid colors. Large pieces of artwork hung above dark, carved furniture polished to a sheen. The faint aroma of orange oil hung in the air.

Following his gaze, Vanessa said, "My parents collected the work of Mexican artists—Frida Kahlo, Diego Rivera, Rufino Tamayo—long before it was fashionable. When my parents died, they left a large part of their collection to a museum near Wilshire and Brea. These are my favorite pieces. They're not as valuable as those from the master painters, but they have meaning for me. I'd like Leo to have them."

Jack was at a loss for words. He looked around, wondering where the boy was.

"Let's sit down," Vanessa said, looking tired. Reading

Jack's body language, she added, "Leo is next door playing with a friend."

Jack eased onto the sofa. "Does he have a skateboard?"

"Why, yes."

"I saw them when I arrived. Good-looking boy." They were wearing helmets, but what else could he say? "Vanessa, this is my fault. I should have been more careful, and I should have called you more—"

"Jack, let me talk." Vanessa reached for a glass of water and took a sip. "I knew what I was doing. Although I hadn't planned on getting pregnant just then, I was happy. I never wanted to get married, though I knew my mother would be thrilled with a grandchild. And she was."

That much Jack could understand. In their profession, many marriages had ended under the stress of too much travel and worry.

Vanessa pressed a hand to her heart and looked at a collection of framed photographs on a baby grand piano in the corner of the room. "Here are my mother and father, with Leo."

Jack rose to look at the photos. "They look like they were having a great time."

Vanessa nodded. "They spent a lot of time together, and Leo loved them so much. I wish they were still with us, but that's life." She smiled wistfully. "I'm so glad you came. I wasn't sure that you would understand."

Jack joined her again, sitting in a chair near her, but being mindful of keeping a safe distance. "Seeing you like this...you don't have to explain. We both know what happened back then."

Vanessa took another drink of water. "Let's be honest. We were never in love, although I always respected you. I could have—and probably should have—told you about Leo, but my parents were very traditional. To make it easy on everyone, I told them I didn't know who Leo's father was. I lied because I refused to be forced into a marriage."

"But, Vanessa," Jack began.

She held up her hand. "Had my father known who you were, I can't imagine what he might have done with that anger. Papa was a good man, but he wasn't perfect. Especially when it came to defending my honor. Nothing good could have come from revealing that you were the father."

Jack nodded. "Okay, I can see that." He had to be honest with himself, too. "Vanessa, if you'd told me, I would have done the right thing. Married you, supported you, whatever you wanted."

"I got what I wanted," she said, lifting her chin in defiance. "I didn't need your money, and I didn't want to be married to anyone. No offense. For me, marriage simply wasn't necessary. My grandmother inherited a large ranch from a 19th-century Mexican land grant. The original hacienda still stands on the property as a historical monument to the time that California was part of our neighbor to the south. My grandparents sold parcels over many years and put the funds in trust. I've been well provided for, as Leo will be. I'm not asking you to support him. I'm only asking you to step into his life now."

Her words chipped away at Jack's masculine view of himself. Yet, she had a point. "I guess you didn't need rescuing."

Vanessa smiled. "My mother might have liked that, and I think she would have liked you, too. Mama always dreamed of a lavish wedding in the church for me. Having a child out of wedlock was hard enough, but I was not going to compromise my principles or what I wanted."

Wiping a tear from the corner of her eye, Vanessa paused for a breath, and then went on. "That makes Papa sound terrible, and he wasn't really. My parents were proud people, and they were worried about me. But they were still clinging to the past."

"I understand," Jack said quietly. The world around them had changed so quickly, and Vanessa was their precious daughter, their future. He might not agree with her on everything, but he respected her views.

"I hope you do," she said, stretching her fingertips toward his sleeve. "As a teenager, I rebelled against tradition. When I discovered I was pregnant, I thought it was time for me to do something for them. And that was to give them the grandchild they'd always wanted. They'd longed for a large family, but after I was born, my mother couldn't have more children. I was their hope to continue the family."

Vanessa paused and blinked back tears. "I'm sorry. I've always felt so guilty about keeping Leo from you. I thought I was independent, but now I realize we all have a greater connection. And we need that."

"Hey, it's okay," Jack said. He spied a box of tissues and handed it to her. "That's all in the past. You did what you thought was right at the time," he said, though it pained him to say that. He would have liked to have had the opportunity to be in Leo's young life. But it was too late to argue.

"I'm not saying what I did was right by you or Leo. I see that now. And that's why I contacted you. Maybe it's not too late to set things right."

Jack considered this. Setting things right would upset his life, but a little boy's life—no, *his son's* life and emotional well-being—was at stake.

She shook her head through her tears. "After my parents died, I could have called you. But by then, I didn't know what to say, and I thought you'd be upset. Or worse, that you might not care. So, I did nothing. I was chicken."

Jack shook his head sharply. "I'd never use that word to describe you. What you did was incredibly brave and thoughtful.

I was just some guy, but you tried to spare your parents and raise a child alone." Jack couldn't deny that he felt a twinge of male-ego resentment, but given the circumstances, he was a big boy. And, unlike the courageous women who sat before him, he'd survive.

"Thank you for saying that." She turned her face up to his. "I told you it was complicated."

The sound of children's laughter floated through an open window.

"Sounds like the kids are in the backyard," Vanessa said, nodding toward a pair of French doors on the side of the house. She pushed herself up and walked to the door. "Leo has grown so much in the last year."

Jack joined her. Together, they gazed out, watching the children through an old chain link fence.

"Denise keeps the hedges trimmed low on their side so I can watch Leo play on the swing set with Samantha. Denise and John have been such good neighbors."

"Are you close?"

"They moved in the year after Leo was born, so our children have grown up together. He's going to miss Samantha." Vanessa touched the glass. "The tech company John works for has been acquired, so they're moving to Oregon at the end of the year."

"About Leo," Jack began, then hesitated. He didn't want to rush her, but he wanted to know what she expected of him.

Vanessa looked up at him, her expressive, dark brown eyes looming large in her thin face. "He's your son, Jack. You have a decision to make, but I can't make it for you."

Imani's advice floated to mind. He had to know what her options were. "But if I don't—"

"Mom, watch this," Leo called out.

"I'm watching, *mi hijo*," she said, lifting her voice, though it sounded strained. Yet she smiled bravely and waved, beaming at her son.

Leo pumped hard on the swing set, his brown hair ruffling

in the wind, and then jumped off the swing, ending in a somersault and tumbling across the yard. He popped up, grinning. "Did it! Mom, did you see that?"

"I saw it, honey. That was great." Vanessa clapped her hands and gave him a thumbs up. As she did, she wavered a little on her feet.

Standing behind Vanessa, Jack slid his hand under her forearm for support. She clutched his arm and looked up. "Thanks. Sometimes I'm a little wobbly on my feet."

"Maybe if you get some rest, you'll regain your strength," Jack said. "You could still beat this. There are a lot of new drugs…" He stopped when he saw the look in her eyes.

"I'm not one to give up, but I know when I'm beaten. I've had surgery and experimental drug treatments. My doctor advised me to organize my affairs and be comfortable for as long as I can. And when the time comes, and the pain is too great, I'll go into hospice."

Jack wiped his eyes and nodded. She had no other options. "I'll do whatever you want."

"I know what I'd like for Leo," Vanessa said softly. "And I know it's an awfully big ask. But it's your decision to make."

Leo raced to the chain-link fence and stuck in the toes of his athletic shoes, hoisting himself up. "Samantha's mom is calling her for dinner."

Vanessa tilted her chin up. "Come on home then. I have a friend I want you to meet. Don't forget your skateboard."

While Leo rushed to get his board, Vanessa turned to Jack and pressed her hands against his chest. Wordlessly, Jack brought his arms around her, and she shivered against him.

"I haven't been held like this in so long," she said. With a soft chuckle, she added. "Just don't get any ideas again."

Gently rubbing Vanessa's back in comfort, Jack felt her fragile bones protruding beneath the large linen shirt she wore. That shirt had probably once fit her, he realized. The magnitude of her situation hit him, and he swallowed hard.

"Don't worry about your son," Jack said, and then corrected himself. "*Our* son. I want you to enjoy the time you have left with him." He helped her back to the sofa, and as she was getting settled, Leo burst in with his skateboard under one arm, and a tin foil-covered Pyrex dish in the other.

"Samantha's mom sent spaghetti tonight," Leo said.

"Put it in the kitchen, and then come back. I want you to meet…" Vanessa shrugged. Leo had already dashed into the kitchen.

Jack had to admire the kid's energy. At ten years old, the boy seemed tall for his age. Leo was solid, with a wavy flop of brown hair.

Like his, Jack realized. *His son*. His hand flew to his breast pocket again before he caught himself. He glanced at Vanessa and saw her shallow breaths.

Sobered, Jack let his hand fall. He rubbed his fingertips together to calm his nerves.

Leo rushed back into the living room and sat next to his mother. "Hi," he said to Jack.

Vanessa hugged her son close. "This is an old friend of mine. Jack Ventana. He's a reporter, and we worked together once."

"Cool," Leo said, sticking his hand out.

Shaking his son's hand, Jack grinned. "You've got a good grip there. Saw you on your skateboard. Pretty smooth."

"Thanks," Leo said, pushing his hair back from his face.

Jack got a good look at the boy's face. Leo had Vanessa's dark brown eyes, but other than that, Jack could have been looking at a picture of himself at that age. He shot a look at Vanessa, and she nodded. She'd been raising a miniature replica of Jack. Nearly overwhelmed, Jack fumbled for a moment.

"Maybe you can stay for supper," Vanessa said to Jack. "Denise always sends plenty."

"Her meatballs are really good," Leo said, leaning his head on his mother's shoulder.

"Did Lupita leave a salad in the refrigerator?" she asked.

"Yeah, I saw it in there," Leo said. "Want me to set the table?"

"I can help you with that," Jack said, and Leo looked pleased.

Vanessa nodded. "Wash up first, *mi hijo*."

Leo hugged his mother before jumping from the sofa and heading down the hallway.

Jack watched him go, still in awe that he had a son. He fumbled for the right words, yet mere words were inadequate for the magnitude of what he'd just experienced. Swallowing hard against his emotion, he simply said, "He seems like a good kid."

"He's the best."

At supper, Jack sat across from Leo, still marveling at the boy's existence and noticing every little detail about him. He also saw that Vanessa couldn't eat much, and Leo doted on her. Jack could hardly keep his emotions reined in, and he fought against a lump in his throat throughout the meal.

"Jack, I'd sure like to see Summer Beach again," Vanessa said. "It's one of my favorite little beach towns. The waves for surfing are excellent." She clasped Leo's hand. "Since you want to try that, I think we should go for a visit soon."

Leo's smooth forehead wrinkled with concern. "We don't have to, Mom."

"I want to," Vanessa said, speaking with urgency. "I want this for you. And don't worry, I'll be fine for a short trip."

Jack wasn't as confident. He could see the pain etched on Vanessa's face, though she tried not to show it. As Vanessa suppressed a yawn, he rose from the table. "Leo, I'll wash the dishes if you want to help your mom. It's getting late."

Vanessa shook her head. "I can manage just fine. You two visit in the kitchen."

After Jack helped Vanessa from the table, he carried the dishes into the kitchen.

Leo tagged behind him with condiments, which he put into the refrigerator. Perching on a stool by the counter, Leo studied Jack. "You've known my mom for a while, right?"

"I have, and I'm really sorry she's so sick." Jack scraped food from the plates into the trash with slow, measured movements, focusing instead on Leo.

The boy jerked his foot back and forth in a nervous twitch. "Mom doesn't know about this, but I heard her talking on the phone one day. I'd forgotten the phone she gave me to carry, so I came back for it. She kept mentioning your name."

Jack grinned with studied nonchalance. "Hope it wasn't too bad."

"She was talking about *hospice*." Leo spat out the word. "I know what that is. Are you here to take her away from me now? Tonight?"

Leo's words were like a knife in the gut. Jack put down a plate, desperately seeking the right words, but there were none. Not in a situation like this.

"Not tonight," he said. "But you're a smart young man, and I think you know what's ahead at some point."

Leo ducked his head and nodded. His little face turned red, and Jack could tell the boy had bottled up his emotions. Without hesitation, Jack held his arms out to his son.

Looking confused, Leo scooted off the stool. But instead of stepping into Jack's arms for comfort, the boy backed out of the kitchen, his face contorted with anger and grief. "No! I won't let you take her. This is our home, and this is where we're staying. Get out!" He turned and ran, slamming the door behind him.

Jack finished washing the dishes and walked in the direction of the bedrooms. Tapping on a door, he waited for a response. He eased open the door.

Vanessa was asleep on the bed. Leo was right beside her, also asleep.

He didn't have the heart to wake her. Instead, he closed the door and let himself out. His heart ached for what Vanessa and Leo were going through.

At his car, Jack ripped a parking ticket from his windshield and got inside. Just when he'd thought that he and Leo were getting along well, Leo had snapped. The poor kid was under unimaginable stress.

A whirlwind of thoughts nagged Jack. Was he the best option for Leo? The boy would need a lot of grief counseling. As Jack started his car, he glanced back at the house.

Even if he was ready to take Leo into his life, would Leo ever accept him?

Chapter 10

"You're giving up your apartment?" Kai asked.

"With the twins in college, I don't need as much room," Marina said, strolling beside her sister on the dock. She still wore her ankle sock, but the sprain was much improved.

Ivy and Bennett had invited them for the Open House at the Marina day, a fundraiser to support her friend Celia's school music program. Marina had braided her sister's thick blond hair, and they'd both put on tank tops and shorts to enjoy the sunshine.

"I've been renting forever," Marina said, pausing by a boat owner selling fruit smoothies. "Housing prices rose so much faster than my income in San Francisco that I could never afford to buy in the city. My agent doubts if she can find work for me there, and I have to stretch my savings to pay college tuition."

Kai slung her arm around Marina's shoulder. "That's a smart move. But won't you miss San Francisco?"

"The kids and I had great times there," Marina said. "We often ate clam chowder overlooking the bay or explored the botanical gardens in Golden Gate Park. It was such fun riding the cable cars to Union Square on the weekends. And we loved taking the ferry to Sausalito for the art festival. But that time has passed." She felt a twinge of regret, but she had to be practical.

Marina and Kai waited in a short line to buy smoothies, admiring boats decorated with different themes. This boat owner was displaying vintage surfboards and blasting Beach Boys music. On another, a man was playing a jazz saxophone and offering New Orleans-style jambalaya. And at the end of the dock, Bennett's boat was adorned with Hawaiian flowers and tiki torches.

While they waited, Kai hummed "Let It Go," a song from *Frozen*. When it was their turn, Marina made a donation for two icy-cold, fruit smoothies. She was enjoying the sunshine and the slower pace of Summer Beach.

"Ginger has managed to live here all these years," Kai said, sipping her mango smoothie.

"She never really worked in Summer Beach, though," Marina pointed out. "She left on assignments all the time. But next week, I'm going to make my debut at the farmers market."

"Oh my gosh," Kai said, sipping her smoothie. "You have to make that chocolate-cinnamon bread you made the other day."

"And a lot more," Marina replied.

Ahead, their grandmother stood by the mayor's sleek vintage boat, waving to them. Ginger was chatting with Ivy, and Scout sat beside her. Two children were petting the dog. A crowd of people was milling around.

"It is just me, or is that dog grinning?" Marina asked.

"Like its owner," Kai replied, laughing. "Have you ever noticed how many dogs look like their owners?"

"Oh, stop," Marina said, though she chuckled along with her sister. "I wonder where Jack is? He's been staying in his cottage a lot. Except for walking Scout in the mornings."

Kai shot her a swift glance. "Look who's keeping an eye on the cute tenant. I think you're interested in him."

"Hardly." Marina poked her sister in the ribs. "He's a writer, so that means he's hard at work."

"Welcome to the luau," Ivy said, calling them over. "We're grilling sliced pineapple and peaches with your choice of coconut ice cream or a side of shave ice." She was wearing a Hawaiian sarong with a flower lei.

"Sounds yummy," Kai said, pulling Marina toward the party.

"Leilani and Roy are the real hosts," Bennett said, who was working the grill. "I'm just the grill master."

Strains of "Somewhere Over the Rainbow" sung by Hawaii's beloved Iz, Israel Kamakawiwoʻole, filled the air, and Kai began singing along. Marina laughed and joined in. Soon, everyone was singing.

Bennett flourished a pair of tongs. "We also have some shrimp on the barbie with your choice of dipping sauces: cilantro and lime, sweet-and-smoky barbecue, sesame soy sauce. Homemade ice cream, too. Leilani's mother's recipes."

Ivy introduced Leilani and Roy. Marina learned they spent part of the winter at Leilani's family home in Kauai.

"So you're Ginger's granddaughter," Leilani said with a smile. "We're happy to meet you. We own The Hidden Garden in the village. I hope Ginger's garden is doing well now."

"As long as we can keep Mr. Happy Face out of it," Marina said, motioning toward Scout.

Another couple Marina didn't know stepped to one side. Behind them, she saw Jack kneeling by a little boy who looked just like him, and a little girl. She felt curiously drawn to Jack, but a lot of women probably were. Next to them was a lovely woman in a bright turban sitting in a wheelchair.

Jack glanced up at her.

"Hi, Jack. Great event." Marina hadn't seen much of him

since they'd replanted the garden together. Recalling the conversation she'd overheard between Jack and Imani at the farmers market, she smiled. "Is this your son?"

A strange expression crossed Jack's face that she couldn't read. His face flushed and he seemed stricken.

"Uh, this is Leo and Samantha," he managed to say. "And this is Leo's mother, Vanessa."

Oblivious to his reaction, the children looked up at her. "Hi," they said.

The woman beside him in a wheelchair smiled weakly at her.

"It's so nice to meet you," Marina said.

"And you, too," Vanessa said. "The children are having such a wonderful time."

A couple she didn't know turned around. "Samantha is ours," the woman said, smiling. "I'm Denise, and this is John."

"How do you do?" John shook hands with Marina and Kai. "Vanessa and Leo are our neighbors. We're all visiting from Santa Monica. And since we're staying at the Seabreeze Inn, Ivy forced us to come."

"How could we resist?" Denise said, tucking her arm through her husband's. "I've been wondering why we don't live here."

"And this is Scout," Leo said, petting Scout, who was still lapping up the attention. "I wish I had a dog like this." He flung his arms around the dog and buried his face into the fur behind Scout's ears. Scout sat patiently, nuzzling the boy.

"We know Scout," Marina said. "He's famous here."

"Not always for the right reasons," Jack said. "Have you seen the garden? The tomato plants have taken off."

They spoke a little about the sweet pepper and cucumber plants, while Kai made a donation and came back with a plate laden with grilled shrimp, peaches, and pineapple.

"You have to try the pineapple with the sauces," Kai said. "Oh my gosh, this is delicious."

Marina dipped a slice of warm pineapple into one of the sauces. The smoky flavor with the natural fruit sweetness, combined with tart lime and cilantro, was a perfect blend. "Appetizer or dessert?" she mused.

"Or a side dish with barbecued vegetables and meats," Leilani said. "Pineapple is pretty versatile. We prepare it a lot of different ways in Hawaii."

"Delicious," Marina said. "How do you manage to leave your business in the winter?"

"We just hang up a sign," Leilani said. "We do a brisk business with poinsettias at the end of the year, and then we close until the first of March. If we have plants left, we hire high schoolers from the garden club to care for the plants until we return." She nodded toward Leo and Samantha. "Our kids are grown now, but we used to enroll them for the winter in Kauai. They loved it and learned a lot from the experience. We work to live the life we want."

"Rather than living to work," Marina added.

Holding a cup of Hawaiian shave ice, Ginger turned around. "And what have I been telling you?"

"I'm beginning to understand," Marina said. People in Summer Beach had a different outlook on life. The pace was beach-slow, but more than that, the locals she'd met seemed to love what they did. Somehow, they made it work in the modern world.

"Maybe we should spend the summer here," Denise said.

"That's a thought." John put his arm around his wife. "I bet I could do a lot of work remotely, and it's just a couple of hours away if I have to go in for a meeting."

Their little girl's face lit. "Could we? And could Leo come, too?"

Leo's mother ruffled his hair. "I think that would work out well. I like it here a lot, too." She mouthed a silent *thank you* to Denise, who nodded.

Marina detected an undercurrent of a story between them.

Denise looked excited. "Ivy, is it possible to rent our rooms for the entire summer?"

"I'm sorry, we're really booked this year," Ivy said. "But you can find summer rentals in town. Bennett can help you with that. He has a real estate license, so when he's not mayoring, he helps people with their property."

Standing by the grill, Bennett waved his tongs again. "Happy to help," he said. "Once school is out, places rent fast. If you want to see some places this weekend, I can probably arrange it."

"School is almost finished for the year," Denise said. "We'd better look now."

Marina listened, sensing an urgency behind Denise's words, but she couldn't quite place why. Maybe, like so many other people, they were burned out and needed to get away.

"I hope to see more of you all then," Marina said to Denise and Vanessa. "Jack is renting the guest cottage on my grandmother's property, so when Leo and Samantha visit Scout, we could have hors d'oeuvres on the patio."

"We'd like that," Vanessa said, taking Denise's hand.

The two women seemed like very good friends who shared a special bond. Marina could see that Vanessa wasn't well, and her heart went out to her.

"Mom, can I have some more fruit?" Leo asked. "This is really good."

Vanessa nodded and reached for her purse.

"I'll get it," Marina said. She made her way to Bennett's grill and dropped some money inside the donation jar. There was something about that little boy that tugged at her heart. He was crazy about his mother, of course, but it was more than that. Marina had brought up two children, and she recognized the sweet vulnerability in Leo.

Bennett looked up at her. "Seconds?"

"For Leo."

Bennett nodded and piled the fruit high on the plate for the boy.

When Marina brought the plate of grilled peaches and pineapple back for Leo, the boy's eyes widened with delight. He thanked her with a hug and offered the plate to his mother, who refused, and to his friend Samantha. The two children scrambled inside the boat—with help from Jack— where they sat sharing their sweet bounty.

"I just love kids at that age," Marina said, watching Leo and Samantha. Feeling Jack's eyes on her, she turned to him and saw deep compassion etched on his face. She could have fallen for him right then, but instead, she glanced away. Grady had done that to her, too. He'd been acting, though she hadn't known it at the time. At the moment, she didn't trust herself to tell the difference.

"Ready to go?" Marina asked Kai, feeling a little nervous.

Kai made a face. "You've got to be kidding. This is a great party." Then, noticing Jack, Kai nodded. "I think I see your problem. But please stay. If you do, I'll go with you to San Francisco to help you pack your place."

Marina couldn't turn down an offer like that. "Next weekend?"

"I promise."

"You're on," Marina said. "I think I'm ready for a shave ice."

Kai tugged her elbow and pointed across to the bow of the boat. "Shelly's mixing her special Sea Breezes. Ask for the fully-loaded variety. Only for friends and family. She told me the password is *woo-hoo*. Let's make a nice donation. It's for a good cause, right?"

"Good thing we're walking." Marina had to laugh at Kai. Her sister and Shelly were about the same age, and they'd hit it off pretty well. They'd met at Java Beach, and Shelly had invited Kai to her morning yoga class.

After Shelly served them cocktails, Marina found a spot in the cabin to sit and elevate her ankle while she watched the crowd. Everyone was having a good time, and she was glad she'd stayed.

Ginger ducked inside the cabin and sat across from her. "Ah-ha, this is where you're hiding."

"Still recuperating," Marina said, sipping her icy drink.

"Kai tells me you're putting your household in storage next weekend."

"That's right."

Ginger leaned forward on her knees. "Good to see you reducing your overhead and committing to a course of action. What's your plan?"

As usual, Ginger was direct.

"I thought I'd start small and gain a clientele at the farmers market," Marina said. "If it's okay with you, I could organize pop-up dinners this summer on the little patio overlooking the beach. When I have enough saved, I could lease space and open a restaurant. I've already talked to Bennett about getting the right permits and licenses. Would you mind? It would just be for the summer. By then, I should know if I have a concept that will fly."

Ginger tapped her fingertips together, ruminating over the idea. "This old cottage was my wedding gift from Bertrand, and we promised each other that we would keep it for our children and grandchildren and their children."

As the boat rocked softly in its harbor, Marina put her hand on Ginger's shoulder. "The cottage means a lot to me, too. And to Heather and Ethan, and Brooke's boys, even if they don't express their feelings often."

Ginger smoothed her hand over Marina's and smiled. "It's funny you should ask about putting on dinners. You might not know this, but after befriending Julia Child, I often dreamed of having a little cafe myself. Summer Beach is a perfect spot, though, at my age, I'm enjoying my freedom."

Marina listened, wondering where her grandmother was going with this. She could always look around and find another place. Maybe at the Seabreeze Inn. She could talk to Ivy and Shelly.

Ginger's eyes sparkled. "I like that you're taking action. Maybe my dream should be yours to exploit. You'd have to figure out your costs, but you're clearly determined. I say, do it. Use the cottage for your dinners."

Marina was thrilled to think of having events there. Gazing from the boat, she spied the cottage from a new vantage point. "Seriously?"

A smile touched Ginger's lips. "Why not? I could use a little more company. Stay here and give it a go."

"I'd love to do that," Marina cried, hugging her grand-mother. "I can just see it, filled with fairy lights and flowers. We'd open just in the evening. Ivy and Shelly will send guests my way, and Ivy wants to buy appetizers for their tea-and-wine hour."

"I think we're all going to have a grand time with these parties," Ginger said. "But, we need a larger patio."

"I've been giving that some thought. Ivy mentioned a contractor who is rebuilding many of the damaged or destroyed homes on the ridgetop. I'll ask her for his name."

Ginger nodded. "Might be costly, though."

"Not the way I'm thinking. If the contractor could handle the framework and electrical, I think we can do a lot of the finish work. I could ask Brooke's boys to help. What I'd save from giving up my apartment would easily pay for this."

"Good ideas." Ginger frowned. "But there's one big condition."

"Anything."

A smile crept onto Ginger's face. "You have to name a dish after me."

Marina sat back and folded her arms. "Only if I can use some of your recipes."

"Deal," Ginger said, and they shook on it. "As long as they're not Julia's recipes. Though I changed many of those," she added with a mischievous grin.

For the first time in years, a new sense of freedom filled Marina. She loved having a new project to direct. This was surely going to be a summer to remember.

On the dock, she could hear Jack calling for Scout, and it made her smile. Even Jack seemed less irritating now. Besides, after the summer was over, he'd be on his way somewhere else, and she'd be free of the awkward feelings that seemed to bubble up whenever he was around.

Those feelings meant nothing, she told herself. Because of Grady, she'd learned that she was a lousy judge of character when it came to men.

She was officially retiring from dating. Never again.

Chapter 11

"Is this it?" Marina asked as she whipped her turquoise Mini Cooper into the small parking lot for the Summer Beach City Hall. The convertible top was down, and Ivy sat beside her.

"I love this little car you have," Ivy said. "I have an old vintage Chevy that Bennett usually keeps in tip-top shape for me, but today that machine decided it was taking the day off. I hope it's just the battery."

"Can't blame it. I sometimes wonder how anyone gets motivated to work at the beach," Marina said.

Ivy tucked her highlighted, wavy brown hair behind an ear and laughed. "If you love what you do—"

"You'll never work a day in your life." Marina smiled at her old friend. "I love that quote."

From their vantage point on the top of a hill, Marina could see boats nestled in the marina, and surfers cruising waves that rolled endlessly toward the shoreline.

This morning, Marina had met Ivy and Shelly at the Seabreeze Inn to discuss tasting trays for their daily events that brought their guests together every afternoon.

"Are you sure Mitch won't feel like I'm moving in on his

business?" Marina asked.

"He supplies the cookies, but his main reason for showing up every day is to see Shelly." Ivy chuckled. "They've been dating for a while now. Our guests will love finding out about your pop-up dinners. I think you're going to be surprised."

"Shelly and Mitch seem like a good couple," Marina said. Shelly had a quirky, yoga-bohemian style, which meshed well with Mitch's relaxed surfer vibe. "Mitch is fortunate to do what he loves."

"Surfing in the morning when the waves are good, then making coffee and chit-chatting with visitors and locals." Ivy picked up her purse. "It's a good life for Shelly, too. Aside from running the inn with Poppy and me, she films lifestyle videos. Over the last year, her vlog morphed from New York chic to a casual beach vibe. Her followers love it. And she covers the landscaping she manages at the inn. She studied horticulture in college."

"The inn is lovely," Marina said. "Did it take you long to renovate it?"

"It's a work in progress," Ivy said as they got out of the car. "We're still working on the lower level, which was closed up for years."

They started toward the City Hall doors. "What do you do for fun around here?" Marina asked.

"There's always something to do," Ivy replied, her lacy turquoise top fluttering in the breeze. "A big Independence Day celebration, plenty of beach barbecues. In between caring for guests and working on the inn, I manage to squeeze in a little painting, which is my passion. We hosted an art show last year that proved popular, so we'll do that again this year."

"Not much has changed here since I was a kid," Marina said. "I wonder if I had stayed how I would have felt about Summer Beach."

Over the years, Marina had brought the twins here when she could, but Ginger usually visited them in San Francisco.

Since Marina had to work, it was easier. Her children had probably spent more time in Summer Beach than she had over the years. After a few weeks, they'd return with their little sunburned noses and happy faces. She'd often wished she could join them. And now, here she was. Possibly forever.

The sun was warm on Marina's shoulders. Although she missed San Francisco at times, she didn't miss the chill that often crept in from the sea, shrouding even summer days with coastal fog. They walked past purple bougainvillea and an assortment of desert-scape plants toward the mid-century modern building.

Shading her eyes, Marina said, "Looks like vintage California architecture."

"Wait until you see inside," Ivy said.

As Marina stepped inside the light-filled structure, the high ceiling drew her gaze. Sunlight spilled through the clerestory windows. A wall of plate glass windows looked out over the bay and beyond. And hung across the edge of the reception desk was a banner that read, *Life is Better in Summer Beach.*

Marina sure hoped so.

A woman's voice rang out ahead. "Good morning, it's a glorious day in Summer Beach. May I help you, hon?"

Ivy ducked out from behind Marina. "Good morning, Nan. Have you met Marina?"

The fifty-ish woman with a crop of red curls burst into a sweet smile. "Why, I'll be. My husband Arthur and I were just talking about you at Java Beach this morning. Welcome to Summer Beach, hon."

Ivy touched the edge of the reception desk, pausing to smell a vase full of garden roses as she concealed a little smile. "Word travels fast in a small town."

Inwardly, Marina winced. The local gossip wire would take some getting used to, but it also meant that news about her baked goods and pop-up dinners would also spread quickly. That was good *and* bad. She couldn't afford to make mistakes here.

"It's hard to believe that it was just a year ago when I was standing right here, asking for a business license," Ivy said.

"That's why I'm here," Marina said to Nan.

"Well, I thought you might be," Nan said, her curls shimmying as she spoke. She leaned in and lowered her voice to a conspiratorial whisper. "Mitch tells me you've got some of Ginger's recipes—the ones she wouldn't share with him. She's our local lady of mystery, that Ginger."

"I don't know if that's true," Marina said. "But Ginger made me promise to name a dish after her."

"Why, you should name dishes after all the locals," Nan said, her eyes dancing with delight. "Wouldn't that be fun?"

"Maybe once I meet them," Marina replied, trying to remain noncommittal. "Where do I go to get a business license?"

"Jim Boz can help you with that. He handles all matters in Planning and Zoning, and business licenses when he's not busy." Nan pulled out a form from a folder and snapped it onto a clipboard. "Fill this out, and walk right over there." She motioned toward a doorway. "I'll let Boz know you're here. And Ivy, is Bennett expecting you?"

"He is, but don't disturb him if he's busy. I'll get Marina started first."

"Nice to meet you, Nan." Marina started toward the doorway, weaving past a robust rubber plant that was reaching toward the light.

"Nan's a real sweetheart," Ivy whispered. "She might gossip a little too much, but she means no harm."

"Unlike the one I used to work with," Marina said, thinking of Babe Barstow, celebrity gossip queen. If she had some news she could pierce you with, so much the better. But now, that was in the past.

"Are you missing your old life yet?" Ivy asked.

"Sometimes. I love San Francisco, but this is feeling more like home every day. Ginger wants me to stay, and I have to think about her, too. She's not getting any younger, even though she's still a force. Are your parents nearby?"

"They are, and they're still active, sailing and throwing parties every chance they get. Shelly and I have twin brothers here, and between them, they have a slew of children. Though all the kids are grown now."

"And how are your two girls doing?"

"Good. The older one is an actress on the east coast, though she sometimes shoots commercials here. A few months ago, she shot a pilot show, but her real love is theater." Ivy shook her head. "My younger daughter is commuting to the university in San Diego for her last year. It was an effort to get her here."

"It's not always easy." Marina thought about her children. Heather had called to say that Ethan had failed an important exam and skipped a few classes afterward to play golf. Marina had been trying to get through to him, but he wasn't answering her calls.

Scanning the application, Marina quickly filled it out while Ivy answered a few texts on her phone. When Marina finished, she turned to Ivy. "Ginger and I were talking about expanding the patio. You mentioned a good contractor who's been rebuilding the homes on the ridgetop. I wonder if he'd have time for a simple job."

"Axe has more than one crew, and he does small jobs, too," Ivy said, scrolling through her address book. "I'll give you his number."

"Axe?" Marina raised her eyebrows. "Should I be worried?"

Ivy laughed. "That's a nickname. Axel Woodson is an exceptionally nice guy from Montana."

As Marina tapped in a number for Axe, a buff, youngish-looking man with a thick head of salt-and-pepper hair appeared at the counter.

"Howdy, ladies. What can I do for you?"

"This is Jim Boz," Ivy said, introducing them. "Marina is one of Ginger's granddaughters."

"From San Francisco, I understand."

"That's right," Marina said. "Bennett suggested I start here for permits. I'd like to sell my homemade food at the farmers market and have pop-up dinners at Ginger's cottage. Maybe a few times a week. After the concept is proven, I'd like to expand as a cafe."

"You're smart to ease into that." Boz shook his head. "Rough times for restaurants right now in this town."

"Why is that?" Marina asked.

"Our neighboring community approved some major chain restaurants last year," Boz said. "They're advertising heavily and offering deals that our local restaurants can't match. Though their food isn't nearly as good, the big boys have brand recognition. Tourists flock there, leaving our restaurants empty."

Ivy nodded in agreement. "At the inn, we refer people to local cafes and diners, but the chain deals are pretty attractive. Still, visitors can get far better meals at local restaurants."

"It's herd mentality," Boz added. "It's a big problem this year. And I don't know if many of our local folks can hang on much longer. The chains are already sniffing around here to buy or lease property from those that fail."

Marina found this disturbing. "That would destroy part of what makes Summer Beach unique."

"That's the problem," Boz said. "Besides hurting a lot of our local people. Java Beach, the Starfish Cafe, Rosa's fish taco stand. These are just a few that have seen business decline."

"Sounds like my timing could be better," Marina said. All the more reason to start small, she decided. The shift in the market was concerning, not only for her but also for local restaurateurs and their clientele. She wondered what could be done about it.

"I see that Nan got you started with the business license." Boz pulled out another sheaf of forms. "We'll have to do an onsite inspection. How's tomorrow?"

"Wow, so soon." Immediately, Marina thought about how much cleaning she'd have to do. Not that the kitchen was dirty, but would they look behind the refrigerator? Or old Myrtle, the vintage red oven?

Boz arched an eyebrow. "Any problem with that?"

From the tone of his voice, she could tell he already had questions. "Will you perform the inspection?"

Boz clicked his pen a couple of times. "We have a contract vendor who'll meet you at the house. I know where the cottage is, but she might not. Address?"

"Oh, right," Marina said, feeling flustered. She'd have to tear the place apart for a good cleaning this afternoon.

The phone on the counter buzzed, and Boz picked it up. "She sure is. Shall I send her over?" He glanced at Ivy. "The big guy's ready for that pastrami sandwich."

"I'll see you later, Marina, " Ivy said. "Thanks for the lift." She hugged Marina and walked out toward Bennett's office.

Boz scanned her application. "Any experience with this kind of business?"

"No, but I've been cooking with Ginger all my life."

"You'll have to pass a food handlers and safety certification exam and follow the California Health and Safety Code Guidelines." He slid a packet of information across the desk. "This contains the details you'll need."

Suddenly, her phone buzzed, and she glanced at it. A text from her agent floated across the screen. *Call me at once. Re: Hal.*

Marina sighed. Thoughts of that vermin clouded her mind. Irritated over Hal, she let out a huff. "How long will all this take? I was hoping I could get started at the farmers market this week." She pressed her lips together. She hadn't meant that to come out sounding quite so snippy.

Boz slapped another form on the desk. "In that case, you'll need a Temporary Food Facility Permit."

Annoyed at the mounting forms, Marina blew a wisp of hair from her forehead. She couldn't believe all the details she'd have to address to sell a few loaves of bread. And she still had to calculate her costs to determine her profit margin. And test recipes. And create menus. Not to mention photographing food for the website and social media. "You've got to be kidding. All I want to do is sell some bread."

Boz raised his eyebrows and inclined his head. "I don't make the rules, ma'am."

Marina pressed her fingertips against her temple. This was suddenly starting to seem like too much. She'd never run a business before. "And if I want to expand the patio area?"

"Depends on what you plan to build. Will you be using a contractor?"

"I think so."

"I'd recommend it, ma'am." He slid yet another form across the desk.

"Wow." Marina didn't mean to be rude, but going into business was a lot different from showing up for a job that she'd been doing for years. "Thanks, I guess."

"If you have any questions, give us a call," Boz said cheerfully. "We're here to help, not hinder your efforts, even though it might seem that way now."

With a grimace, Marina bundled up the paperwork and headed back to her car. Thankfully, the cheerful Nan was away from the reception desk. Marina could stand only so much help in one day. Yet, she was here to build a business.

In the parking lot, she paused by her car, breathing in to calm her frustration. Remembering the text that Gwen had sent, she tapped her agent's number. Her call went straight to voice mail. If this was concerning Hal, it couldn't be good. She left a message, shuddering just at the thought of her old boss.

Pausing, Marina looked out over the community from her vantage point. The sunshine warmed her face, and the expansive view of the ocean from this hilltop soothed her spirits. As each day passed, she felt a little lighter. So far, she had to admit that life was good in Summer Beach.

No more Hal, no more Babe, no more Grady. She had a chance to reboot her life. She chuckled to herself. Not that she had much choice. Her agent had made that clear.

But now, she was determined to be proactive and make the best of her situation.

Pulling her phone from her pocket, she dialed the contractor's number. He picked up right away.

"Axe here," came the confident, upbeat answer. "What can I do for you?"

Marina quickly explained who she was and what she needed. "When could you come over to look at the patio?"

"How about this afternoon?"

Deep voice, baritone, Marina noted. A voice meant for radio or voice-overs. "Sure. I'm on my way there now."

"Then I'll meet you there in half an hour," Axe said.

Marina agreed and got into her car. There was a simplicity to life here that she found appealing.

When Marina arrived at the Coral Cottage, she saw Kai outside sunning herself. She had a broad floppy hat protecting her face and a gold-colored, retro bikini that showed off her toned body and long legs. Dancing in her musicals kept her in great shape.

Marina had kept her figure out of necessity for her job, although she'd noticed a little weight creeping onto her hips as she baked and sampled recipes. But she didn't care. She liked the way she looked now. Not as gaunt and much happier. Here, she could be whoever she wanted.

Preferably, herself.

She walked toward her sister. From the corner of her eye, she saw Jack on the front porch of the guest cottage. He was bent over his laptop computer working, and Scout was snoozing by his feet. A funny feeling tugged at her, and she quickly shifted her attention back to Kai, who was humming along to a song in her head.

"Hey, you," Marina said, tapping her shoulder. "Company is coming."

Kai lifted an edge of the hat. "Are my services needed?"

"I have a contractor coming over to look at the patio. He's going to give me a bid for work. I want to finish what we can on our own to keep the costs down."

"And who, exactly, is this *we* of whom you speak?"

Marina perched on the edge of Kai's chaise lounge. "Me, Brooke's boys, and you."

Kai raised herself on one elbow and reached for a thermos beside her chaise lounge. She sipped and arched an eyebrow at Marina. "First time I'm hearing about this."

"Come on, Kai. It'll be fun." Marina held her hand out for the thermos. "I'm parched. Share your water?"

Kai hesitated. "It's juice." She passed the thermos.

Marina took a big sip and sputtered. "Wow, what is that?"

Laughing, Kai said, "It's Shelly's specialty. A Sea Breeze cocktail."

"You didn't tell me it had vodka in it."

"Surprise. Just like you surprised me with the patio work." Kai reclined and pulled her hat over her face.

"Come on, Kai. Think of all the times I've helped you with things like homework."

"Are you going to hold that over my head forever?" She reached out a hand and wiggled her fingers. "May I have that back, please?"

Marina took another sip. *So refreshing.* She took one more sip and handed the thermos back to Kai.

In the distance, Marina saw a truck turn onto the lane that led to their property. "I think that's the contractor. Get up. Besides, you're burning."

"No, I'm not. Wake me when it's over."

The truck came to a halt beside Marina's car, and a tall, Montana-sized man stepped out. His sun-bleached hair was brushed back, and aviator sunglasses obscured his eyes. Axe wore a sport shirt with nice-fitting jeans and boots. All that was missing was the cowboy hat.

Marina poked Kai in the ribs. "You might want to see this."

"Leave me out of this."

Axe strode toward them. "Are you Marina Moore?" His deep voice matched his build.

Marina rose. "I am. And that's my sister under there."

Kai peaked out from under her hat. "Well, hi there," she said, surprise evident in her tone.

"Hello." Axe touched his forehead with a finger as if a hat often sat there.

Cowboy hat, Marina bet.

Marina saw Axe's eyes flick toward Kai—she was a difficult vision to resist—but to his credit, he snapped his gaze back to Marina. "Where's this patio?"

"I'll show you," Marina said.

Beside her, Kai sat up abruptly. "I'll come, too."

"You don't have to, Kai. We've got this." Marina smothered a laugh.

Kai stood. Or rather, she tried to stand. All of a sudden, her sister crumpled toward the ground, and her sunhat rolled off.

"Whoa, there," Axe said, catching Kai before she fell.

"Oh, I'm so sorry," Kai said, flushing even beneath her sunburn. "My legs went to sleep."

"Or maybe that juice got to you," Marina remarked.

As Kai shook out her legs, Axe stood beside her,

supporting her while trying to keep a respectable distance. "You might want to sit down, ma'am."

Kai turned a radiant smile toward him. "My sister's the *ma'am*. I'm quite a bit younger, so I'm still a *miss*."

Marina rolled her eyes. "My sister is a stage actress. Can you tell?"

"I've heard you were in town again this summer," Axe said as he bent down to retrieve her hat. "Years ago, I used to sing and act in a little summer stock myself. Now, about this patio?"

With a rich voice like his, Marina could just imagine. And she saw Kai visualizing that, too. "The patio is this way." After Kai shot her a scathing look, Marina started for the patio, with Kai limping behind them.

"Kai, dear, you might want to put something over that." Marina motioned toward Kai's barely-there bikini. "You don't want to burn, and our guest has already seen the merchandise." She wanted Axe's full attention on the patio job. And she couldn't resist teasing Kai a little more.

"Oh, Marina, really!" Kai tore off her hat and flounced inside.

While Marina described what she envisioned, Axe walked around the small patio. "We'd have to grade the property or extend the space with a deck."

"A deck sounds nice, and I'd like to string up lights overhead to give it a cozy ambiance. Under the stars and softly lit. And maybe a firepit, while we're at it."

"We can do whatever you want." Taking off his sunglasses, he flipped open a small photo book he'd brought with him. "Here are several that we've done. You might like one of these, or if you have images or photos of something you like, we can probably recreate it."

As Marina glanced through the photos, she raked her teeth over her bottom lip. "I'm afraid my champagne taste might exceed my budget, though. I'd hoped that I could do some of the finish work, string up the lights, that kind of thing."

"Sure, I'd be happy to work with you on that." Axe's eyes crinkled at the corners.

Marina guessed that he was about Kai's age. Mid-to-late thirties. "You've done a lot of work. Have you been in Summer Beach long?"

"Long enough to call it home now." He grinned. "My folks still live in Montana, and I go back to see them on the ranch and get in some snow skiing nearby, but it's a different life."

"They must miss you," she said.

"I've got five brothers and sisters still there. My folks don't have time to miss me much. And they come to visit when the snow gets too deep there."

Idly, Marina wondered if he was married. Not for her, of course. She didn't see a ring on his finger, but that didn't necessarily mean anything.

Marina tapped a photo. "I like this deck."

"You can keep the cost down by buying a ready-made firepit."

"I appreciate that."

"Anything for Ginger," Axe said. "She's done a lot for the community." His phone buzzed, and he turned it off. "You can let me know if you see something else, and I'll send you a proposal for this one."

"I will, thank you."

As Marina watched him get into his truck, Kai emerged from the house. She'd put on a partly sheer flowing caftan with kitten heels, brushed her hair, and put on makeup and perfume.

Kai saw Axe's truck pulling away. When he saw her, he waved but didn't stop. "Why didn't you keep him here?"

"I didn't know I was supposed to."

"You knew I'd be back. Some sister you are."

"Sorry, I left my lasso in San Francisco. But aren't you engaged?"

"The ring is in my purse, not on my hand." Kai flopped down on a step, picked up a stick, and drew a squiggle in the sand. "You must think I'm silly, and maybe I did have too much to drink in the sun. Or maybe I'm addicted to attention." She passed her hands over her face.

Marina sat beside her. "Don't be so hard on yourself. I'm sorry that I teased you. But I can't blame you; Axe is a good-looking guy."

"Was I being too obvious?" Kai asked, leaning her head on Marina's shoulder.

Marina smiled. "Just a little."

Squeezing her eyes shut, Kai let out a little scream. "I always do that. And it chases them away."

"I can't imagine you chase away too many men."

"A couple of them have called me clingy."

Since Kai was young when their parents died, Marina imagined a therapist might link that behavior. It wasn't surprising. And of all the sisters, Kai had spent more time at Summer Beach with Ginger than she or Brooke. But then, they had families to look after.

"It's okay," Marina said, patting Kai's arm. "If the price is right, he'll be back to build a deck."

Kai sniffed. "I have to make a decision for Dmitri, don't I?"

"No, you have to decide for yourself."

Chapter 12

*J*ack called for Scout, who'd run ahead of him on the path up the ridgetop chasing a squirrel.

"Dang dog." As Jack trudged through the brush, the scent of wild, rambling rosemary crushed underfoot rose in the air. He stuck two fingers in his mouth and whistled—the piercing whistle he used at baseball games.

That did it. Scout stopped and spun around with a funny little backward jump. Fixated on a spot obscured by brush from Jack's vision, the dog whimpered. He paced back and forth as if he had a critter cornered.

"Come on, boy." Jack huffed as he climbed higher through the underbrush. He was determined to restore his lung capacity as much as he could.

A voice cracked the quietness. "He's got a rattlesnake." A woman's voice, calm and steady. "Don't move."

Jack whirled around. Ginger sat on a massive boulder, staring out to a shimmering blue-gray sea in a sort of meditation. She wore jeans and a windbreaker.

The wind up here was bracing. Jack zipped up his sweatshirt.

"How do you know it's a rattlesnake?"

"Listen for it, farm boy." She winked at him. "Or has it been too long?"

"Ouch." But he grew quiet. And there it was—a soft, distant sound like a sprinkler sizzling to life. Instead of water, venom waited to spurt into your veins. As a boy, he'd once been rushed to the hospital in a race against a snake bite. Ginger signaled for him to come over. "Impressive whistle. But call him slowly."

Jack did, and when Scout saw Jack, he left the snake with reluctance and padded toward his human with his funny gait.

Jack eased onto the edge of the massive, flat rock that looked like it had been heaved toward the sea by some ancient volcano but just missed its mark. Around them, brilliant orange poppies with silky petals swayed on slender stalks, their dark eyes turned toward the sun. Yellow goldfield flowers and purple lupine bloomed in tandem, spilling along the hillside like paint on a palette.

"What an extraordinary perch," Jack said, still catching his breath. Ginger was almost twice his age, and yet, there she sat, perfectly composed, long legs outstretched, her spun-ginger hair like a halo around a barely lined face.

"I've been climbing this hill for almost six decades," she said. "In between traveling the world with Bertrand."

"What was it like here then?"

"Quieter. Fewer cars. Simpler times." Her fiery green eyes lit under a fringe of pale lashes. "I loved the thrill of exploring new places, but coming back here was always a welcome return to nature."

"A chance to recharge." Jack picked up a dry stick and snapped it, hurling half of it away from the snake's vicinity for Scout. "Did your husband write his books at the cottage?"

A half-smile touched her lips. "Why, yes. Quite often. In those days, we used the guest cottage for our work. The girls knew not to bother us there."

"I read his book on leadership and diplomacy as background for an article I was writing. That's when I discovered your work, too." Jack had finally had the chance to go through his old notes to refresh his memory on Ginger's name. What he'd found had proven interesting, yet there was still so much he didn't know. Bertrand and Ginger Delavie had been an amazing power couple in their day, but Ginger's work was mostly behind the scenes.

"Oh, you did?" Ginger shrugged a slender shoulder that belied her strength. "Well, if it's a book you want to write…" Her voice trailed off, and the comment hung in the air like a challenge.

She probably meant her husband, but that's not who intrigued Jack. "Women weren't recognized for their efforts back then."

"I didn't work for the notoriety."

"No." He tossed the other half of the stick for Scout. "Did you study mathematics in school?"

"High school. Didn't go to college."

"Why not?"

"In the 1950s, in some circles, it was considered extravagant to send a woman to college. My older brothers—rest their souls—had gone, and I'd read their schoolbooks in greater detail than they did, so there was no point, you see."

Jack had a hard time accepting this explanation, but then, much had changed in the intervening decades.

"How did you come to work for the C.I.A.?"

"Who says I did?"

"I'm an investigative reporter," Jack said. "Some have called you the Ace of Codes. How did you come to do that kind of work?"

A hawk soared overhead, gliding over the hillside, looking for small prey. Scout perked his ears and watched, enthralled with this strange new creature.

"It all started with Bertrand," Ginger said, before snapping out of her reverie. "Did you come here to write about me?"

"No, ma'am, I did not. But you've made a lot of contributions in your career. Maybe it's time to share some of your perspectives." Jack held his breath. *Would she talk?*

She narrowed her eyes. "So, how did you find Summer Beach?"

"One day, I took a fortuitous turn off the highway. And I thought, if I ever decided to write a book someday, this would be the place to do it." Jack clasped a knee and looked out to sea, where the waves curled in with relentless force.

"You won't find your inspiration out there."

"Maybe you'd like to tell some stories of your work." Jack reached for his phone, thinking he might even record her.

"Oh, I have plenty of stories, but not for the book you might be thinking about. I have another project in mind I think we should talk about." The timer on Ginger's watch went off. "That's for my massage appointment. See you around."

With that, she slid off the rock with a nimble motion and started back down the trail, walking brisker than he had.

Jack watched her go. He had stumbled across one of the truly brilliant minds of the twentieth century. And her equally intriguing granddaughter. Were Marina and her sisters aware of their grandmother's accomplishments, or only of the long shadow that her husband cast?

Marina.

She wasn't helping him focus on his work. Nor was the boy who'd quickly stolen his heart. Fortunately, Leo had warmed up to him again after his outbreak in the kitchen the first day he'd seen the boy. Leo was a good kid, but Jack could tell he was taking his mother's condition hard. No one knew how much time Vanessa had left.

Jack had never imagined this summer unfolding quite the

way it was. And in the recesses of his mind was the notion that nothing would ever be quite the same again.

Chapter 13

*M*arina pulled another batch of mini-tarts from the oven and placed them on cooling racks. She swept her sleeve across her forehead, feeling the heat rising from Myrtle, the old red oven. Fortunately, the kitchen had passed the inspection.

Marina had been working all day. First, finishing the paperwork from City Hall, and then deciding on recipes, buying groceries, and baking. She was concerned that Gwen still hadn't returned her call, even though she'd tried reaching her again.

Kai sauntered into the room, humming an old Broadway tune.

"Irving Berlin?"

"Very good." Kai spread out her fingers, making jazz hands on either side of her face. "'There's No Business Like Show Business.' But from which show?"

Marina made a face. "*Seven Brides for Seven Brothers?*"

"Nope. *Annie Get Your Gun.*"

"Are you homesick for the stage?" Marina asked, blowing stray strands of hair from her face. She'd been baking for the last couple of days, and she couldn't wait to claim her little corner of the table at the farmers market that Cookie had promised.

"I miss the excitement." A wistful look crossed Kai's face. "What have you made today?"

She had made several types of bread: French baguettes, rosemary, and olive, and the chocolate cinnamon babka. She'd made little blueberry and strawberry fruit tarts, and on a whim, she'd decided to whip up saucer-sized chocolate chip cookies. Nothing too fancy, just good, homemade food.

And a lot of dirty dishes. "Unless you want to help clean up," Marina added.

"Actually, I'm on design duty," Kai said, wrinkling her nose. "You need a website where people can register for your next pop-up dinner. I'd much rather work on that."

Making a face at her sister, Marina pulled the last sheet of chocolate chip cookies from the oven. As she did, her oven mitt slipped, and she bobbled the hot cookie sheet. In a flash, warm cookies careened across the floor. "Noooo!"

"Five-second rule," Kai shouted, diving for a cookie.

"What's going on here?" Ginger asked as a cookie slid in front of her feet.

Behind her, Jack swept up the cookie like an outfielder. "Anyone looking for this or is it a free agent?"

"Don't you two dare eat those," Marina said, making a face. "I have others I just took out."

As Jack knelt to scoop up damaged cookies, he glanced around. "I'm impressed. I haven't seen this much baking since I was a kid on the farm."

"Ginger taught me most of what I know." Marina threw crumbled cookies into the trash. The soft chocolate chips, warm from the oven, left streaks on the floor.

"I'll clean that," Jack said.

"You don't have to," Marina said, stooping over with a rag.

Not giving up, Jack caught one end of the dishrag, his

hand brushing hers. "You cleaned the slipcovers after Scout climbed all over them with his dirty paws. Washing dishes is the least I can do." He jerked his chin toward the pile of dishes in the sink. "Bet you need help with those, too."

"He's right about that," Kai said, waving several pieces of paper. "I've got the sticker mock-ups for you when you're ready."

Marina sank back on her heels and reluctantly let go of the dishrag. Jack's hand was warm and sure against hers. *What kind of guy offers to help like that?* Not any she'd met in the last two decades. Arching an eyebrow, she said to Jack, "You just want free food."

"Maybe," he replied. "But not for myself."

Marina couldn't quite figure out Jack, but she wouldn't dismiss the help.

As Marina and Jack spoke, Ginger lifted the leopard-rimmed half-glasses she wore around her neck to inspect Kai's work. "These mock-ups are very nice, indeed. You have a talent for this, Kai. As I've always said, those who are creative in one area are often creative in others."

Marina stood up and turned back to Kai. "Let's see what you've got, sis."

Kai sat beside her grandmother. "While the show was running, I'd fill time by helping other cast members create fan pages and merchandise. It's fun." She spread out several designs on the red Formica table. "I've made up one with a cottage, another with seashells and coral, and this one with flowers and a table setting. Which one do you like?"

Marina fanned her warm face. "They're all beautiful, but I like the cottage. It will reinforce the name in people's minds."

Both women looked at Ginger. "You've got my vote for that one, too."

Kai beamed. "That was my favorite, too. The other images will be good for the website. I'll print these and put them on the paper bags and cellophane you bought for your bread."

"Then we'll pack it all and off I go early in the morning." Marina picked up a platter of blueberry tarts and offered them to everyone. "Try this one."

"Maybe you should start a tab for me," Jack said, taking a tart.

"If I keep this up, I won't be able to fit in my costumes in the fall." Kai bit into one. "Mmm, delicious. You'll sell out of these for sure."

"I sure hope so," Marina said. "This is my first test market. And I made some for Ivy and Shelly for the inn. Ginger, would you like to try one?"

"Absolutely—with my tea later," Ginger said. "These remind me of the ones Bertrand and I used to have in London. Made by the Queen's personal chef trained in French cuisine, mind you."

Grinning, Kai said, "I'd better get out of here and print these stickers. I'll make business cards for you, too."

After Ginger and Kai left, Jack stayed back. Without being asked, he began to heft mixing bowls and baking sheets into the large sink. "Dishwashing liquid?"

"Below the sink to the right. You don't have to do this," Marina said.

"If you say that one more time, you might lose me," he said.

Marina made a zipping motion across her mouth. Despite their rocky beginning, Jack was proving himself to be a likable sort after all. She swept the dirty dishes from the counter and plunged them into the sink of soapy water Jack had going. "I can dry, too."

"You're on," he said.

Marina whipped a cotton dishtowel from a drawer. Soon, she and Jack were working in unison. Since the luau on

Bennett's boat, Marina had been thinking about the little boy she'd seen with Jack.

"It was good to see you at the marina the other day," she said. "Writing at such long stretches must be tough."

"It's not that bad," Jack said quickly. "Scout reminds me when it's time to take a walk."

Steering the conversation back, Marina said, "I enjoyed meeting your friends that day. Denise and John and their daughter. And Vanessa and Leo."

Jack was quiet for a moment as if weighing his reply. Marina waited.

"They're good people," he finally said.

"And Leo is adorable," Marina said. "You two seemed to have a special bond."

Again, Jack hesitated. "Vanessa is an old friend and colleague. It's painful to see her in such a fragile condition." He drew in a breath. "Anything I can do for her son, I will. He's a fine boy."

Marina sensed a finality to Jack's comments on the subject, though she couldn't help but feel that there was more to his story. Leo bore such a strong resemblance to Jack.

"You and Ginger seem to be getting on well," Marina said, breaking the silence. She'd seen them outside talking on the patio several times.

"Your grandmother has had an amazing life," Jack said as he scoured a pan. He seemed to relax with the change of subject.

"Her stories are certainly entertaining," Marina said with a light laugh. "Has she shared much with you?"

"She talked about how she got into her line of work."

"Most people think being a statistician is fairly boring, but she seems to have enjoyed it, especially after Grandpa passed on. It's taken her all over the world."

"A statistician, huh?" Jack looked at her with a funny grin. "Is that the family story?"

What is he getting at? Marina bristled at his comment. "That's the truth."

"I wrote a story a few years back on one of the women she trained. They don't talk much, you know. But I remembered her name."

"I'm not following."

Jack drew his eyebrows together. "You do know what Ginger does, right?"

"Of course. I just told you." Slightly irritated, she dried a pan and put it away.

Amused, Jack handed her another pan dripping with water. "I don't think you do."

She flicked water droplets toward him. "I think I know my grandmother." The fine hairs on the back of Marina's neck were bristling with irritation. Just when she was beginning to like the new Jack, the old one re-emerged.

"Do you?"

Ginger appeared at the doorway. "Heard you two bickering in here."

"We're not bickering. Jack is simply mistaken." Marina whipped her towel around, drying a pan before shoving it into a cupboard.

Folding her arms, Ginger said, "Actually, he's not."

Marina jabbed a hand to her waist. "Would one of you let me in on the secret?"

Ginger nodded toward Jack.

"A few years ago," Jack began. "I interviewed one of the top code-breakers in the country. She revered your grandmother, who taught her everything she knew."

Marina stared at Jack. "I'm sorry, I think I misunderstood—"

"No, you didn't." Ginger arched a brow with modesty. "Though others have surpassed me. Except most of them use computers."

"What are you talking about?" Marina asked slowly.

"Actually, artificial intelligence is the next frontier," Ginger said. "Still, someone has to develop the algorithms and train the machines."

"That's not what I mean," Marina pressed a hand to her temple. She tried to remember a story she might have heard, too. Female code-breakers. Women who ran the effort during the second world war. But Ginger would have been too young for that.

Ginger sat down and laced her fingers on the table as if waiting for Marina to catch up.

"Why have you never mentioned this?" Marina asked.

"I didn't do the work to bring attention to myself," Ginger said, lifting a shoulder and letting it drop. "Few people would understand what I did. And we weren't to talk of it." Her lips curved. "No one wants to hear what a statistician does. That's always been safe."

"Safe?" Marina intoned. Suddenly, her grandmother was sounding like a spy or something. "You sound like you worked for the C.I.A."

"I wouldn't put it quite like that," Ginger said with a quick, self-effacing quirk of her mouth. "You might say that I was on call. A consultant. Why, what with dear Bertrand's schedule—"

"Wait, you did this when Grandpa was living?" He'd suffered a heart attack while swimming at the Paris Ritz Hotel in the eighties when Marina was a teenager.

Seeming slightly impatient, Ginger tapped a neatly manicured nail on the table. "That's how I got into it, don't you see?"

"Through Grandpa?"

Ginger turned up a corner of her mouth in an enigmatic smile. "More or less, dear. We were in the midst of the Cold War. For decades, really."

All thought of Jack and Leo and bread for the farmers market vanished. Feeling her pulse quicken, Marina threw her dishtowel down and turned on Jack. "I can't believe you weren't going to say anything about this."

Jack stepped back and put up his hands in defense. "Ginger just told me. I thought you knew."

"Now, you two, simmer down." Ginger stood imperiously, brushing the creases from her slacks. "I can't imagine what else you'd want to know, Marina. I worked with a few codes. It was more like solving puzzles. That's all there was to it."

Ginger paused, looking at them cryptically. "Life is a puzzle, and you can put it together or take it apart in many different ways. Now, if you'll excuse me, I have a bridge game." With a wave of her hand, she left the kitchen.

Marina advanced on Jack. "What gives you the right to delve into our private business?" she demanded, trying to ignore that she had been doing the same thing to Jack just minutes ago.

Jack passed a hand over his face, trying unsuccessfully to hide an amused expression. "C'mon, you can Google her name."

"Who Googles their grandmother? She once taught math —did you know that? Right here in Summer Beach," Marina said, pointing toward the town. "A small-town math teacher is not some sort of spy, and that's that."

Jack pressed his hand against his chest. "I never said that."

In the distance, Scout barked.

"You're being called." Marina opened the back door for Jack.

Shaking his head, he strolled out and made his way toward the guest cottage. Marina slammed the door behind him.

Stalking through the house, Marina saw Ginger driving away. Stopping by the study where Kai was, she folded her arms and leaned against the doorjamb. The knotty pine-paneled walls still seemed imbued with her grandfather's vanilla pipe tobacco—or maybe it was the vanilla incense that

Kai liked to burn here. "Just how much do you know about our grandmother?"

Kai pulled a sheet of printed stickers from the printer. "What kind of question is that?"

Marina flung her arm toward the guest cottage. "Mr. Know-It-All-Investigative-Reporter just implied something about Ginger that makes me very uncomfortable."

Kai smiled. "You forgot Pulitzer Prize winner."

"I'm not kidding."

"Like what?" Kai popped her head up. "That Ginger used to be an exotic dancer?"

Marina's lips parted. "Are you serious?"

"What do you think?" Kai laughed.

Marina rolled her eyes. "I need to use your computer." Before her sister could answer, Marina sat down in front of Kai's laptop on the desk and began typing.

Moments later, the computer screen flashed. Kai turned around, and the two sisters stared at the screen.

Chapter 14

"Who is Grandma COBOL?" Kai asked, leaning toward her laptop screen in the study. "And that looks like Ginger beside her." She read the caption under the photo. "That hulking machinery is a Univac computer, early 1960s. Way before PCs."

"In the age of the dinosaurs in computer terms," Marina said. "Say, that's about when Ginger and Grandpa were living on the east coast, isn't it?" The old photo uploaded to a website was a little blurry, but Marina could make out Ginger. "Let's see," she said, clicking on the other woman's name. "Grace Hopper. Commodore Hopper, that is. Recipient of a Presidential Medal of Freedom. I think that's the highest honor in this country."

"For what?" Kai asked. The sisters sat huddled in front of her laptop in the study. They'd almost forgotten about the new stickers that Kai was making for Marina.

Marina clicked again. "Wow. Grace was an amazing woman. Ph.D. in mathematics from Yale, Navy Reserve, and this." She pointed to the screen. "She was known for translating mathematical notations into machine code. She wrote the very first computer compiler."

"And invented the programming language, COBOL." Kai pressed a hand to her forehead. "That's huge. Wonder if Ginger worked with her?"

"Maybe. Evidently, Jack knows more about our grandmother's professional life than we do. And she confirmed it. But that's about all she said." Marina folded her arms. "Have you ever noticed that Ginger is sometimes vague about the trips she takes?"

Kai nodded. "I never really thought of Ginger as more than a math teacher or a diplomat's wife."

"Those are both important positions," Marina said, shooting her sister a look.

"I know, but hanging out with people like Commodore Hopper. And Julia Child, and princes and barons and who knows who else. I used to think she made up all her stories, but maybe our granny had another life we didn't understand when we were younger."

"Perhaps she still does," Marina said, musing over what she saw on the screen. "Jack said she was a code breaker. A cryptologist. That's easy to believe. We all played her games with codes and ciphers when we were little."

"Looks like she knows more people in high places," Kai said. She tapped another link. "There she is again on the grounds of the C.I.A."

"But Grandpa's work took them everywhere, and they would have met many high-ranking people." Marina squinted at the image. "She's standing in front of a sculpture that looks like alphabet soup. Wow, it's beautiful, like a high, verdigris scroll unfurled with row upon row of letters. And she's with the head of the C.I.A."

Kai read the headline. "*Kryptos: An Undecipherable Code?*" Sitting back, she said, "Why do I feel like I'm Alice stumbling around in Wonderland?"

Marina laughed. "Or Forrest Gump, where our grandmother seems to have inserted herself into history, and we knew nothing about it." She rested her chin on her hand. "But this sort of makes sense. Remember those clues she used to leave for us that led to birthday surprises? We had to solve them to find the gifts."

"That was so much fun," Kai said. "I remember the Caesar cipher she taught us. She'd hidden our new summer clothes and made us unscramble the code to find them. I think I was about seven years old." Kai grinned. "Maybe Ginger has left more encrypted messages around here."

Marina glanced around. "You never know." Ginger often had reasons of her own for what she did. *Enigmatic*, that's what people often called her. Although to Marina and Kai and Brooke, she was simply the fascinating grandmother they loved.

"Enough of this," Marina said, slightly overwhelmed. She closed the computer browser, wondering if Ginger would share more with them later. "Right now, we've got work to do if I'm going to make it to the farmers market early in the morning."

Back in the kitchen, after checking to make sure the baked goods had cooled, Marina and Kai worked together at the table to package the loaves and baked goodies. Marina wrapped while Kai put on labels.

"How much are you selling these for?" Kai asked.

"While I was at the market, I looked to see how other people had priced similar items." She flipped open a notebook. "Here you go."

Kai glanced at it. "Good prices. Are you sure you're making money?"

"After the city fees, supplies, and ingredients—barely. But my initial costs will be defrayed over time. And I need to buy my ingredients in bulk—once I figure out what's selling."

As Kai listened, she drew her eyebrows together. "You're serious about this, aren't you? I thought you'd go back to work in the fall."

"I might have to, but that would depend on someone offering me a position. Right now, I'm *persona non grata*. You've seen my meme."

Kai sighed. "You were trending on social media."

"I didn't need to know that," Marina said, carefully sliding a loaf into a bag and closing it. "There's a difference between popularity based on your work and notoriety from making yourself look like a fool."

"I think a lot of women feel sorry for you."

"That won't pay the bills."

"Now you sound like Ginger."

Marina closed the notebook. "I have two children in college."

"Maybe you're putting too much pressure on yourself about that. If you can afford to pay their way, that's great. But you did it by yourself."

"That was difficult." Marina recalled juggling work at a cafe to pay for her tuition. "And yet, that was also one of the happiest times of my life. Before Stan, before the kids, when I was on my own."

"I hate to point this out, but you've come full circle. I love Heather and Ethan, but they can take care of themselves if you can't. They're eighteen, so they're adults, too."

Marina frowned at Kai. "Barely." She thought about Ethan and what a difficult time he was having.

"You're such a mom," Kai said, shaking her head. "Let them stand on their own."

"You have no room to criticize me. My children are the most important thing to me." Marina stopped herself. Kai might never know what it was like to be a mother. And she knew that worried Kai.

"You don't have to rub it in," Kai shot back. "Just because you've been supermom until now."

"I'm under a lot of pressure," Marina snapped back. "You have no idea what it means to be responsible for children and their development into functioning human beings." As soon as the words left her mouth, she was sorry.

"It's not for lack of trying, is it? At least I have an engagement ring, and what do you have? A meme. And everyone is laughing at you." Kai shoved away from the table and stormed outside.

"No, no, no," Marina mumbled against a rush of regret. "Why did I have to go there?" She'd always been the big sister, the one who was supposed to make everything all right. She knew Kai's sensitive points. "What's wrong with me?"

The stress of unemployment, public humiliation, and worry about her children was getting to be too much to handle—and making her do things she wished she hadn't.

"I need to apologize," Marina mumbled, blinking back tears of anger at herself. Gazing from the wide kitchen window, she could see Kai angling toward the water's edge. Her sister paused to kick off her shoes. Gripping a flip-flop in each hand, Kai started running, kicking up sand and gaining speed as she went.

Even from childhood, Kai often ran when she was upset, pounding her feet against the sand to relieve her anxiety.

Kai might have a lot on her mind, too, but Marina couldn't help but feel responsible for her sister's breakdown.

"FRESH BREAD," Marina called out to the throngs of people passing by at the farmers market though no one stopped. She felt a little embarrassed, like a carnival barker.

When no one paid attention to her, Marina went back to organizing her offerings. She must have shifted her loaves of bread with packages of cookies and tarts a dozen times. Nothing seemed to help.

She hadn't sold anything in two hours while the two high school girls next to her had almost sold out of Rice Crispy treats. She was happy that they were learning entrepreneurial skills, but if they gave each other one more high-five after a sale, she would scream. And Cookie, the manager of the market, wasn't impressed. She'd never get a table this way—or be able to pay for it.

What was she doing wrong?

"Fresh bread," Marina called out in another attempt.

"Oh my gosh, you sound like you're apologizing for taking up space." Kai leaned against the edge of the table. "Don't state the obvious."

"Well, when did you get home last night?" By midnight, Kai hadn't returned home.

Kai quirked a corner of her mouth. "Checking up on me?"

"No, I just noticed. That's all."

Kai picked up a loaf and a package of cookies. "Want me to show you how it's done?"

"You've never sold anything at a farmers market." Marina shrugged a shoulder, but if anyone could move the merchandise it was probably Kai. Being younger and blond couldn't hurt. "Go ahead, charm them all with your gorgeousness."

"You think that's what it's about?" Kai looked a little hurt as she opened a loaf of bread. "Do you have gloves?"

"For what?"

"How did you manage to get this space? I'll be right back." Kai crossed the aisle to another vendor, who, after a few words, gave her a pair of thin, food safety gloves, a knife, and a paper plate. Kai slid her hands into the gloves, then set about cutting up the rosemary bread, chocolate chip cookies, and a blueberry tart. Once she'd piled the samples high, she turned toward people streaming by.

"Homemade rosemary bread," Kai called out in her confident stage voice. "The world's best chocolate chip cookies. Blueberry tarts to die for."

"You can't just give it all away," Marina said, watching people stop for samples, then walk away. One couple, who

looked like they'd just stepped off their yacht, helped themselves to double samples. Marina rolled her eyes. She supposed
she could always write off the loss on her tax return. That was
thinking positive, right?

"Just wait." Kai kept passing out samples.

The yacht couple got to the end of the aisle, and then they
turned around.

The woman strode back to Marina's table. As she pointed
toward the rosemary bread, her armful of gold bracelets
jingled. "That bread is horrible."

"Excuse me?" Marina wanted to crawl under the table
and disappear.

The woman peered over the top of her dark sunglasses.
"Because it's going to be responsible for me having to add an
extra day at the gym." She smiled. "But it will be worth it. I'll
take two loaves. Imagine grilled cheese sandwiches with that."

Her husband walked up behind her. "Don't forget the
chocolate chip cookies. Get a dozen."

Marina gaped at them, hardly knowing what to say. Were
they serious?

"Of course," Kai said, darting beside Marina. "And have
you tried the tarts? I like mine with whipped cream and a
sprinkle of cinnamon. They're marvelous with champagne
cocktails for brunch on the boat, or dessert as you watch the
sunset."

"I vote for a scoop of ice cream on them," the husband
said.

"We could serve them this evening at the dinner party,"
the woman added. "We'll take six of those."

Marina was dumbfounded and flustered. Real customers,
actually buying what she'd made. "Don't you want to know
how much they are?"

Kai and the woman looked at each other for a moment
and then burst out laughing together.

"Just add it up," Kai whispered.

Marina's face burned with embarrassment. She was clearly out of place here. Had she been talking to a camera so long that she'd forgotten how to converse with people?

Kai slid one of Marina's new cards into the couple's bag. "Be sure to call or email when you want to reserve your purchases because we sell out so fast," Kai said in a confidential tone. "I'd hate for you to be disappointed."

"Why, that's so kind of you," the woman said. "And do you take special requests?"

"As long as I can make it," Marina said, hesitant to boast of skills that were still rusty.

"My sister is too modest. She can make anything."

After the couple left, Kai turned to her. "You almost had it right in the end, but you'll get the hang of this."

"You're a natural," Marina said. "I feel like such an idiot." She could stare at a camera and read a news broadcast to a million or more people, but her personal interaction muscles had atrophied.

Kai flipped her hair over her shoulder. "Remember, I'm a professional. This is just another stage."

With Kai passing out samples, Marina sold out of her stock before the farmers market closed for the day. Watching her sister, Marina thought about how much she loved Kai. She realized she was not alone, that even when they argued, the bond they'd woven since childhood was still strong.

As Marina cleaned the table, she touched Kai's shoulder. "Did I tell you I'm sorry for my remarks yesterday?"

"You don't have to," Kai replied, taking her hand. "We're both on edge, and I'm sorry, too."

"Watching you out there, I thought of something," Marina said, easing into a thought she'd had. Would you like to come in on this enterprise this summer? I'm better in the kitchen, and you're a natural with people."

"Don't sell yourself short," Kai said. "You've been on the air for how many years?"

"That's different. As a news anchor, I had to contain myself and bottle up my emotions and opinions. Here, I have to learn to relate to real people again."

Kai's expression softened. "Honestly, I've noticed that about you."

Marina went on. "I know my talents, and I know yours. I might never work in television again, and I'm not even sure I want to. For once in my life, I want to love what I do, even if I don't make a lot of money. That's not too much to ask at my age. But what if I dream bigger? And team up with the people I admire the most, like you and Ginger? We're all stronger together."

"I'd like that, but you know that I'll be gone soon." Kai motioned at the crowd around them. "This is your stage, not mine. But if I stayed anywhere, it would be here with you and Ginger and Brooke."

"Keep my offer in mind, would you?" Marina paused, looking out over the ocean. "Now I understand why Ginger never wanted to get rid of the cottage, even when she and Grandpa were working elsewhere. This place is a slice of heaven. I can do a lot of good here."

And it wasn't only about her. Marina had been thinking about what she could do to help other restaurant owners here. What Boz had said about the deep-pocket competitors in the neighboring community had disturbed her. She hated seeing hard-working, dedicated people who'd built their dreams being taken advantage of. Business people would say it was merely the survival of the fittest, but some fights weren't fair.

Kai returned the platter and knife to the neighboring vendor and thanked them. When she came back, she asked, "What will you do about Heather and Ethan and their college tuition?"

"I'll do what I can. Maybe you're right. My kids are old enough to understand that life can get complicated. I plan to

have a talk with them about applying for financial aid."
Marina nudged Kai. "So, are you in?"

Kai lowered her eyes. "I can't. I just made another commitment."

"You got a part? That's great." Though disappointed, Marina was truly happy for Kai. She knew that Kai was feeling antsy being away from her work and the stage.

"No, but I will in the fall, I'm sure." Kai bit her lip, hesitating. "Don't yell at me, but I called Dmitri last night. We had a long talk, and I agreed to marry him this summer." As Kai spoke, the light in her eyes dimmed.

Marina took her sister's hand, which was trembling. "Are you sure?"

Kai hesitated before nodding. "You were right about a lot of things, too. I'm probably too old to start a family anyway. It's time I settled for what I can get." She winced. "I didn't mean that the way it sounded. Dmitri is a good guy, and he has a great relationship with his children."

Marina saw Kai's shoulders slump. Fifteen minutes ago, the confident Kai was full of joy, chatting with strangers and turning them into friends. "Do you have to act so quickly? You've only been dating for a month."

"But I do," Kai said. "If I don't meet him in Chicago, he says it's over."

As Marina wiped down the table, she made a face. "That's an ultimatum. Don't fall for it."

"You're suggesting I abandon a decent man who wants to marry me, which—news alert—doesn't happen every day?"

"Just because you've got the proverbial bird in the hand doesn't mean it's a good one for the long term. I sure learned that."

"But Grady left you," Kai said.

"You don't have to remind me," Marina said. "But I've given that situation a lot of thought, and I've learned from it. What if I'd decided to try to get Grady back? Would he have been worth it? Some mistakes can be forgiven, but he was way past the age of rehabilitation. It's a rare old bird that can do that. I'm not saying it's impossible, but the odds are against it. You have to come to terms with abandoning your dream of a family. I'm not sure you have. That's the crux of the problem, and you have to be honest with yourself."

Kai grew quiet, and Marina knew she'd hit her sister's most sensitive nerve. They left the market, got into the car, and drove the short distance to the cottage. They could have walked, but the car had been full of baked goods that morning.

Marina reached across to Kai and touched her shoulder. "Thanks for all your help today. I couldn't have done it without you. And don't worry, you'll figure out your relationship with Dmitri." She smiled. "There's always Axe."

"He is easy on the eyes," Kai said. "And he did summer stock."

"The singing contractor." Marina pulled the car in front of the cottage and stopped. "The fact that you're even noticing other men should mean something."

As they went inside, Marina noticed a car parked in the front of the cottage. She figured that Ginger might have company. After putting down her purse, a knock sounded at the door, and she opened it.

An older man wearing sunglasses and a sport shirt stood before her. "Marina Moore?"

"Yes?"

He handed her a sheaf of papers. "You've been served."

Marina threw up her hands. "Oh, for heaven's sake," she said, her throat constricting with anger. Hal was behind this for sure.

Kai raced back to the front door. "What's the matter?"

"Please take them, ma'am." The papers shook in his hand.

"Let me see that," Kai said, snatching the stapled packet from the man, who immediately scurried away. "What a vile little man." She flipped the pages. "These are from the company that owns the station. They're suing *you*?"

Marina watched the man jump into his car and peel out. "He's just doing his job on behalf of that lecherous fool at the station," she said, jabbing the air to punctuate her words.

Just then, her phone rang. Answering it, she said, "Gwen, I just got served with a lawsuit."

"I was calling to warn you. I've been in touch with your attorney, who says you should start getting prepared. Your contract calls for mediation. When can you be here for that?"

Marina gulped. Just when her life was looking up, legal complications were the last thing she needed. "I have to close my apartment next week. I can do it then."

"I'm not sure the attorneys can act that fast. You should call your lawyer."

After hanging up, Kai hugged her. "I'm so sorry. But I'm coming with you to San Francisco."

"What about Dmitri in Chicago?"

Kai tightened her arms around Marina. "You're my sister."

Chapter 15

*J*ack leaned back in his chair and stretched his fingers. His Monterey-style, carved wooden desk was positioned in front of a large window overlooking the beach—one of the most incredible views he could imagine for inspiration.

The guest cottage was conducive to inspiration and furnished in early California beach-style. White canvas slipcovers clothed threadbare sofas, throw pillows with pink flamingos and palm trees were strewn comfortably about, and braided rugs in sandy shades covered the Saltillo tile pavers. And in the kitchen, vintage melamine dinnerware was still perfectly serviceable. The guest cottage was a time-capsule of mid-century California beach living, which was fine by him.

Jack tapped a few more notes before closing his laptop. Although he was making progress in his research, he was still at a loss on the angle he wanted for a biography of Ginger Delavie. He had to prepare the first three chapters and a detailed outline before pitching his project. If only Ginger would answer his questions, but she still wouldn't talk about her work.

Scout knew that when the laptop closed, he had a shot for a walk on the beach. He rose and pawed Jack's leg, curling his lips into what looked like a grin.

"Hey, boy," Jack said. "Now that's a great expression. Hold that a minute."

Jack picked up his sketch pad and flipped it open. Drawing had always been relaxing, and he often sent his pictures to his little nephews and nieces. Scout was his latest subject. Jack sketched a few quick lines on the paper, smiling at the personality in Scout's face that he was capturing.

"You're famous in Texas," Jack said, reaching down to scratch Scout's neck. The kids had been clamoring for more cartoon-like Scout illustrations. Jack sometimes wondered what it would have been like to have followed this first passion he'd had. He would have lived a different, quieter life, that was for sure.

One thing was clear now. While Jack was known for investigative journalism that often took him on the road, he would need to change his working style to accommodate young Leo. That quiet path might have been better. With Vanessa and Leo, everything had happened so quickly that Jack was still processing plans and feelings.

Jack closed his sketch pad, satisfied with his work. He'd finish the drawing later.

Clucking his tongue, Jack grabbed a lightweight windbreaker. Mornings were crisp on the beach, especially with the onshore winds. At his signal, Scout leapt up from his position beside Jack's desk and trailed him to the door. The dog sat, wagging his tail and waiting.

"There's a good boy," Jack said, snapping a leash onto Scout's collar. "Who knew you were so smart?"

Jack liked to work early in the morning as soon as the sun rose. By this time, he was often ready for a break with a walk on the beach, though today, he had a meeting. The last few days, he had been easing into a trot. Although he was far from being as fit as the local mayor, he could feel his lung capacity increasing, which felt good.

This morning, Jack was meeting Bennett at a property not far away. He snapped his fingers for Scout. "Come on, boy. Let's go."

After a short walk, Jack saw Bennett waiting in front of a house a few blocks from the beach. The elevated house had a good view of the ocean.

"Get your run in this morning?" Bennett asked.

"A little later. I'm picking up speed, though."

"We have a 10k race through town soon," Bennett said. "You should join us." He leaned down to rub Scout's neck. "Your sidekick is welcome, too. It's a fundraiser for the animal shelter." At the sound of a car, he glanced up. "Here they are."

Denise and John stepped from the SUV, and together they helped Vanessa from the back seat. Leo and Samantha scrambled out, looking sleepy.

"I have a nephew about their age," Bennett said. "Maybe they'd like to go snorkeling off the dock together."

Leo and Samantha brightened. "Could we?" Leo asked his mother as he fell into step beside her.

"That sounds like fun," Vanessa said. She stopped at the clapboard house in front of them. "What a pretty summer place. It reminds me of the houses I used to see on Nantucket."

Bennett fished a key from his pocket. "It has two suites and a third bedroom, plus a loft that leads out onto an observation deck. I thought that configuration might work well. The owners were going to sell it, but they decided to rent it for the season. It needs some work, but it's comfortable."

Denise hooked her arm into Vanessa's. "We're going to have a good time this summer sharing a beach house. I don't know why we haven't done this before."

As they walked through the house, which was a mid-century home furnished in fresh shades of white and turquoise, Bennett pointed out features.

"Ceiling fans throughout, just open the windows and let the sea breezes in. You can easily walk to the beach and the village." He opened the door to a suite, which had a patio off to the side. A wisteria-laden trellis shaded the sunny area, and gardenia flowers sweetened the air.

"This would be lovely for you," Denise said to Vanessa.

"I like it very much," Vanessa replied, looking around with an expression of delight.

Jack guided her to the patio, where a lion's head fountain trickled in one corner.

"I can just imagine sitting here and reading," she said, holding her hand out to Leo. The boy kept close to his mother.

Jack's heart went out to her. Denise and John and the children looked at the rest of the house, and they all claimed rooms. Samantha liked a bedroom decorated with mermaids.

"The loft is amazing," Leo said, his eyes rounded. The spacious area had a nautical theme of blue and white. A circular staircase led to the roof, where a viewing platform was setup.

"Then it's yours," Vanessa said. "We could put a telescope on the roof for you to explore the stars. This beach house is perfect for us."

Jack knew the hospice wasn't far away and thought that having Denise and John and Samantha nearby with Leo was a good plan. He hated to think of what was ahead, though he was looking forward to seeing more of Leo.

"Then we'll take it," John said, shaking Bennett's hand.

Bennett locked the house and turned back to them. "I have all the paperwork at my office if you want to fill it out there or take it with you."

"Might as well do it now," John said, putting his arms around Denise, who clutched Vanessa's hand.

"As long as I can sit down somewhere," Vanessa said.

Jack thought Vanessa looked better than she had the first time he'd seen her in Los Angeles. He hoped that she might improve and maybe even beat this illness, although he doubted that was realistic. Still, Jack could hope. He respected Vanessa and the path she had chosen. It hadn't been easy, he was sure of that, but she seemed content with her decision.

Vanessa and Leo had consumed his thoughts since meeting her again in Santa Monica.

Scout whined beside Jack and thumped his tail. Jack scratched his head. "While you guys tend to that, I can take the kids to the beach with Scout." This bittersweet summer was Jack's opportunity to get to know his son.

Leo and Samantha looked excited, and their parents gave their permission.

Jack started toward the beach with the two children and Scout. When they arrived, he let the kids kick off their shoes while he bought a frisbee from a souvenir shop.

Not many people were on the beach. Surfers were returning from a morning on the waves, and a few people strolled on the sand. A lifeguard sat in a perch high above them, watching the remaining surfers and a couple with children racing through the water's edge.

Jack handed the frisbee to Leo. "Do you know how to throw one of these?"

"Sure," Leo said. He and Samantha giggled.

Stupid question for kids that lived at the beach, Jack figured. "Scout's new at this, so tell him to sit and stay. Throw this as far as you can. Then, give him the command—*fetch it up.*"

Scout's ears pricked up. He was taking in everything. As if he understood, he trotted to Leo and sat, panting with excitement.

"Look at him," Leo said, his eyes widening. "He knows what's going on."

"He's alert and learns quickly. Now give it a good throw."

Scout tilted his head, watching the frisbee spin in the air and settle on the beach. He panted after the new toy.

"What do you say?" Jack asked. "Add a motion, like this." He pointed at the frisbee.

"Fetch it," Leo said, mimicking Jack.

Scout took off running so fast he could hardly stop and skidded around the frisbee. He nabbed it with his mouth and happily padded back.

Soon Leo and Samantha were taking turns and having a great time with Scout.

"Have either of you ever had a dog?" Jack asked.

"We have a cat," Samantha said. "It's with my aunt right now."

"I always wanted one," Leo said. "But my mom says they're a lot of work."

Some of Jack's fondest memories as a boy were with his dog, Buster. "Well, you guys can hang out with Scout this summer if you want. I'm staying in the guest cottage over by the Coral Cottage just on the other side of the village. You can pick him up anytime you like."

"Uh, we'd have to ask our parents," Leo said, and Samantha nodded.

"Oh, sure. I understand." Jack would have to learn a lot about parenting.

"But that would be so cool," Leo said.

"Let's try something different with Scout," Jack said. Taking the frisbee, he whirled it into the air, but before it landed, he gave Scout the command. The dog hesitated, but when Jack repeated the instruction, Scout took off. Moments later, Scout leapt into the air and snatched the frisbee. The dog was so excited at this new twist that he galloped back and circled them twice before settling down.

"Wow, he liked that," Leo said.

Jack rubbed Scout's neck. "He's a smart dog. You can teach him a lot. Just be sure to keep him out of vegetable patches and flower gardens. He loves to wreak havoc in those."

Leo and Samantha were having so much fun with Scout that Jack stepped back and watched the kids, thinking about everything he had missed. He couldn't blame Vanessa, especially now, but he felt a pang of sadness that he'd missed so much.

And yet, Jack was also grateful that Vanessa had called. The alternative was that someday, when Jack was an old man, he might have opened the door to a grown-up Leo, informing him that Jack was his father.

No, better to have part of Leo's childhood than none at all.

I'm a father now. Jack let that sink in, feeling the magnitude of that responsibility. And yet, it was still complicated. Leo had no idea, and the little boy would soon face the tragic loss of his mother. Jack knew he would be a poor substitute for Vanessa.

What could he offer his son? Jack had spent his life chasing stories across the country and around the globe. He had plenty of stories to tell, but now he was having a hard time deciding which direction to take this manuscript. Sometimes he wished he'd become an illustrator, but he was entirely self-taught in that field.

Maybe it was the difference between writing an article and the longer form of a book. Whatever it was, Jack was having a hard time focusing. Whether it was Leo and Vanessa on his mind, Scout tugging on his leg to go for a walk, or Marina distracting him, he'd had a hard time sorting out the notes he'd jotted down over the years.

And then there was Ginger. On the trail, she'd teased him with another project. Could there be something there?

Whatever he chose, he had to send a proposal to his agent soon.

Now that Jack was responsible for Leo, his life would change. Leo would start school somewhere in the fall. He wondered how Vanessa would be then. Maybe in future summers, he and Leo could take off in the van and camp out across the country.

"Watch out," Leo called out.

Jack ducked just in time to avoid a low flying frisbee with Scout in hot pursuit.

Behind him, he heard a scream. Whirling around, he saw Scout sprawled across Marina licking her face, the frisbee slowing to a stop on the sand behind her. Scout had collided with her, overjoyed to see her.

"No, Scout, wrong!" Jack jumped up and rushed to Marina's aid. Behind him, Leo and Samantha were racing after him, screaming for Scout.

Jack pushed Scout away and helped Marina sit up. "I'm so sorry. Did he hurt you?"

"Not really, unless you count the sand in my hair." She shook out her hair and brushed sand from her dress. "Look at Scout," Marina said. "I think he's grinning at me."

Jack brushed a little sand from her face. Her skin was soft, not that he should have noticed.

Leo took a step toward her. "Ma'am, I'm sorry. It was all my fault."

Jack put his arm around Leo. "Those frisbees can sure go sideways on you." He tousled Leo's hair. "That was nice of you to apologize."

"Apology accepted, though not necessary," Marina said. "I should have been looking where I was going, but I was so deep in my thoughts."

"Don't get up. You might have hurt something. Your ankle again?" As Jack gazed at her, a thought bubbled up. She was the kind of woman who became more beautiful with age.

"I'm fine. But that darn dog…" She shook her finger at him. "We're going to have a talk."

As if Scout understood, he slunk toward Marina with his head lowered. She smoothed her hand over his silky, golden fur.

"Apology accepted," she said.

Jack picked up the frisbee and tossed it back to Leo. Scout raced after it with his gangly, lopsided gait.

"He's quite something," Marina said, clasping her arms around her legs. "Though I'm not sure what."

"Like an overgrown kid," Jack said, easing next to her on the sand. The sun brought out golden highlights in her hair.

"Cute kids," Marina said, tossing her hair back over her shoulders. "Ivy told me that Bennett was showing Denise and John a place. Along with Vanessa and Leo, right?"

"Bennett is writing up the lease for them right now, so I thought I'd give the kids something to do."

Marina tented her hands to watch the children. "They're good kids. I remember when my sisters and I used to visit our grandmother here in the summer. We would spend all day at the beach and only go in to eat. Or we'd roam the village, saving our pennies for ice cream."

"Sounds like an ideal childhood."

"In many ways, it was. Summer Beach is a great place for families."

"And for single people of a certain age?" Jack raised his brow.

Marina laughed—a little nervously, he noted. "I don't know about that." Abruptly, she switched topics. "How is your writing coming along?"

"Slower than I'd like," Jack said.

"I know what you mean," Marina said. "I wrote a lot of my material for the news, and I never had time to second-guess myself. Without a deadline, I'd flounder."

"We've both been chasing the news, just on opposite sides," Jack said, changing the conversation. "Do you miss it?"

Clasping her legs, she rested her chin on her knees. "I thought I would, but I'm not. But then, I fell into my career by accident."

"Are you taking the summer off?" he asked.

"Not like you. No, I've left that position…" She paused and shook her head. "I'm changing careers. It's time I do what I want with my life."

"And what's that?"

Marina's eyes lit with happiness. "I just had a great test run at the farmers market. With Kai's help, I sold out. That's part of a larger plan. See, I'm going to organize dinners at the cottage. And someday, I plan to open a cafe here in Summer Beach."

"Impressive. That's quite a career change." For the first time, Jack felt at ease with Marina, and she seemed a lot more relaxed, too. He leaned in toward her, and she didn't move.

Marina tucked a strand of hair behind her ear. "It's funny, but as soon as I took the time to slow down here, a lot of my problems became much clearer. And having family around—people who really know you—helps, too."

"You're lucky that way," Jack said.

Resting her gaze on him, she asked, "No family nearby?"

Jack gazed across the beach, watching Leo. Technically, that was no longer correct. "It's complicated."

Marina nodded as though she understood, and she didn't ask any more questions.

As they chatted, Jack found himself enjoying the ease of their conversation and hoping it wouldn't end. When Denise and John waved toward him that they were ready, disappointment gathered in his chest.

"Looks like I have to get the kids back to their parents," he said. That last word hit him. Clearing his throat, he asked,

"Would you be up for coffee one day? I often have breakfast at Java Beach."

"I hear that's gossip central," Marina said. "But I'm going to drop off some hors d'oeuvres at the Seabreeze Inn in a couple of days for their tea and wine reception." She paused as if considering this. "You could join us there, I'm sure. Since you're a former guest."

"I'd like that," Jack said. A tingly feeling coursed through him. He hadn't felt like this in ages. He rose and extended his hand to Marina to help her up. Her hand felt soft, yet her grip was firm.

"Any more sand on me?"

"Just a little." Jack brushed her shoulder, not because she had any sand there, but because he couldn't resist touching her silky skin. "There. All gone."

"See you later," Marina said with a little smile, setting off to continue her walk.

While Jack watched Marina stroll away, he called for Leo and Samantha. "Come on, time to clean up for supper." He'd have to get all these parent-type phrases down, but he figured kids would always be hungry after playing on the beach.

It worked. Grinning, Jack guided them in.

Scout bounded after them with the frisbee in his mouth. Jack helped the children rinse off their sandy feet at a spigot on the beach while Scout played in the water. A wet dog was better than a sandy dog, he figured.

"Is Marina going to have supper with us?" Leo asked. He and Samantha looked at each other and giggled.

"She has other things to do," Jack replied.

Samantha piped up. "She's pretty. She's your girlfriend, isn't she?"

"I've only just met her," Jack said, mussing the kids' hair. "It takes a while to get to boyfriend-girlfriend status. Put your shoes on, and let's go find your parents."

As Jack considered this, he realized he didn't know much

about Marina, though he'd like to know more. As he slung an arm around Leo, he wondered how dating might work as a single father. And how would Leo react to that?

And most important of all, when was Vanessa planning on telling Leo about Jack?

Chapter 16

*S*an Francisco

Dusting her hands on her jeans, Marina stood in her vacant apartment at the crossroads between her old and new paths. She and Kai had been sorting and packing almost two decades worth of her life.

Once a grand Victorian home, the three-story house was divided into flats. Though the rooms were small, Marina had enjoyed the location near the Golden Gate Park, where she and the twins had spent countless afternoons. Here is where Heather and Ethan had gone to school. Marina would be leaving many good friends behind, but she was eager to begin a new chapter in Summer Beach. And all of her friends promised to visit her there.

"Isn't it time for you to get ready?" Kai asked.

Marina hated putting on a suit again, but she had to meet her attorney, Yasmin, at the opposing counsel's office.

"I'm not looking forward to it." Marina picked up a journal she'd found while packing. "I have a feeling Yasmin will be interested in this, though." She tucked it into her purse so that she wouldn't forget it. What Marina had in mind was a long shot, but it was worth trying.

After parking, Marina looked for her attorney in the downstairs lobby of the towering skyscraper, one of the tallest in San Francisco. She spied her sitting on a sofa, reviewing notes. Marina made her way through the crowd toward her.

As Yasmin rose to meet her, she smoothed her dark suit and adjusted her red-framed glasses. "We're almost ready to begin."

According to Marina's employment agreement, she had to submit to mediation. Although California laws were changing in favor of employees, she still had to go through this process.

Marina followed her to a bank of elevators, and soon, they had arrived at the attorney's office for the television station. With a billion-dollar company, Hal's father probably had an army of lawyers across the country.

From their perch on the fortieth floor, they could see the Golden Gate Bridge in the distance. The décor was a study in steel-gray and gray, an overwhelmingly masculine atmosphere meant to intimidate.

It's working. Marina sucked in a breath and thought of all she had endured at the station, and decided that she would no longer be intimidated. *Not anymore.* She checked her purse to make sure her journal was still there.

"The higher the floor, the higher the fees," Yasmin said, looking around. "I think they might be scared of you. This can be a long, draining process, but the goal is to get a favorable settlement."

Marina was trying to breathe in the snug skirt that had once fit her hungry, rail-thin body. Setting her jaw, she brought the journal from her purse.

"As Kai and I were packing up the apartment, I came across some notes I'd kept over the years. I thought this might be useful today." Marina handed the journal to Yasmin. "See what you think."

Before Yasmin could look at it, an assistant appeared to escort them to a meeting room where the process would begin. As they walked through the office, thick carpet muffled their steps.

A plate glass window into a conference room broke the long hallway. Inside, Hal was hunched over the table with a team of dark suits. *His attorneys*, Marina figured. Beside him sat Babe, attired in a tight-fitting dress with a deep V-neckline. Just what Hal liked to see on women. When the pair glanced up, Marina quickly turned away.

Having to submit to such a process was mentally taxing, but Marina had signed the agreement when she'd been promoted to an anchor position years ago. While she was relatively happy for a long time, Hal came on board after the station was acquired, and everything changed. Hal was committed to bringing the show into the twenty-first century, as he often reminded everyone.

Marina agreed in concept, but she did not agree with the shenanigans that began taking place, which is why she'd kept a record of incidents she found distasteful and unfair. Hal played a starring role, but even Babe was in there. She'd started writing as a way to vent, never intending to show these writings to anyone.

After Marina and her attorney sat down to wait in another meeting room, Yasmin opened the journal. As soon as she began reading, her eyes grew wide.

"Has anyone seen this?" Yasmin asked.

"Except for my sister, no one. I wrote these incidents down as an emotional release. I thought they might prove helpful today." Marina knew what she had, but only Yasmin could determine the value.

A look of determination settled on Yasmin's face. "You could sue for harassment with this. Or use it as a bargaining tool."

"I want these jerks out of my life," Marina said. "I can make my own money. But don't let them know that."

"Got it," Yasmin said. "Wait here. I'm going to have a chat with Hal's boys."

Marina sat listening to the wall clock ticking in the conference room. As she waited, she reeled back the last two decades in her mind, comparing her life then to her life now. Except for the regular paycheck, Marina was infinitely happier in Summer Beach. She could see a future filled with family and friends and doing what she loved. Her future would be what she was willing to make of it.

If only she could get rid of Hal and Babe and the legal entanglements.

Presently, Yasmin returned. She stuffed a paper into her briefcase. "We're going now," she said evenly.

When Marina started to ask why, Yasmin winked and headed toward the door.

They rode the elevator in silence, and after they reached the ground floor and emerged into the sunshine, Yasmin turned to her.

"Congratulations," Yasmin said, breaking into a broad smile. She handed the journal to Marina. "You're a free woman. They went for the deal and agreed to call off everything. Plus, I negotiated a good settlement for your troubles." Yasmin named a number that made Marina smile.

This was more than Marina had hoped for, but certainly what she deserved. She could use that to get her new business off the ground and stretch out her savings cushion. Marina pressed the journal to her chest. "How can I thank you?"

"Thank yourself. By keeping such a detailed record with dates, places, and events, you nailed them." Yasmin smiled. "As I was leaving, Babe caught up to me and gave me her card. I think Hal has a huge problem on his hands."

"That's the best news I've heard," Marina said. Maybe

Babe realized Hal would treat her no better than he'd treated Marina. But that was of little concern to her now.

Marina hugged Yasmin before they parted. Marina strode back to her car with renewed lightness in her step. She was free. On the way back to her apartment, she called Gwen and Ginger, and each woman was elated for her. Marina burst through the door of her old apartment and flung her arms around Kai. "It's over," she cried.

After telling Kai what happened, her sister did a crazy little happy dance for her while Marina laughed. She quickly changed and joined Kai, ready to finish packing.

Kai emerged from the kitchen with a box. "Here's the last of your dishes." She placed the box on a stack of others that lined the living room.

THE NEXT MORNING, Marina and Kai cleaned the apartment while they waited for the movers. Marina wrung out a mop. "After the truck is loaded, we can head to the hotel, shower, and start the drive back to Summer Beach."

"Now we have something to celebrate," Kai said.

"Have you heard anything from Dmitri in Chicago?"

Sadness washed across Kai's face. "He's giving me the silent treatment."

"Life isn't all hearts and roses. It's important for couples to work through disagreements before they get married."

Kai leaned against the old mantle. "Did you and Stan ever fight."

As Marina recalled their arguments, she laughed. "The things we disagreed on seem so trivial now. Stan once forgot to pay the electric bill, and the lights were shut off during a party. Someone chided Stan, and I was mortified. We dug out candles, and everyone had a great time, but I didn't speak to him for two days. Now that seems so childish."

"I'd be upset, too," Kai said.

"It's one thing to be disappointed over someone's mistake that inconvenienced you, but those two days were before Stan went on a mission for a month. I had a lot of time to think and put things in perspective. By the time he returned, I'd changed. We'd both learned to take things in stride, solve problems, and move on. Life is too short not to laugh. And I'm glad we did."

Kai put her arm around Marina. "And now, here we are."

"Older and wiser—just making different mistakes now." Marina wrinkled her nose.

"Leaving your job here was not a mistake. Wait until we return. All those recipes you've been testing and the menus you've been working on will prove your skill."

"Did anyone ever tell you you're the best?"

"Right back at you," Kai said. "And next time I talk to Dmitri, I'm going to tell him that I'm glad we're arguing because we need to get to know each other better before we commit to a lifetime together." She paused and passed her hands over her face. "He's not going to like it, but I'm going to postpone the wedding. He rushed in a little too fast."

"I think that's wise," Marina said. "Even though I know it's painful."

The doorbell downstairs rang, and Marina buzzed in the moving team.

Three burly men appeared at the front door. "Everything here goes into storage?" one asked.

"Except for the boxes along that wall," Marina said, motioning to a few boxes that would fit in her car.

As the men began carrying out the remnants of her life, Marina's phone rang, and Ethan's image appeared on the screen.

"Hey, Mom. How's the move going?"

"Pretty smooth, sweetie. I'm putting our belongings into storage for six months until I get situated in Summer Beach."

"You're really staying there?" His voice held a note of disbelief.

"I'm sure Heather shared that meme with you," Marina said, making a face. "My agent says I need to cool my job search. But I love Summer Beach, and I have a brand new venture that's going to put me right back on top." Marina bit her lip. She needed to be more realistic with the kids.

"As long as you're happy, Mom," Ethan said.

"I'd meant to talk to you about this in person," Marina said, diving into the subject she'd been dreading. "It's important that we make preparations for the coming school year."

"What do you mean?"

"I've contacted Duke to get the financial aid paperwork going. You and Heather will stay in school, and we'll simply pay the loans later. The two of you must stay on track with your education."

"Yeah, about that…" Ethan's voice trailed off.

"Have you found a summer job yet? If not, there's room at Ginger's. I can help you find work here."

"Mom, please." Ethan blew out a breath. "I called because I need to talk to you."

Marina's mom-antenna sparked a warning. "I'm listening."

"See, it's like this… Duke's a great school, but it's not for me."

"If it's your grades, you can get another tutor," Marina said quickly. "As many as you need to get through. We've faced this before, and you can do it again. I know you can, Ethan. Heather is there to help, too. Don't quit now."

"Mom, listen to me. Please."

As the movers hurried around her with boxes, Marina frowned and gripped the phone. "Go on."

"This is not a problem that you have to race in to solve," Ethan said earnestly. "I'm not a kid anymore, and I know what I want. Golf is all I've ever wanted to do. If I put the time in to practice that I put into schoolwork, I think I can step up several levels."

"But your education—"

"I can always go back to school, and it doesn't have to be Duke. I know it's expensive."

"Sweetie, don't even think about that. I will do anything for you and Heather."

Ethan expelled a great sigh. "I've already quit school. I'll find a friend to stay with where I can practice every day. I want to go pro, and I don't want to wait until after I graduate. Golf is the only thing I can do well."

Marina chewed on a fingernail. "You might find other subjects you like."

Sounding exasperated, Ethan burst out over the phone. "I have dyslexia. But did you know that some other top golfers do, too? I know I can do this. I'm not going back to Duke. It's over."

Marina pressed a hand to her face to stem the tears that sprang to her eyes. *What would Stan do?* She could hear the earnestness in her son's voice, yet she was still a parent who wanted the best for her children.

She tried again. "You know that your future job prospects will be limited without an education."

Ethan let out a frustrated cry. "Haven't you heard anything I've said? Geez, Mom, why can't you listen? I suck at school, but I'm a solid golfer. I can always find work at golf clubs."

Marina paced the floor, trying to think of a way to get through to him. This wasn't what she'd planned for him. She'd worked hard to give her children the education they would need.

And then it hit her.

Here she was, making changes in her life to do what she truly wanted. Couldn't she give her son the same benefit? Marina caught Kai's empathetic expression. As difficult as it was to let go of her dream for him, she had to let her son live his dream.

Catching her breath, Marina said, "I do understand. If there's anything you need…" She'd already told Ethan and Heather that she would put their boxes in the storage unit in the front so that they could get whatever they needed.

"Thanks, but I got this," Ethan said. "I've been working at a country club course here in Durham, so I've got some money saved."

"You didn't mention that before." Nor did Heather.

"No one knew. I wanted to see if I could actually get a job in golf. And I did."

Marina was impressed. "You've really thought this out?"

"Yeah, I have. Don't worry about me. I've got this."

Sighing, Marina said, "I admit I was shocked at first, but I want you to know I'm proud of you for following your heart." Her son was no longer a child, and he was taking his first steps to secure the future he wanted.

"Thanks for saying that, Mom."

She could hear gratitude in her son's voice and wished she could hug him. After telling him how much she loved him, she hung up.

"Wow," Kai said, arching an eyebrow. "I gather Ethan has dropped out of school. I wonder what Heather will think of that. She might feel abandoned."

"I hope not. I left a message for Heather to make sure. But I'm sure she will want what's best for Ethan." Still, Marina couldn't help but feel that Kai might be right.

"Once all this is packed, let's eat," Kai said. "I'm already starving."

Marina withdrew some cash from her jeans and handed it to Kai. "My treat. You know my favorite places. Bring anything to tide us over."

"Sushi, Thai rolls, cannoli, or tacos?"

"Surprise me. And before we leave, I have more foodie research to do. Are you up for staying another day?"

"Yum, I like the sound of that. I don't have to be anywhere," Kai said, hurrying out the door.

After Kai returned, Marina sat with her sister in a corner of the living room. They ate sushi while the movers loaded the van and talked about the summer ahead.

Once the van was packed, Marina closed the door to the apartment and delivered the key to the landlord upstairs. Marina and Kai showered at the inn they had booked while the apartment was torn apart, and then they spent the rest of the day and the next morning visiting many of Marina's favorite hole-in-the-wall restaurants. Having lived in the neighborhood for years, she knew many of the owners. After sharing her plans in Summer Beach, several offered to help and told her to call anytime she needed guidance.

"What's the most challenging aspect of running your restaurant?" Marina asked one owner.

"Consistency in food preparation, hiring the right employees—and standing on your feet most of the day." The woman placed her hands on the counter and beamed. "But I like making good food that people enjoy. Food is love—and you have to love to serve others."

"I think that's true of many professions," Marina said. In her former position, she got up early every morning, eager to share the day's news with viewers. Many contacted her through social media or wrote to her to thank her for her friendly, even-toned reporting style. When Hal arrived at the station, he had complained, saying that she was too nice—a dinosaur, in fact—and that today's viewers wanted edgy shows.

Edgy shows and sexy young women, that was the news show Hal wanted.

He sure paid for that mistake. Now, Marina could laugh at that comment, although it had cut deeply at the time. If she were a dinosaur, that was fine with her. She was too old and experienced to go against her principles of journalistic integrity.

Once again, she found herself eager to get up in the morning and ready to serve others. Only this time, instead of the fare being news, it would be good food and a relaxing setting by the sea.

Marina couldn't wait to get back to work.

When Marina's tiny car was packed, she and Kai drove by her old apartment one more time. With one hand resting on the steering wheel, she looked up at the old Victorian building. "This is the end of an era, isn't it?"

"It's someone else's turn to start fresh here," Kai said. "You have Summer Beach."

"And the summer to kick off this crazy idea."

Kai put her hand on Marina's arm. "It's not crazy. I'd intended to spend a few weeks relaxing in the sun while Dmitri hammered out deals in Chicago and New York, but I'm all in with you on this project."

"You can go anytime," Marina said.

"I know, but I'm liking this vibe." Kai drummed her hands on the dashboard. "Let's go. It's time that you got back to work."

"That reminds me." Marina tapped a quick text to Ivy. *On our way back from SF. Okay to deliver the first batch of hors d'oeuvres to the Seabreeze Inn tomorrow?*

Ivy's reply came quickly. *Can't wait! Drive safe, and see you then. Guests will be excited. When are you open for parties?*

With a frisson of excitement in her chest, Marina showed Kai the text. "Looks like we're really in business."

Kai bounced in her seat. "Want me to make a shopping list for you as you drive?"

"That would be great. I want to create standard shopping lists for certain dishes. That will save a lot of time in the future, and I can project costs for the dinner so I'll know what to charge, and what kind of profit I can expect from each event. From that, I'll calculate my return on investment and on time."

"Smart." Kai stretched her arm into the back seat to grab a notepad out of her purse. "You already sound like a business owner."

"My visit to City Hall was a wake-up. At first, I found all those forms daunting, but that's what it takes to be a professional."

"One step at a time, as Ginger always says." Kai clicked her pen.

As Marina recalled what Boz had said, an idea struck her. She quickly explained the stiff competition local Summer Beach restaurants were facing. "I know I'm the new kid in town, but the right media coverage to illuminate the issue would help."

Listening, Kai shook her head. "The problem seems deeper than that. Restaurants in Summer Beach have great food, but visitors don't know it. That could be part of the reason they're visiting, aside from the great beach."

"That's public relations," Marina said. Tapping her fingers on the steering wheel, she turned to Kai. "What if there were an annual event that showcased local restaurants? Like a giant tasting party."

"Maybe a famous chef that could rate the local restaurants?" Kai's eyes widened. "Who's that chef with the spiky white-blond hair and the cool car?"

"He gets a zillion requests," Marina said. "We need something we can count on, something fast and effective."

Kai flipped open the pad of paper and clicked her pen. "Brainstorming time. Ready when you are."

"Let the ideas flow," Marina said, pulling into traffic. "We're on our way."

. . .

ON THE DRIVE back to Summer Beach, Marina dictated shopping lists, menus, and even recipes she had in her head. The more she could standardize from the beginning, the easier the tasks would be, especially once the business started growing.

Marina and Kai brainstormed ideas that could help the local restaurants and the entire community of Summer Beach. Marina couldn't wait to share her ideas. She'd start with Ivy and Mitch.

When they parked the car in front of the cottage and began removing boxes from the small trunk, Jack emerged from the guest cottage.

"Welcome back," he called out. Scout raced eagerly in front of him. "Need help with those boxes?"

"Sure do," Marina said. Scout circled her legs, begging for attention. "Hey, you, did you miss me?" She knelt to rub Scout's neck, and then the dog whined to Kai to join in.

"He sure did," Jack said as he picked up a couple of boxes. "Tell me where to put these."

"Thanks," Marina said. "In the garage. I made some space on the side before I left. Hit the opener in the kitchen by the back door. If Ginger's here, the door is probably open."

After waiting until Jack was out of earshot, Kai said, "I think he missed you more than Scout."

"I doubt that."

"I don't know," Kai said with a little grin. "What's going on with you two?"

"Absolutely nothing." Still, even as Marina uttered the words, she felt a little pinch in her chest. There was something about Jack that made her pulse quicken when he was near. "I don't have the time to think about him."

"There's something," Kai said. "I know that look in your eyes."

"Okay, we had a good talk before I left. Jack was on the beach playing frisbee with Leo and Samantha, and the frisbee got away from Leo. Scout was chasing it, and we had a little run-in. Anyway, after we sat and talked for a while, Jack helped me up then dusted me off."

Kai's eyes flashed. "In the theater, we call that the meet-cute scene."

"Oh, stop it. There was nothing meet-y or cute-y about it. Shh, here he comes." Marina paused to watch Jack stroll back. Scout heeled beside him, looking up at Jack with adoring eyes.

"Got another one for me?" Jack scratched Scout behind the ears.

Marina leaned into the back seat to pull out another box. "Got it. Here you go. And those on the other side, too."

Jack loaded up the next round of boxes and took off.

"What did I tell you?" Kai let out a little squeal. "Did you see that? He was enjoying the view when you reached into the car."

"Kai! He was not. He wasn't even looking my way when I brought that box out."

"Well, he wasn't obvious about it, but I can tell. I'm trained to read body language. He looked away out of modesty. You know what that means."

"Cut it out right now." Marina remembered a promise she had made to Jack and passed a hand over her face. "Look, Ginger's waving at you from the window. Better see what she wants."

Kai turned around. "No, she isn't. I'm not six years old anymore."

Jack returned with Scout prancing beside him. "What else do you have?"

"Just these." Marina pointed to the last boxes. Kai was leaning against the car, intent on staying right where she was.

Marina cleared her throat. "Say, I'm going to cater the tea and wine gathering at the inn tomorrow. You mentioned you might want to check it out."

"Sure," Jack said, his face brightening. "I need to get out from behind the computer."

Marina hooked a thumb into her jeans pocket. "How's the writing?"

"Still organizing my notes. But I'll get there."

"Okay. Well, thanks for the help." After what Kai said, Marina felt awkward. "See you tomorrow?"

"Wouldn't miss your debut for the world." He snapped his fingers and pointed toward the cottage. Scout raced ahead of him toward the guest cottage.

Once the sisters were inside the house, Kai burst out laughing. "Jack's interested, no doubt about it."

Marina thought of the conversation they had on the beach. She could feel herself falling for Jack, but she feared stepping into another insta-love mess as she had with Grady.

"I don't have time for this nonsense," Marina said, feeling flustered. "Especially after Grady. Kai, I'm no kid, and I'm raising two of my own."

Ginger emerged from the kitchen. "I saw Jack helping you with those boxes. Is everything okay between you two now?"

"Just fine, except my sister has it in her head that I'm interested in him."

"Okay, if you insist," Kai said, shrugging. "Although what I actually said was that he's interested in you."

Ginger raised her brow. "He's a fine specimen of a man. Might make someone happy."

Marina's mouth opened. "I can't believe you just said that."

Ginger whipped around, her zebra-striped caftan fluttering in the breeze off the ocean. "Well, I ain't dead yet," she said before returning to the kitchen.

Marina swept her hands over her hair. "I don't know what's gotten into the two of you, but I've got to shop for groceries." Picking up her purse again, she headed outside to her car.

Having an interest in Jack—or any man right now—was the last thing on her mind. And Jack had problems of his own.

She didn't know what they were, but there was something he was hiding. She could just feel it.

Marina wanted no part of complicated problems. *I have enough of those, thank you very much.* She started the car.

Kai came running out waving a list they'd made on the drive home. "You forgot this."

Marina rolled down the window and snatched it from her. "I don't want to hear any more about Jack Ventana. I have work to do. Ethan might have quit school, but I still have to provide for him and make sure Heather stays in school. This is my life, Kai."

Kai folded her arms on the car door. "Exactly my point. Tough stuff happens, but if you're not at least trying to make every day special, then what's the point? As for Jack, I know you're just getting over Grady, but isn't it nice to know there's someone who finds you attractive? Do with that what you will." She made a face and whipped a hand around in a theatrical gesture. "And that's all I've got to say about that."

Marina started laughing. She didn't want to be angry at Kai. "This is one crazy family, you know that?"

Marina was including herself in that statement. Still, Jack was creeping into her thoughts more often. With all that she'd endured with Grady, she wasn't sure that was wise. One summer, that's all this was.

Chapter 17

The next morning, Marina went to work in the cottage kitchen, preparing the hors d'oeuvres for Ivy's afternoon event at the Seabreeze Inn. After taking her chilled pie dough from the refrigerator, she pulled out Ginger's old wooden rolling pin from a drawer.

Sprinkling a little flour on the dough and the roller to reduce the stickiness of the dough, she pressed the rolling pin down, smoothing out what would form the crust for the miniature mushroom and walnut tarts she'd made many times.

"That old rolling pin has seen almost as many years as I have," Ginger said as she walked in the kitchen. "That was a wedding gift from one of my aunts, and it traveled the world with me."

Marina tapped the rolling pin on the counter. "The first time I remember using it was to flatten modeling clay."

"Isn't it interesting to think that mere objects will enjoy a longer life than we will," Ginger said, glancing around the kitchen.

Marina raised her head. That kind of talk from Ginger made her nervous. "Are you feeling okay, Grandma?"

Ginger put an arm around Marina and kissed her cheek. "I'm fine, sweetie. You don't call me Grandma very often."

Marina was grateful that she and her sisters still had Ginger. "Maybe I'm feeling nostalgic. I was thinking about when I first made these tarts for you and Grandpa. I think I was about eighteen."

"Perhaps I should have encouraged you more toward the culinary arts back then. Why, Julia Child would have loved to have met you and shared some of her dishes with you."

"But I had you, and you had her recipes, even her special ones. Which ones are your favorites?"

"One can't go wrong with her Boeuf Bourguignon or Quiche Lorraine. And her Crepes Suzette are always to die for. Those recipes are in her books that I gave you." Ginger filled a kettle with cold water for tea and put it on the stovetop. "Watching her cook with Jacques Pepin on *Cooking in Concert* was such a treat. That show always reminds me of the time I spent with her in Boston."

Marina pressed a round cookie cutter into the dough before fashioning the small rounds into a miniature muffin tin. When that one was full, she filled a second one.

Ginger inspected the areas where Marina had organized and measured her ingredients at different stations. "Very nice *mise en place*."

"You taught me to start organized and stay organized. Sure helps the process."

"Need help with anything?"

"Thanks, but I've got this," Marina said. She was in the flow and enjoying herself.

Ginger measured out loose Earl Grey tea, and the citrusy bergamot aroma wafted through the kitchen. She poured the leaves into a mesh ball and snapped it shut before hanging it inside a teapot. "What type of hors d'oeuvres are you preparing?"

"This pie dough is for mushroom and walnut tarts with

fresh thyme from your herb garden. There was plenty, so I thought you wouldn't mind. I'll also serve cucumber curls with crabmeat, topped with an avocado emulsion, and a dollop of tobiko."

"Good choices. You'll serve the cucumber crab first? It's lighter on the palate."

"Of course," Marina said. "Along with pear slices topped with goat cheese and crispy pancetta—all drizzled with honey. I'll have ingredients ready for final assembly at the inn."

Marina motioned to a glass dish. "And I'll finish with my luau spare ribs, which I'm marinating now. I'm using rice vinegar, soy sauce, ginger, and garlic, and then I'll sprinkle the spare ribs with sesame seeds and slivered green onion stalks. I'll also serve my rosemary and olive breads with olive oil."

"Sounds delicious. I'm sure the guests will enjoy it." Ginger brought two antique teacups from the cupboard. "When do you think we'll have our first dinner here?"

"Ivy is going to make an announcement at the gathering." Marina paused to stir a mixture of mushrooms, walnuts, thyme, and onions on the stovetop. "As for other marketing, I'll pass out flyers at the farmers market this weekend, Kai has the website ready, and I'm going to test some local ads on social media to drive traffic. I'm aiming for two weeks to get dinners underway. In the meantime, I'll keep selling at the farmers market."

Ginger warmed the teacups with hot water. "Events like this one at the inn will send the word around Summer Beach in no time."

"I hope so." Marina recalled the list of ideas that she and Kai had brainstormed on the drive from San Francisco. "Has Summer Beach ever had a food festival showcasing local restaurants?"

"Not that I recall. Why?"

"I've been thinking about what Boz said at City Hall, about chain restaurants stealing business from local places.

Wouldn't it be interesting to organize a tasting festival here? We could make Summer Beach a destination for foodies and support the local economy."

"I think it's a marvelous idea," Ginger said. "And where would you have this event?"

"Ivy mentioned that they had an art show on the grounds of the Seabreeze Inn last year. We could do it there."

"Or here," Ginger said. "The yard is certainly large enough. People can easily walk from the village, and we have plenty of street parking. That would bring attention to your work."

"Kai has offered to handle the entertainment, which we could set up on the deck. I can contact the local and regional news to gain coverage." As she spoke of the idea, Marina was growing more excited. "We might call it Taste of Summer Beach, a food festival. Kai can whip up a website fairly quickly, and I'll pitch it to local restaurateurs."

"Cookie could probably help you, too," Ginger said. "I like your drive and enthusiasm. So, what's stopping you?"

Marina laughed. "Guess I'd better get to work. I'll talk to Bennett to confirm a good date on the summer calendar. I imagine we'll need at least a month to pull it together."

Ginger arranged the cups and teapot on the red Formica table. "What's the latest on the patio addition?"

"Axe can start at the first of the week. He called while I was in San Francisco and sent the proposal. I want to go over it with you first."

Marina still had an uneasy feeling about burdening her grandmother by running a business out of the cottage. "Are you sure you don't mind a lot of activity around here? Between building a deck and giving dinners, I'm afraid of infringing on your privacy and relaxation."

"You sound as if you don't know what I like," Ginger said. "Since when have you ever seen me in a rocking chair in the corner?"

With that image in her mind, Marina suppressed a laugh. "I didn't mean that."

Ginger lifted her chin with determination. "We've got to live life as if it's the greatest gift ever granted to us—because it is. I've loved every minute that's been afforded to me, even the tough ones. I don't plan to slow down for a long time, so let's get this show underway." The tea kettle whistled, and Ginger removed it from the stove and set it aside to rest. "Can you sit for a moment?"

"I'd like that." Marina turned off the mushroom mix and put the tart shells into the oven while Ginger poured hot water into the teapot to steep the tea.

"There, I have a few minutes," Marina said, sitting down to join Ginger.

"I'm looking forward to having a lively household again," Ginger said. "Bertrand and I always did so much entertaining—and with such fascinating people from all over the world. I couldn't be happier about what you're doing."

Marina could just see Ginger welcoming the guests like Auntie Mame, infusing the evening with a theatrical element. Seeing Ginger having a good time would almost be worth the effort alone.

Ginger poured tea while they talked about the new deck. Marina showed Ginger the one she liked. "This will be a beautiful addition, even if the pop-up dinners are a flop—"

"Don't you dare put that vibe out into the universe," Ginger said, bristling.

Marina laughed. "You sound like Kai."

"Where do you think she got it from?" Ginger huffed. "Now, I won't have that kind of talk. You will be successful, so charge ahead full speed."

"I'll call Axe and tell him to begin the construction," Marina said as she sipped her tea. Ginger was always exacting in how she made her tea, and Marina had to admit it was worth it. "Axe said the entire process won't take long at all."

"He's a good man, from what I hear."

The timer for the oven went off, and Marina rose. "Back to work."

Ginger glanced at Marina's jeans and T-shirt. "I know this is the beach, but you will change before going over there, right?"

"If I have time," Marina said, noticing the clock. "I'll spend most of the time in the kitchen prepping dishes. Ivy is going to make the announcement."

Ginger shook her head. "You'll do that before everyone arrives. You must be the spokesperson for your company. No one better than you. After I finish my tea, I'll help you assemble the cucumber and crab while you make the avocado emulsion. And I'll keep an eye on the spareribs. That way, you'll have time for a quick shower and dress. I'll get Kai, and we'll help you set up at the inn. Best foot forward, dear. Always."

AFTER SHOWERING and changing while Ginger was finishing in the kitchen, Marina took the first trays of hors d'oeuvres to put into the car. When her phone rang, she leaned against her car and answered. "Hi Heather, what's up?"

Her daughter's voice exploded across the line. "Mom, what in the world are you thinking?"

"Excuse me?"

"You gave Ethan permission to leave school? After all your lectures about how important college is, how could you do that?"

"That was his decision to make, and he did." Marina bit her lip. She could tell this wasn't going to be a quick call.

"No, it isn't," Heather wailed, becoming even more distraught. "Ethan has left me here at school all by myself. Going to Duke wasn't even my idea. I did it only because he got a golf scholarship. He begged me, told me he needed me to help him, and now he's bailed on me. I have a final exam tomorrow that I know I'm going to fail because of him."

Marina thought she knew what was behind this. Somehow, she had to diffuse her daughter's outbreak and get her on track for her exam. "Heather, is there someone you can call to study with?"

"How could I make any new friends here with Ethan dissing every single person I met? No one was up to his standards. It was like he wanted me to stay with him all the time. So no, there's no one I know to call."

"I wasn't aware of that, honey." Heather and Ethan had had arguments in the past, but nothing like this. Marina needed to calm Heather, but she was aware of the minutes ticking by, too. She didn't want to be late for her first event, but she had to support her daughter.

"Ethan abandoned me. When he needed me, I was there, but when I begged him not to leave, it didn't matter at all to him."

"I understand why you feel that way." Marina knew what it was like to feel abandoned—and on national television, no less. But this was about her daughter. Thinking fast, she said, "School is almost over for the year. This is when all your hard work and careful notes count." Even though Heather prepared well for tests, she was often nervous. Maybe her hysteria over Ethan was due in part to that.

"I haven't been able to study because of Ethan," Heather cried as she broke into a sob.

Marina wished she could be with Heather to put her arms around her and soothe her. The first year away from home had been rough on the kids, and Heather and Ethan had never been separated.

Still, Ethan had made his decision. Even if Marina didn't fully agree with it, she could see his point. Maybe he'd change his mind and go to another school in the fall. But where did that leave Heather?

On her own for the first time in her life.

Marina saw Ginger look through the window. She was clearly concerned about the time, too. "Heather, honey, is there anyone you can talk to there?"

"No one. Ethan never liked my new friends. He said they were shallow rich girls, and the guys were even worse. And the smart ones he called show-offs." She sniffed. "I hate it when he's so right."

"It's a challenging school with high academics," Marina said, wondering if she'd made a mistake in sending her children across the country. "But for you, I thought Duke would be a good fit."

"It's not Duke, it could be anywhere. Ethan's gone, and I can't focus on anything else. I'm going to fail my exams, and that will be all his fault."

Now Marina understood. Heather had been Ethan's support for schoolwork. On the other hand, Ethan, with his ability to make friends easily, provided the social support that Heather needed. "Sweetheart, you can do this without Ethan. I know it's too late in the year to make friends and get the support you need, but right now, you have to take a deep breath and put everything in perspective."

"I don't know what you mean by that."

Marina looked back and saw Ginger at the door, tapping the watch on her wrist. Marina nodded. While her food debut was important, Heather needed her now.

"Show Ethan what you're made of," Marina said. "He looks up to you and your academic ability. Maybe he's even intimidated by it, or a little jealous. Golf might be the right choice for him, but for you, your academic record has always been a source of pride. You have the ability to excel in whatever you put your fabulous brain to work on. Can you find a different place to study? Someplace where you can focus, but you're not alone?"

Heather sniffed. "I think so."

"I know you're so angry you feel like smashing Ethan right now, but remember, he's also your biggest cheerleader. And he will feel horrible if you fail out of school. So will you, sweetie. Just set your mind on what must be done—nothing else—and get through this next week. I know you can do that. After you finish your finals, come to Summer Beach. You've earned some beach time."

"But what about next year? I don't want to stay here without him."

"I'm sure there's a solution, maybe one we haven't even thought about. But for now, go for a run and try to clear your mind. Worry about you right now, not Ethan. I know you can pass your exams with high grades, but you'll have to focus and commit the time to study, starting now. Can you do that?"

Heather sniffed again. "I guess so." Her voice sounded small, but at least she had stopped crying.

Despite the minutes slipping away, Marina had to stay calm for Heather. This moment could change the course of Heather's academic career. "I love you, honey, no matter what. But if you allow this to drag you down, you may regret it. Can you pull out those running shoes I gave you for your birthday?"

"Yeah, I guess so."

"Do that, and I'll wait." Marina prayed that she could help Heather out of this. If she failed her exams, it would be harder for her to transfer schools, if that's what she wanted. Not impossible, but failing courses would devastate Heather.

Marina saw the front door swing open as Ginger and Kai hurried out with trays of appetizers covered in plastic wrap. Marina pressed a hand against her heart. "Thank you." Pointing at the phone, she added in a whisper, "It's Heather. She's upset about Ethan."

"We've got this," Kai said. "Just take care of her."

Heather came back on the phone. "I've got them," she said, sounding stronger.

"Okay, put them on." Marina could hear the sound of Heather doing just that.

"Now, grab your keys and headphones and ID."

"Mom?" Heather sounded calmer.

"Yes, darling?"

"I think I've got this now. I'm still mad at Ethan, but I'll show him that I can do this without him. I'll be okay. I'm going for that run now, and then I'll head to a coffee shop and start jamming on the books. Thanks, Mom. I love you for understanding."

"I love you, too, sweetie. You've got this." Marina sent her a couple of air kisses before hanging up. Being clear across the country was challenging, but at least Heather sounded better. As for Ethan, she'd have a talk with him, too.

Between them, Ginger and Kai had finished loading the car for her while she was on the phone.

"We can still make it just in time," Kai called out. "We'll take the rest of the food. Now go, and we'll meet you there."

Marina slid into her little car with her heart pounding. Just in time was good enough.

Chapter 18

*D*riving as quickly as she dared without jostling the trays of hors d'oeuvres in the back seat and trunk of her car, Marina wound through the streets of Summer Beach. Heather's call had her running behind, but Ginger and Kai had stepped up to help, and she was so grateful. She eased into the rear parking area behind the Seabreeze Inn and came to rest where Ivy had told her to park—right next to Ivy's cherry red, vintage Chevrolet convertible.

Marina turned off the car and gripped the steering wheel for a moment to gather herself. She hadn't been this nervous since her first day on the air reading the news. Creating food that people loved is what she yearned to do now. Still, everyone had different tastes in food.

Too much salt to some was merely a good start to others.

Marina glanced in the back seat to check on her trays. She'd made a variety of appetizers to appeal to different palates, but she knew there could be harsh critics among the strangers. She'd also taken special care in creating her sample dinner menus to take into account health and dietary restrictions.

Ivy emerged on the back steps of the grand old house and

waved. She wore a flowing, flowery top with a turquoise necklace, jeans, and leopard-print kitten heels. The effect was casual but carefully coordinated with stylish pieces. "Need a hand?"

"Sure. Kai and Ginger are right behind me, too." Marina hugged Ivy in greeting. She was so happy to have reunited with her old friend in Summer Beach. And she was glad she'd heeded Ginger's advice and changed clothes. She'd found a canary-yellow sundress that still fit around her pleasantly expanding waistline and borrowed coral accessories from Ginger.

"I'm excited for you today," Ivy said. "I'm sure you can make a go of this venture. Your intimate dinners can be highly personalized to diners. People will enjoy that. But it's a little selfish on my part, too. I want to see you stay in Summer Beach."

Marina opened the door to the back seat. "That will all depend on if I can build this business."

"I understand that," Ivy said, taking a tray that Marina handed to her. "Was Boz helpful at City Hall?"

"He gave me a flurry of forms and sent me on my way. I'm afraid I might have been a little overwhelmed and frustrated that day, but it didn't have anything to do with Boz. Still, I gained valuable insights from him." She brought out another tray.

Marina and Ivy hurried up a ramp to the rear door, and Shelly held it open. "When I first met Boz, I didn't make the best impression either," Ivy said. "I think he's used to stressed-out city people when they first arrive in Summer Beach."

"But we all get our chill on after we've been here a while," Shelly added. She wore a short white sundress with her long chestnut hair piled high in a casually twisted topknot.

Marina noticed that Ivy and Shelly were as different as Marina and Kai were. And then there was Brooke, the earth mother of the three Moore sisters, who was so busy with her family that Marina and Kai hardly saw her anymore. Brooke barely had time for an occasional text, but Marina was determined to see her soon.

Inside, the kitchen was a vintage throwback to the 1950s. Twin turquoise refrigerators hummed away. She and Ivy placed the trays on long counters that must have been used for large dinners and catering in the old home.

"I've made room in Gertie if you need to put anything in the fridge," Ivy said.

Marina looked at the old units. "You've named the refrigerator?"

"And the other one is Gert," Shelly said. "Gert and Gertie just seemed to fit them, though Gertie is the harder working one of the two."

"We weren't always this nutty," Shelly said. "You'll see. Once you relax and get in the groove here, you'll forget what your uptight old self was like."

Thinking of the old oven Ginger called Myrtle, Marina laughed. "I think I'm going to like living in Summer Beach."

"You have to come to my yoga class," Shelly said. "I gave you a pass when you stayed here because of your foot. But that ankle looks pretty good now."

"Most of the time," Marina said. She glanced at a large kitchen clock shaped like a seashell. She didn't have much time to set up. "We'd better get the rest of the hors d'oeuvres in here."

Between the three women, they quickly unloaded Marina's car, and Marina shared her idea of a food festival with Ivy, who agreed to mention it to the crowd to build interest. Ivy excused herself to check on guests while Marina set up in the kitchen.

"We have some large platters if you need them," Shelly said. "That's what Mitch uses for his cookies. Might save you some trips back into the kitchen."

"That would be better," Marina agreed. She was short of

supplies, but she was trying to conserve expenditures, especially with what the deck would cost, even though Axe had quoted a reasonable price.

"I'll get them from the butler's pantry." Shelly disappeared and then returned with an armful of beautiful antique platters. "They came with the house, among other treasures."

Marina turned on the oven to warm the walnut-mushroom tarts and the luau spareribs.

Just then, Ginger and Kai arrived. "Tell us what to do," Ginger said.

Marina directed them to place the cold cucumber and crab rolls on a platter while she assembled the pear and crisp prosciutto, being careful in stacking them. They worked quickly, and soon everything was ready.

"Let's go," Marina said, hefting a platter onto her shoulder for support. Inside the music room, she placed it on a table where Ivy directed her.

Antique chandeliers lit the graciously appointed room. A grand piano stood on one side, and a marble fireplace flanked the other. French doors stood open to the veranda, letting in the late afternoon breeze. A few guests reclined by the pool, and beyond them, waves rolled onto shore. Marina couldn't imagine a better place for her debut.

"These look sensational," Poppy said, surveying the hors d'oeuvres. "I'm glad you brought extra. We invited some local people and new summer residents to help spread the word."

"That's wonderful, thanks," Marina said. This event could cement her future in Summer Beach. Or, if the guests hated her food, it could spell the end of her new career. Anxiety gripped Marina, and she glanced up at a French, gilded ormolu clock ticking loudly on the fireplace mantle. She'd soon find out which it would be.

After setting up, Marina clasped her hands to keep them from trembling. Guests were arriving at the afternoon tea-and-wine event, with outfits ranging from stylish beach cover-ups to cocktail dresses. A teenage girl sat down at the piano and began to play "What a Wonderful World," and Marina could feel the mood in the room instantly lift.

She watched the guest's reactions as they selected her handcrafted hors d'oeuvres from a platter and tried them. This was the best market research she could have. Mitch rushed in with a tray of fresh oatmeal cookies studded with cranberries, macadamia nuts, and white chocolate. Evidently, these were a known favorite, as guests immediately scooped these up, too.

Standing beside Marina, Ginger greeted people she knew, while Kai hummed along with the music. Marina smiled when she saw Leilani and Roy

"How is the new garden doing?" Leilani asked.

"Everything is thriving," Marina said, spotting Jack at the door with his friends Vanessa, Denise, and John. The two children darted toward the cookies, and then made their way to the open doors to the veranda. "As long as Scout stays out of it."

"What's this about Scout?" Jack asked, joining them along with Vanessa, who had threaded her arm through his for support. "He's more popular than I am."

Marina's heart went out to Vanessa. "Would you like to sit down? There's a comfy-looking wingback chair where you can sit and still watch the kids outside."

"I'd like that," Vanessa said, and Jack helped her get settled.

"Can I bring a plate of hors d'oeuvres for you?" Jack asked. "Marina made them."

"I don't have much of an appetite right now, but I wish I did. The food looks delicious." Vanessa touched Marina's hand.

"Another time," Marina said softly.

When Jack left to get a glass of water for her and check on the children, Vanessa trailed him with her eyes. "He's such a good man. I don't know what I would have done without him."

Taking Marina's hand, Vanessa went on. "He saved my life once, you know. We were reporting on a dangerous situation, and he threw himself over me to protect me from bullets whizzing overhead." She gazed after Jack. "I'm afraid I might have underestimated him in the past."

Vanessa's words tore at Marina's heart. This woman was suffering, and Marina felt for her and her son. More than that, Vanessa seemed very much in love with Jack.

Marina chatted with Vanessa for a while. "Will you be staying in Summer Beach long?" Marina asked.

"I'd like to stay as long as I can." Vanessa glanced through the doors that stood open to the beach and the sea beyond. "All I want is to feel the sun on my shoulders and my son's arms around me."

Jack returned with a glass of water for Vanessa, and her face bloomed when he handed it to her. After Denise and John joined them, Marina excused herself to check on the food. She made a mental note to ask Denise what Vanessa might be able to eat so that she could make something special for her.

Marina caught a glimpse of a guest picking up a few of the appetizers. She watched as the man ate a mushroom-walnut tart and nodded with pleasant surprise. He said something to the woman he was with before returning to get another plate for her.

Marina let out a sigh of relief. She would have to replenish the food shortly.

Ivy signaled to her, and Marina joined her.

"I'm going to welcome everyone and introduce Celia's student musician, and then I'll introduce you. Did you want to say a few words?"

"I'd like that, thanks." Though Marina was a seasoned speaker, this was all new to her, and she felt jittery. She smoothed her yellow sundress and lifted her chin, summoning her professional presence.

After the applause subsided for the young pianist, Ivy turned to Marina. "Today we're enjoying appetizers from Marina Moore, who has recently returned to Summer Beach. She's organizing a food festival called Taste of Summer Beach this summer, and she has a new venture that I'll let her tell you all about."

"Thank you, Ivy," Marina began, projecting her voice so those standing on the veranda could hear her. "Ivy and Shelly and Poppy invited me to share some of my favorite recipes, which I hope you're enjoying. Along with the food festival, I'm also creating a fun, new concept in dining—pop-up dinners. Some will be held here at the inn, and others will be at the Coral Cottage—my grandmother Ginger's home on the beach. I can also bring delicious dinner concepts wherever you like, in your home, or on your boat. The menu is ever-changing and customizable, and—"

Marina froze. She heard a male voice ring out. *That's her, the woman in the meme.* And then the small group began laughing.

Struggling, she went on, "And we can accommodate…"

Imani turned to quiet the snickering guests, who looked like college students, but someone else picked up on it, too. Soon another group was laughing. Others were turning to look at them.

"Most any dietary…" Marina felt her face growing hot. She was accustomed to cameras and crews, not live audiences. With her heart racing, she gestured toward the group of people who could hardly contain themselves now.

"It's true," Marina said, acting more confident than she felt. "I'm the meme lady. The anchor from San Francisco that people have been laughing about all over social media." People were laughing louder now. She had to wrap this up. "Well, I hope you enjoy the food."

Mortified, Marina managed a wan smile and hurried toward the door to replenish the trays and escape the spotlight of humiliation. As other guests shifted uncomfortably, the entire mood in the room seemed to plummet along with hers.

Kai stopped her at the door. "I'll get this party back on track for you. Maybe the young pianist knows some show tunes or Disney songs."

"That would be great," Marina said. As she made her way through the hall, she could hear the strains of "Cabaret," and soon, Kai was belting out the song to rival Liza Minelli. *Thank goodness for sisters.*

Ginger followed her into the kitchen. "That was quite rude of those people," she said, folding Marina into her arms.

Marina blinked back hot tears of anger and hurt. "People have been so mean online, making ugly remarks. I don't look at their comments anymore, but to say that to my face? When I'm speaking before a group? I don't understand people like that."

Ginger smoothed her hair and kissed her cheek. "If you're in the public eye, people forget you have feelings. You can remind them of that, but they seldom care. They only feel powerful when they can crush another person."

"I should know that from my old job." At times, viewers had complained about a story they didn't like or made comments about her clothing or hair. "But it always hurts."

Ginger gestured with her hand. "Rise above it. When they go low, you go high."

Marina managed a crooked smile. "That's what you used to tell us when we were kids." Ginger had always been there for her, just as Marina had supported Heather earlier today. As she thought of this, she saw her place on the ribbon of life.

Ginger placed her hands on Marina's shoulders. "Same advice. Hasn't changed."

"I'll try to remember that. I guess every industry has its critics." She opened one of the refrigerators and pulled out another tray of canapés. "The cucumbers and crab spirals are going fast."

"That's it. Focus on the positive, my dear."

"I'll imagine that my first clients are out there." Marina made a face. "Except for that young crowd."

"That's the spirit," Ginger said. "You're doing what you love. Now get back out there and spread your joy and good food throughout that room. And know that the people who matter love your work."

"Rise above," Marina said, freshly determined. She lifted the heavy platter onto her shoulder for extra balance and started through the hallway.

As Marina was turning into the music room, one of the twenty-something guys who'd been laughing at her suddenly reeled out of the doorway.

"Right behind you," Marina called out, stepping back to avoid the young man. *Spoiled frat boys,* she thought. Then, *when they go low, you go high.*

He careened through the hall, probably drunk and oblivious to her. Marina pushed herself against the wall, but there was nothing she could do with the tray. He lurched against the platter, and suddenly, every cucumber roll took flight.

"No," Marina cried as the silver platter clanged to the floor. "Why are you out to ruin my day?"

He turned and shrugged. "You should've gotten out of the way, meme lady."

"And what if I'd been an elderly person? You have to watch where you're going in this world." Her mom instinct kicked in, and she pointed at the splattered food. "Now get down there and pick that mess up."

The young man—who'd probably started drinking early that day—snorted. "You're the help now, meme lady. You do it." He spun to leave.

But Jack was blocking his way. "It wasn't enough to insult

this woman in front of a crowd?" He put his hands on his hips. "Do as the lady asked."

"Oh, yeah? And if I don't?"

Chief Clarkson, who was in uniform this time, stepped behind Jack. "How does a charge of drunk-and-disorderly sound? Because we can do it that way, or you can make amends. Right now."

Bennett and Mitch stepped up, too. Grumbling, the young man began scooping up food and slapping it onto the platter.

His friends spilled out of the music room, wide-eyed. But none of them lifted a hand to help him.

"I'd like an apology, too," Marina said, folding her arms. She was grateful that Jack and the others were standing up for her.

"Sorry."

"Like you mean it, you little scumbag," Jack said.

The kid waved a hand. "Alright, I'm sorry. Happy?"

Ivy pushed through the crowded hallway. "You're not staying here at the inn. Who are you with?"

One of the young women in the group slowly raised her hand. "My friend and I checked in this afternoon. We met the guys on the beach."

"Either they go, or you go," Ivy said. "And I suggest you find a higher class of men next time."

Marina was silently cheering Ivy on. She watched while the young man slopped the rest of the food onto the tray.

Poppy appeared behind her. "I've seen you picking up girls on the beach. You should be ashamed of yourself." She plopped a roll of paper towels down before him. "Don't forget to wipe the floor before you go," she added, tossing her hair over her shoulder.

Marina turned to Jack and her other new friends. "Thank you," she said, grateful for their intervention. Not that she couldn't have ignored the situation and taken Ginger's high road, but it meant a lot to her that her friends held that young man accountable. Maybe he even learned a valuable lesson.

Satisfied, Marina went back to the kitchen for another tray of food.

Jack followed her. "Rough debut. Are you okay?"

Nodding, Marina said, "Thanks for what you did back there."

"The kid had it coming to him. Too much sun, too much beer, but no reason to act like a jerk. At least he didn't ruin that beautiful dress." He touched her hand and held her in his gaze a little longer than usual. "Your food is truly a work of art—and delicious. What can I do to help you now?"

Jack's simple touch sent a spark through her, and she took a step forward, toward the warmth and safety that his arms seemed to promise. But then she thought of Vanessa and how the poor woman looked at Jack with so much love and admiration. Marina would never do anything to hurt a woman who had such a heavy burden to shoulder.

Catching herself, she averted her eyes and stepped back. "I've got this."

Looking at her with concern on his face, Jack reached for her arm again. "Marina, you're not alone."

Outside, a child's scream drew their attention, and they both dashed to the window, alarmed.

"You're *it* now," Leo cried, having found Samantha hiding behind a chaise lounge.

Samantha dissolved with laughter and then covered her eyes and started counting.

"Whew," Marina said. "Looks like a rousing game of hide-and-seek."

"Glad they didn't see that fiasco in the hall," Jack said, clearly relieved. "Not the kind of role models they need."

"Kids learn from witnessing good and bad behavior. I'm glad they're having fun." Marina returned to the counter and lifted a tray. Jack picked up another one and followed her to the music room.

After the gathering had thinned out, Marina stood at the sink to wash the serving dishes she had borrowed.

A glass of red wine appeared on the counter beside her.

"I think you've earned this," Kai said. "Wish I'd been there in the hallway to give that snotty kid a piece of my mind. But I was well into the *Phantom of the Opera* score by that time."

"I'm glad you distracted the crowd." Marina shook soapy water off her hands and took a sip of wine, breathing a sigh of relief. "Now, I just have to wait and see if this event generates any business."

Kai brightened. "Denise asked if you could prepare picnic baskets for the beach. I told her I was sure you could. She's going to call you."

"That's wonderful, thank you." Marina hugged her sister. "I don't know what I would've done without you and Ginger here today."

Shelly joined them in the kitchen carrying an empty platter. "I'd hoped for leftovers, but the guests didn't leave a scrap. That's a good sign."

After the kitchen was clean, Ivy and Shelly walked Marina to the car. Shelly glanced at Jack and Vanessa, who were sitting on the terrace with Denise and John watching the children. "Jack and Vanessa both seem so nice, and it's sad that she's ill. At least they're on good terms for Leo's sake. A lot of exes never make up. Poor kids."

Marina listened, intrigued.

"I don't think they're a couple," Kai said. "Just old friends."

Shelly shrugged. "Maybe not anymore, but Leo looks exactly like Jack. And the way Jack looks at that boy with such pride, there's no doubt that's his son."

Marina had noticed the resemblance, too. And Vanessa

204 | JAN MORAN

seemed besotted with Jack. He was warm and respectful, but that was all. She wondered what had happened between them.

Ivy poked her sister. "No gossiping about guests."

"He's not a guest anymore," Shelly said, making a face.

"That doesn't mean he's fair game," Ivy shot back. "And you will not repeat that, especially not at Java Beach. People deserve a little privacy, even if this is a small town. Do you want everyone gossiping about you and Mitch?"

Shelly dipped her head, looking sheepish. "Forget I said anything."

But Marina couldn't. *Is that what Jack is keeping secret? And if so, why?*

Chapter 19

$\mathcal{J}$ack threw covers over the bed, stashed a pile of dirty dishes in the oven, and stuffed dirty clothes in the closet. He didn't usually clean house like this, but Ginger would be here any second.

Jack had called her to ask if they could meet to talk about his book proposal this morning. He suggested coffee at Java Beach, but she didn't go for that. *I have time now. If you're decent, I'll be right over.*

As Ginger knocked on his door, he kicked Scout's ragged chew toys under his dog bed. Scout cocked his head in confusion, so Jack ruffled the dog's ears. "Sorry, bud. You'll get them back later." He pointed to Scout's bed and snapped his fingers. "Stay."

With reluctance, Scout curled up on the dog bed.

Jack ran his hand over his hair and opened the door. "Good morning. Come in."

"Hard at work, I see." Ginger chuckled and gestured at his desk.

Jack felt his insides implode. Cartoon sketches he hadn't thought to put away littered his desk. Hardly the work of a serious writer.

"Ah, that." Jack shuffled the pages together in a stack. "Some silly drawings for my nieces and nephews."

"May I?" Ginger held out her hand and wriggled her fingers.

Jack could hardly refuse. Justly cornered, he gave her the pages.

Ginger slipped on the half-glasses she wore on a glittery chain around her neck, magnifying the intelligence glimmering in her eyes. *The color of Colombian emeralds*—that's how he'd describe them in his book.

"Why, these are delightful drawings," Ginger said. "This is Scout, isn't it? And Leo and Samantha. How charming. Have you ever done anything with your illustrations?" She looked up expectantly.

"That's just for fun." Jack hooked his thumbs in his jeans and rocked on his heels. "I never had any formal training, but I enjoy it a lot. Makes the kids happy."

Ginger tapped the pages. "Creative in one area, creative in others. The forms creativity can take are exciting, don't you think?" Without waiting for a reply, she went on. "Drawing, writing, singing, cooking. The sciences and maths. Even international business and diplomatic negotiations. Today, that's called thinking outside of the box. Every generation has its buzz words, I suppose." She shrugged and continued to flip through his drawings.

Remembering what else might be in that stack of sketches, Jack reached out. "I'll take those now. There's nothing much more."

"No?" Ginger came to the last sketch. "Now, if I didn't know better, I'd think this might be Marina." With a little smile, she handed the pages back to him.

The tips of Jack's ears were burning, a sure sign that she'd gotten to him. He'd sketched Marina one day while she was outside. That wasn't a cartoon character, but one of his more serious drawings.

Jack cleared his throat. "Now, about this book I'm working on. I'd like to schedule some time for interviews to talk about some of your accomplishments."

"Enough of that," Ginger said. "I'm not interested in that project. As I told you, I'm not finished with my life yet, so what's the point?"

Jack felt like a helium balloon with the air whooshing out. He'd already pitched this concept to his agent. However, he could still go ahead without Ginger's involvement, but that would make him feel uneasy—as if he was sneaking around. "Won't you reconsider? I'd like to work with you on this."

Jack heard something and looked down. Scout had chosen this inopportune moment to drag out his chew toys from underneath his bed.

Ginger dismissed the thought with an imperious wave of her hand. "I've heard that Denise and John are thinking of staying in Summer Beach. Leo, too?"

"That's right, but—"

As Ginger glanced at his illustrations again, a smile grew on her face. "Perhaps I have another idea." She paused by the door, looking at Scout, who was happily shredding a chew toy. "What a wonderful companion. I have a fastidious housekeeper who comes every other week. Perhaps she can fit you into her schedule. After all, you'll soon have a great deal of work ahead of you."

"But I—"

Ginger held up a hand. "I must be off now. Let's chat later."

After she shut the door, Jack plopped into his chair. Ginger had to be one of the most evasive interview subjects he'd encountered.

That's when he realized Ginger would have had a clear view of bright orange mugs through the glass pane on the oven door.

"Give me that," Jack said, tugging a toy from Scout's

mouth. He scooped up the stuffing Scout had tossed around. "Making me look bad. As if I can't do that myself."

Then he thought about what Ginger had said. *A great deal of work ahead of you.* What did she mean by that?

LATER THAT MORNING, Marina dropped off a picnic basket lunch that Denise had ordered.

"Want to come to the beach with us?" Jack asked.

"Thanks, but I have a busy day ahead," Marina said before dashing back across the yard.

With such an abrupt departure, Jack couldn't help but wonder if Ginger had mentioned his sketch of her. But there was no time to worry about that. He had to meet Vanessa and Denise and John at the beach.

"Have you secured that side?" Jack called out as he jabbed a stake into the sand. If he let go, the breeze off the ocean would lift the beach canopy like a sail. The kids might like to see that, but it was no way to start a day at the beach.

"Got it," John replied.

Under the awning, Jack set up a folding table for the food. Denise covered it with a beach tablecloth printed with shells and starfish and spread out an assortment of food that she'd ordered from Marina. This morning, Marina had sent Jack off with a beach basket filled with prosciutto and melon, cold turkey and avocado sliders, and homemade sweet potato chips with truffle oil.

"That looks delicious," Jack said. He was already starving.

"Help yourself," Denise replied. "Marina is such a real treasure. We're looking forward to her food festival, too. What a good idea that is."

Jack selected an assortment and dove into the delicacies with gusto. Knowing Marina had made them somehow made this simple picnic even more special.

He paused in mid-bite. How did *that* thought blow through his mind? As he ate, he stared out at the sea in thought.

The truth was that Marina was intruding on Jack's life with increasing frequency. At the recent event at the Seabreeze Inn, he'd stepped in against that young, privileged thug who'd made fun of her, ruining the debut she'd worked so hard to prepare. He'd wanted to take her in his arms, but instead, he'd assured her she was not alone.

Lame, he told himself. But then, his life was growing increasingly complicated—not that he was complaining. Marina had just sent two children to college, and now he was on the verge of becoming a full-time father. Looking ahead, would she be up for sharing such a life with him? As a formerly freewheeling bachelor nomad, he wasn't used to considering others in his life. These thoughts were new to him. First, a dog, then a child, and now…

No, too complicated.

After finishing his snack, Jack tented his eyes against the morning sun. The thick morning fog that the locals called June gloom was burning off, and rays of sunshine were peeking through the shifting clouds. In the distance, sets of waves were rolling into the shore, and wet-suited surfers were rising on their boards. Jack longed to give surfing a try. Maybe he and Leo would take lessons this summer.

Vanessa was relaxing in a chaise lounge next to the canopy, where she could feel the sun on her face, even though she was wrapped in a blanket for warmth. She smiled broadly. "I've been longing to do this. Summer Beach is so peaceful. Nothing like Santa Monica, which is overrun with crowds." She waved to Leo, who was running along the surf with Samantha, chasing shorebirds. "*Mi hijo*, come get your sunscreen."

Leo bounded over, panting, his little chest heaving from exertion and excitement. Vanessa smoothed on sunscreen with soft, loving strokes. She kissed his forehead, and he hugged her before racing back to Samantha.

Jack grabbed a sketch pad from his backpack and eased into a chair. When words wouldn't come, he enjoyed sketching. Today was that kind of day. Watching the children at play, he made a few strokes, and then began to fill in the details, humming as he worked.

"What an enjoyable lifestyle," Denise said, popping open a can of sparkling water and passing it to Vanessa before opening one for herself.

Sitting in a beach chair, John clasped his hands behind his head. "Why don't we stay in Summer Beach?"

"If only you were serious," Denise said, laughing.

"I am," John said, gazing at the horizon. "I've been talking about opening a technology consulting firm for years. Why not now?"

A smile bloomed on Denise's face. "Samantha would be so excited. She's been so sad about moving away from the beach, though this is a world apart from Santa Monica."

"That means Leo and Samantha could start school together here." Vanessa's face shimmered with hope. "Oh, Denise, that would be perfect for him."

"Assuming I stay here," Jack said, but as soon as the words left his mouth, and he saw the expression on Vanessa's face change, he regretted them. "Though I'm committed to making that happen."

Inwardly, Jack winced. He sounded like the double-talking politicians he'd interviewed, but he was serious. Now, Jack needed to remain flexible for the coming change in Leo's life.

He put his sketchpad down. "I hear there's an opening at the local Summer Beach paper for an editor." Bennett had mentioned this at the cocktail party at the inn. It wouldn't pay much, but it was something Jack could easily do. "And the cottage has a second bedroom that Leo can stay in."

"Unless he wants to stay with us," Denise said softly.

Jack's heart lurched at that comment, but then, Leo had grown up next door to Denise and John. "We need to have that conversation with Leo soon."

A wave of emotion crossed Vanessa's face. She chewed her lip as she watched the children playing in the sand a little distance from them. Finally, she said, "When Leo was a baby, I thought it would be easy to raise him on my own. But once he started school, he began asking questions. He wanted a father, and he wanted to know where his father was. I didn't have the heart to tell him what I'd done."

Jack felt a twinge of warning in his neck. "What did you tell him?"

Denise and John looked away, and Vanessa bowed her head. "I told him that his father and I separated when he was very, very young. Before he was even born, before he knew I was pregnant. That was a little bit true."

"That makes me the bad guy. As if I left you." Jack ran a hand through his hair. This was going to be even more difficult than he thought.

"Jack, I'm sorry," Vanessa said. "I never thought we'd be in this position. As Leo grew older, it became more difficult to tell him the truth." A silent tear trickled down her face. "I'm afraid he'll be angry, and I can't face that. He's all I have."

Jack wanted to be understanding, but this had to be sorted out. Kneeling beside Vanessa in the sand, he folded his hands around hers. "You're stronger than that, Vanessa. I know you are. Together, we can tell him the truth."

"We'll be there for him, too," John said. "He's your son, and we don't want to interfere with your relationship with him. But I hope you understand that Leo is going to be fragile. He'll need familiarity."

Vanessa laid her head on Jack's shoulder, and together they watched Leo and Samantha scraping sand into a bucket for a sandcastle.

Although Jack had only just met Leo, his attachment to

the boy was growing stronger by the day, like a fast-growing vine twining around his heart. Yet the question remained: Would Leo accept him?

Chapter 20

*a*fter pouring her morning coffee, Marina sat at the red Formica table in the kitchen, checking her email. She was delighted to find an order from her first customers at the farmers market. They wanted to reserve bread, tarts, and cookies for the next market.

An email from a woman who owned the Starfish Cafe, a popular hillside restaurant in Summer Beach popped up. She'd heard of the Seabreeze Inn event and asked Marina to come by one afternoon to share her baked goods. That would be a perfect time to pitch her on the food festival. Mitch had already committed Java Beach.

Outside on the patio was Kai, who'd volunteered to take over the management of the new deck off the patio. Marina could see why. A swarm of men and a couple of women were offloading lumber and supplies onto the patio, and at the center of it was Axe, directing his workforce.

The sound of hammers and drills filled the atmosphere with the beat of new progress, and Marina welcomed it. She loved watching her dream take shape.

Marina put a call through to Brooke, hoping she could catch her sister at home. Instead, she got her message again.

"Hey Brooke, maybe you're in the garden. I'm building a new deck at Ginger's, and I was hoping that Alder, Rowan, and Oakley could come over to help finish it. I'm offering all the food they can eat, which I know is a lot. We could have a family beach barbecue like the old days. Love to see you soon."

Ginger sauntered into the kitchen. "Good morning, sunshine."

"Hi, I just left a message for Brooke. Is she always this hard to reach?"

"Between the boys and her garden, she's pretty busy. When Alder starts driving next year, that should help."

Marina remembered the days of chauffeuring the twins around. She put her phone down and sipped her coffee.

Her grandmother was dressed in yoga gear for her bracing morning hike up to the ridgetop, where she frequently meditated. Marina had gone with her a few times. Perched on Ginger's favorite flat boulder, one could see boats plying the ocean waters and whales on migratory paths. The expanse was awe-inspiring.

Glancing outside, Ginger said, "Kai is certainly exhibiting good management skills."

"She's exhibiting a lot more than that," Marina said, arching an eyebrow.

Kai wore a white shirt with one too many buttons open. The shirttails tied at the waist, where a little skin peeked out above her slim-fitting white capris. On her feet were black patent kitten mules, and she wore ebony bangles and hoop earrings dangling beneath her long hair, which was pulled back into a loose braid. Her sister had good fashion sense, but judging from the careful makeup application, Marina knew something was on Kai's mind.

Marina watched her sister hanging onto Axe's every word. "Kai was belting out Gershwin tunes in the shower this morning, so you know something's up."

"Heard it, too. A rousing rendition of 'I Got Rhythm.'" Ginger stirred cream into her coffee. "She seems fascinated with Axe. Imagine if they sang together. He has a beautiful baritone voice. Last year he sang at the Independence Day bonfire on the beach." She tapped the spoon on the side of her cup. "Have you met this Dmitri?"

"I haven't, but he gave her a ring that says hands-off-the-lady's-mine."

"Kai hasn't shared that with me," Ginger said, surprised. "You'd think he'd want to meet the family first."

"I get the idea that he's a me-me kind of guy who expects the world—and Kai—to revolve around him."

"Well, that's not going to work." Ginger shook her head.

"I hope she doesn't break her heart out there," Marina said, angling her head outside.

Ginger sighed. "It's not Kai I'm worried about."

Marina caught a glimpse of Jack and Leo on the beach with Scout. Ever since Denise and John and Vanessa had rented the beach house, Leo had been coming over to see Jack every day. Sometimes Leo was with Samantha, and other times, he was on his own.

Marina couldn't get Shelly's comment from the debut event at the inn out of her mind. Could Leo be Jack's son? If he was, why didn't Jack simply say so? She couldn't imagine what was so secretive about that.

"You've been watching Jack an awful lot," Ginger said, a slight smile playing on her lips.

"Have I?" Marina had told Ginger about Shelly's comments. If anyone could keep a secret, it was her grandmother. "I'm still thinking about why he doesn't tell us if Leo is his son."

"Maybe it's none of our business. Or perhaps Leo is a relative. Could be a nephew."

"I didn't think about that," Marina said. That would explain a lot.

Later that afternoon, Marina was outside inspecting the framing for the deck after the workers had left. The smell of lumber was fresh in the air, and she couldn't wait to see the finished project. She had already determined where she would place tables, and she was scouring garage sales and ads for used patio furniture.

She heard Scout's playful bark and turned around. Jack had just emerged from the guest cottage, where he'd probably been working since Leo left. Not that she was keeping track of him or anything like that.

Jack jogged after Scout.

"Hey," he said, slowing down beside her.

"Haven't seen you running on the beach before."

"Bennett inspired me. Went for about a couple of slow miles this morning." He patted his stomach. "Getting back in shape."

With all the baking Marina was doing, she was heading in the opposite direction, but she didn't mind a little extra weight. However, she made a point to walk on the beach almost daily. Maybe she'd drop into Shelly's yoga class or go for a swim, she thought.

"Saw Leo here today," she said.

"Yeah, he's a great kid. Samantha, too." Jack drew a tennis ball from his pocket and tossed it ahead of them onto the beach. Scout took off after it.

Marina fell into step beside him, and they slipped off their shoes, carrying them as they walked. Strolling beside him like this felt like the most natural thing to do. They'd taken a few walks with Scout now.

During that time, they'd found they had a lot in common. They'd both come from news backgrounds. Whereas Marina had delivered news on the air, Jack had been dedicated to in-depth investigative projects. They shared a quest for the truth.

That desire to know the truth was itching at Marina now.

As the waves pounded the beach, the chilly water sent

brown-spotted sanderlings scurrying before them on their little legs. Overhead, gulls squawked and soared and dipped into the surf, scooping small fish from the waves.

Marina ventured into the conversation. "With Vanessa being so ill, it's good that Denise and John can help her with Leo. And you."

Jack nodded. "That's a real shame."

"Have you known Leo since he was a baby?"

"Um, no." Jack shoved his hands into the deep pockets of his long beach shorts. "Just met him this summer."

"Really? Gosh, the first time I saw you two together, I could have sworn you two were related." Marina gulped at her audacity, but she couldn't help asking.

Jack arched an eyebrow. "And what gave you that idea?"

"Leo looks a lot like you." She was so close now.

However, Jack didn't respond. They walked a little farther, the sea rushing around their ankles.

Marina couldn't resist forging on. "Sorry, did you say you and Leo were related?"

"Look, I didn't say anything." Jack's voice held an edge she had never heard. He stopped and heaved a sigh.

"I'm not following." Marina blinked as if in confusion. *So close now.*

Turning to face her, Jack put his hands on his hips. "Leo's my son, okay? Is that what every nosy gossip-monger in the town wants to know?"

She'd touched a nerve. "Jack, I didn't mean to pry." But she had.

And Jack saw through her plea of innocence. "Yeah, you did. You, I understand. That's our nature. Find the story and report it. But it's no one else's business. When we're ready to tell people, we will."

Suddenly, a thought dawned on Marina. "Leo, he doesn't know, does he?"

Casting his gaze down, Jack shook his head. "It's complicated."

"When did you…"

"Find out? A few weeks ago. Vanessa's parents wouldn't have approved of me, and she didn't want to get married. I had no idea. Leo was the result of a one-night encounter that neither of us much remember."

"It happens," Marina said, trying to be understanding.

"Not usually to me. I've never been that kind of guy." Jack seemed a little self-conscious. "Vanessa and I were working for different newspapers, covering a dreadful hostage situation on a cult compound. It stretched on for weeks, and the tension was almost unbearable. There were kids inside, too. Eventually, the children were released unharmed, but in the meantime, we had some close calls. One night a bunch of us news jockeys passed around a bottle of tequila to blow off some stress." He shrugged. "You can figure it out from there. But I always had great respect for Vanessa."

"Did you see her again?"

"No, but I followed her byline. Then Vanessa switched to softer, local news. Lots of people burn out on tough assignments, but at the time, I was kind of surprised that she did. She's always been a strong woman."

Marina nodded thoughtfully. "We spoke some at the event at the inn. I admire that about her."

"So, here we are," Jack said. "I want to tell Leo, but Vanessa is afraid he'll be upset with her."

"That's why no one else knows."

"And shouldn't," Jack said firmly. "Not until we tell Leo. I hope there's no speculation going on. I know how small towns can be. I grew up in one before it got swallowed up by suburbia."

Before Marina could answer—and she had to make sure Shelly didn't spread her conjecture—an icy wave splashed them to their waist, knocking them off balance with its force.

Marina cried out, and Jack gripped her around the waist as she stumbled to her knees in the strong current.

"Hang on," Jack yelled, reaching for her.

"Trying," Marina cried out. The giant wave had caught her off guard. She flailed against the force, gulping saltwater. Another wave crashed over them and dragged her into deeper water. Overwhelmed, she fought for balance as kelp swirled around her ankles, inhibiting her movements. The flip-flops she'd been carrying were swept away.

Now on his knees, Jack wrapped his arms around her and pulled her onto the shore. As they stumbled into a soft dune, Marina leaned forward, coughing up the water she'd taken in.

"Are you okay?" Jack tossed the seaweed aside. He rubbed her back and smoothed her tangled hair from her face.

"Uh-huh," she managed to say before she dissolved into another hacking round of coughing. Finally, she rolled over and flung herself on the sand. "I can't believe that happened so fast."

Jack leaned over her. "I'm glad you're okay. For a moment, I thought…"

"Me, too…" He was so close she could see his dark lashes damp against his skin, his lips just a few inches away. Having just escaped the prospect of death, she felt a crazy need filling her. She tilted her head and brushed her lips against his.

The connection was so much more than she'd ever dreamed, and a rush of warmth coursed through her, sending tingles all the way to her toes.

Suddenly, Scout burst between them, knocking Jack to one side. The dog licked her face with great enthusiasm and doggie concern.

"Ow, wet dog," she cried, laughing as she pushed Scout away. "I'm okay, you overprotective pup."

"Out of here, you mutt," Jack said, picking up the ball Scout had dropped and throwing it as far away as he could.

Once Scout was satisfied that Marina wasn't hurt, he loped happily away. Jack turned back to her.

"Listen, I'm sorry about that," he said, lifting wet strands of hair from her cheeks. "I don't mean Scout. Well, Scout, too, of course. But I didn't mean to take advantage of the situation, and I—"

"You didn't." Marina's heart beat with such force that she was sure he could hear it. She was tempted to pull him toward her again to finish what they'd started, but the moment had passed.

Jack pulled her up beside him and put his arm around her. "Got to watch those rogue waves. We could've lost a lot more than our flip-flops."

"Hardly a monster wave, though it sure felt like it." Marina leaned against him, enjoying the warmth of his skin on hers. She was shivering from the perennially frigid Pacific waters.

"We should get you back inside and into some warm clothes," he said, rubbing her hands between his.

"You're soaked, too."

"I'm a guy. But a roaring fire sounds good right about now." The late afternoon breeze had kicked up, carrying damp ocean mists in the wind.

"We'll have a fire pit soon," Marina said. She needed Brooke's boys to help with that.

"Why don't I build a fire in my little fireplace?" Jack offered. "You haven't seen what I've done to the little cottage, and I have some soup that's crying for fresh bread."

As much as Marina ached to join him, she was unsure. Her heart was still freshly wounded. "I'd like to, but this could be a little awkward, right?"

"Guess so." Jack's hopeful expression dissolved. "Your grandmother is my landlord. And I'm a pretty complicated guy, aren't I?" He stood and took her hands to pull her up. "Come on. I'll help you back to the house."

Picking their way barefoot back to the Coral Cottage, Marina leaned against Jack, enjoying the sensation of his arm around her. And yet, disappointment gathered in her. If only she hadn't been so quick to reject his offer.

Chapter 21

"*B*rooke, I'm so glad you and Chip came," Marina said, hugging her sister and her husband, Charles, who was still known by his high school nickname.

"I brought plenty of fresh produce for you," Brooke said, directing her sons to put the bags on the kitchen counter. Three tall, gangly teens dutifully complied. "This morning, I harvested a bunch of herbs, tomatoes, peppers, lettuce, and kale from the garden, along with lemons, oranges, and grapefruit. Ginger tells me you're doing a lot of cooking these days."

"I've been selling baked goods at the farmers market, and catering some small events at the Seabreeze Inn. My friend Ivy and her sister Shelly are running it."

"Why, isn't that clever of you? I'm glad you've found something to do that you love." Brooke brushed back her mane of light reddish-brown hair haphazardly braided down her back. "This crew devours practically everything I can coax from the garden. Sure helps on the grocery bill. And this year, I planted twice as much."

Brooke wore a T-shirt with a tiered, ruffled cotton skirt with Birkenstock sandals to match her husband's. Both were salt-of-the-earth types, and Chip was now in charge of a fire department in a rural area just east of San Diego. They'd been high school sweethearts, with Chip, the captain of the football team, and Brooke, an avid gardener even back then.

"I forgot the strawberries," Brooke said, her face falling. "You would have loved those."

Marina hugged her. "Brooke, it's okay. There's enough here to feed a baseball team."

"Those kids sure eat like one." Brooke pressed a hand to her forehead. "I don't know what's gotten into me lately." She threw up her hands and let them fall by her side.

Marina took her sister's hand. "If you have excess from your garden, I'll buy it from you. I'm going to need a lot of fresh produce, and yours is so healthy-looking."

"Sell it to you?" Looking hesitant, Brooke raised an eyebrow. "I can't accept your money."

"Put it in the boys' college funds," Marina said. "Or take a vacation."

"It's been years since we've done that," Brooke said, looking haggard.

Ginger and Kai sailed in to greet Brooke with a round of hugs, and Marina saw Brooke rest her head against Ginger's shoulder for a few moments as if she was thankful for the brief respite. Marina was concerned; her sister seemed in emotional disarray today, but then, it was little wonder with three active boys at home. Marina recalled how Heather and Ethan had filled her every free moment when they were young.

"Let's see that deck," Chip said, his commanding voice carrying through the room. "Come on, boys."

"I really appreciate you and the boys pitching in to help," Marina said.

"Hey, that's what family is for," Chip said. "Just wish Stan were still here with us."

"I know," Marina said. Chip and Stan had been good

friends and often went fishing together. It was thoughtful of him to remember all these years later.

"Heard about what that fancy boyfriend did to you up in San Francisco," Chip said, lowering his voice. He pulled Brooke to his side and put his arm around her. "Brooke told me you called. We're sorry about that mess."

"I'm okay now," Marina said, lifting her chin. The more time she spent in Summer Beach, the more Grady was receding into her past. Right where he belonged. And then there was Jack. She wasn't sure if falling for him would be a good idea, but she couldn't deny her growing attraction.

Marina led them outside to where the deck stretched over the sand. Axe had left a truckload of brick pavers that Marina planned to use for a pathway from the deck to the firepit, safely away from the house and anything else flammable. Summer Beach had strict regulations.

Axe had left instructions for them, and he'd also marked out where to lay the bricks. That had been nice of him, and he'd been mindful of her budget.

Chip took charge, showing the three boys how to position the bricks, tamp them down, and spread sand over them to lock the herringbone pattern in place.

"You look like you've done this before," Marina said.

Chip leaned a hand on his thigh. "A few times. Always helping out my buddies at the firehouse." He glanced around the property. "Be sure to keep vegetation well away from the firepit."

"We sure will," Marina said. "I heard about the Ridgetop fire last year." She started back toward the deck, and Kai joined her.

"Axe did a great job," Kai said. "But his crew worked at lightning speed."

Marina picked up on a wistful note in her sister's voice. "Any luck with him?"

Kai shook her head. "Maybe I overdid it. I heard his last

girlfriend was part of a pro sailing crew. Maybe that's what he prefers."

Marina didn't know what to say. Kai had come on kind of strong, dressing up and flirting with him. "Or maybe he'd rather do the chasing."

Kai angled her head. "You think? Maybe I'll try that next."

"It's not a game, Kai. Just relax. If he wants to see you again, he'll reach out to you. I think you've made your position known."

"I guess so." Kai sighed. "With that gorgeous baritone voice, I could listen to Axe talk all day. I'd love to hear him sing."

"Come on," Marina said, slinging her arm around her sister. "Help me string up these fairy lights."

As the day wore on, the brick pathway and the flat area for the fire pit took shape under Chip's direction. The oldest boy, Alder, was a quick study, while the two younger boys continued moving bricks and sand.

Kai had asked Axe to leave a tall ladder that they could use to string the lights above the deck. He'd built a crisscross design that was open to the sky and could be beautifully lit at night. Marina and Kai took turns climbing the ladder and feeding each other strings of lights to weave through the latticework.

Marina paused to survey their handiwork, satisfied with their progress. "Where did Ginger and Brooke go?"

"I saw them walking toward the village. Maybe they went to the market." Kai glanced toward the town. "They were deep in conversation, too. Did something seem off with Brooke to you?"

"It's no wonder. She's got a houseful of testosterone. It's good that she's talking to Ginger." Still, Marina was concerned about her. "I asked Brooke to sell me part of her harvest. I can see her more often, too."

"That's a good idea."

A few minutes later, a truck loaded with plants and pots pulled in front of the house.

"Special delivery," Ginger called out, waving from Roy's vehicle. Brooke was squeezed in the middle, looking much happier.

"What's all this?" Marina stepped down from the ladder.

Ginger got out, and Brooke followed her. "I thought the deck looked a little bare," Ginger said. "A few palms and ficus trees will make all the difference, don't you think? Just imagine ferns with red and pink geraniums spilling from these fabulous urns that Leilani had just put out."

Marina hugged Ginger. "Thank you. Those plants will bring everything all together."

"These aren't from me," Ginger said. "Jack sent them. He's probably not too far behind us."

"Jack?" That was a surprise.

"We ran into him at the grocery store," Ginger explained. "He suggested we go to the Hidden Garden because he wanted to get something special for you. Said you'd shown him the deck and mentioned that plants would look nice."

"That's a beautiful nursery," Brooke said. "All the plants are so healthy. Leilani and Roy are passionate about plants, too. My kind of people."

Marina noticed Brooke seemed calmer than when they'd arrived. Maybe she'd had a good talk with Ginger, or perhaps the nursery had a settling effect on her. At any rate, it was good to see the old, smiling Brooke.

Behind them, Roy had opened the truck and was unloading the plants when Jack arrived. He and Leo were riding shiny bikes that looked new.

Marina waved Jack down and walked toward him and Leo. They were windblown and slightly sunburned, but happy. She felt a tug of emotion as she approached the pair. "That was so thoughtful of you, Jack. Thank you." She saw that Leo was beaming. "Are these new bikes?"

"Yeah, I needed some exercise," Jack said. "Leo agreed to come along and help me pick out a couple. He tried to talk me into a skateboard, too." Pausing, he tousled Leo's hair. "Maybe next time. I'm still getting back into shape."

"We rode all over Summer Beach, and it's so cool," Leo said. "Did you know that Samantha's going to school here in the fall? Instead of regular gym classes, they have swimming and sailing and surfing. Mom said we might stay, too. I'd like that."

The little boy seemed excited, but Marina detected a note of sadness behind his words, which was understandable. She held out a hand to him. "Come on over and meet my nephews. The youngest, Oakley, is close to your age."

Jack nodded his assent, and Leo jumped off his bike. He followed Marina toward Chip and the boys while Jack parked the bicycles.

As Marina and Leo made their way toward the others, Leo asked, "So are you Jack's girlfriend yet?"

Marina looked into the boy's earnest eyes and smiled. "Not really. Where'd you hear that?"

"Jack said it takes a while to get to boyfriend-girlfriend status, and since that was a couple of weeks ago, I was just checking in to see if you guys had made any progress."

"I see." Since Leo was so serious, Marina smothered a laugh. "And does he keep you updated on this status?"

"Nah. That's why I'm asking you. I know girls like to talk about love stuff more than us guys. That's what Samantha says."

"And are you and Samantha girlfriend and boyfriend?"

"No, we're best friends. But we still might get married when we're older. We haven't decided yet."

"I think it's wise to put off your decision," Marina said thoughtfully. Glancing behind her, she noticed Jack following them and eavesdropping. "Being best friends is perfect right now."

"We can be friends, too, right? I like you a lot. So does my mom. And she's a great judge of character, that's what she says. Samantha's mom agrees. They agree on almost everything, except when they don't, because they're best friends, too. I figure that if I had a dad, he'd probably be best friends with Samantha's dad. I'm pretty sure that's how these things work."

"You're quite smart," Marina said. "I can tell that you're very thoughtful, too. We can talk anytime you want." By then, they'd reached Chip and the boys, and Marina introduced them. Chip folded Leo right into the process, pairing him with Oakley to begin putting the firepit together.

Jack bumped Marina's shoulder. "What was that all about?"

"Leo likes to talk," Marina replied. "He's very observant. Like his—" She stopped herself, embarrassed at her near slip. "You know what I mean."

Jack touched her hand. "I like that he's comfortable talking to you."

"He's a sweet boy." Marina gazed after Leo. "He's going to need a lot of support one day."

Roy signaled to them that he had finished unloading the plants and planters. "That's all, folks. Let us know if you need anything else."

"Will do," Jack called back.

Brooke joined them. "Chip and the boys have made huge progress. Want to help me put those plants in the urns while they finish?"

Marina and Jack agreed, and Ginger went inside to get gardening tools and gloves for them. The set that Marina had borrowed before were part of Ginger's kitchen decoration, and they'd laughed about that.

"Here you go," Ginger said. "I'll finish stringing the lights with Kai. I can't wait until nightfall to turn them on."

Marina went to work with Jack and Brooke to plant what he'd bought. She still couldn't get over his thoughtful gesture. As the three of them worked, Marina noticed that Jack and Brooke got on well. Both understood plant care and nurturing. However, they lost her when they started talking about soil and bugs and composting.

When they finished, Jack placed the plants around the deck, and then he helped bring out all the garage-sale patio furniture Marina had rescued and restored. Most had only needed a good cleaning and fresh pillows. She had a few tables and groupings of loveseats and chairs. As they moved the furniture around, Jack brushed her hand, and she felt the same twinges she'd felt on the beach. She met his gaze and sensed that he was thinking the same thing.

"Now the Adirondack chairs," Marina said, feeling heat rising on her neck.

"Sure thing," Jack said with a lingering gaze.

At Antique Times in the village, Nan and Arthur had given her a good deal on Adirondack chairs, which she and Kai had painted in a vivid coral shade to match the cottage. She planned to cluster these and benches around the firepit she'd bought to accommodate large parties.

Finally, the deck project was complete. Marina hugged her two sisters to her sides. "Couldn't have done this without you and the rest of this crazy family."

Ginger began passing around chilled Prosecco to the adults and ginger ale for the kids. "I think a toast is in order."

Once they each had a glass in their hand, Ginger raised hers high. "Here's to having the courage to follow dreams. To Marina for kicking off this venture, and Kai for pitching in to make it successful. What a team you two make. *Salut!*"

"And Brooke, who's now an official produce vendor," Marina said.

While Chip looked surprised, Brooke beamed at being included.

Marina looked around at all the faces she loved and wished Heather and Ethan could be here, too. She hoped they'd visit this summer, even if they had internships.

And then she looked at the new additions, Jack and Leo, and wondered where their journey would take them. As she sipped her bubbly Prosecco, she studied Jack over the rim of her glass, wondering if they might ever have anything more between them.

What would Jack do when his sabbatical was over at the end of the summer? Leo had talked about going to school here, but did that mean he was staying with Denise and John?

With questions swirling in her head, Marina drank the rest of her Prosecco. Dusk was just settling over the beach. They'd had plenty of food during the day—Brooke had made sure of that. But Marina was in charge of dessert.

She tapped her glass to get everyone's attention. "Now, let's turn on the lights and start the firepit."

When Marina flipped the switch for the lights, everyone cheered. The fairy lights created the perfect ambiance. With the ocean waves crashing in the background and the new palm and ficus trees swaying gently in the breeze, the new deck was as lovely as she'd envisioned. All she had to do was to fill it with people.

"Now, I have a surprise for everyone. Gather around the firepit and get it started. I'll be right back." Marina hurried inside for the ingredients to make s'mores. She'd baked ginger snaps and bought flavored chocolate squares from a local chocolate shop. And the biggest bags of marshmallows she could find.

While Marina was in the kitchen, her phone rang, and she answered it.

"Hi, Marina, this is Denise again. Your beach picnic basket was delicious, so we wonder if you might have next weekend open for one of your dinners? Jack said you have a new deck with plenty of room on the beach. It sounds like such fun."

"I think the schedule is open," Marina said calmly, while silently wiggling a hand with excitement. "Shall I email you some menus so you can decide what you want?"

"Perfect. We're planning for eight people, but I'll confirm the number of guests for you."

Marina made sure she'd hung up before letting out a cry. "Whoop, whoop!" She was on her way, and it felt so good. Even after the disastrous debut at the inn, her food had proven its worth. *Next weekend. One week to get ready.* Could she pull it off?

Actually, she had little choice.

Chapter 22

*J*ack was working at his desk when Scout scratched his leg and whined to go outside.

"Again? You just went out. Bored, I'll bet." He ruffled the fur on Scout's neck. "Later, boy."

Jack had been working on the proposal for a book that his agent had asked for, even though Ginger didn't want to participate. Yet, he had to produce something. He was still turning over titles in his mind, though he liked *The Ace of Codes*. Or maybe, *Ginger Delavie: A Life Deciphered*.

That is, if he ever could decode Ginger's life. There was still so much missing information. He had researched her husband Bertrand's diplomatic service and the countries where he'd worked. He'd read about Ginger's friendship with Julia Child, who had worked for the O.S.S. during World War II—the precursor to the C.I.A. But what he couldn't make out was how Ginger had made the leap from diplomat's wife to brilliant code-breaker.

And Ginger wasn't cooperating with him. She simply didn't want to talk about it. *Plenty of more interesting people*, she'd said.

What did that mean? Was she still working?

Ginger was an enigma. And never more so than in the phone message she'd left for him. *Enough of that stuffy old book you want to write. I have another grand idea, my dear. Do hear me out. I'll be on the ridge in the morning.*

Jack couldn't imagine what Ginger had in mind. But he would meet her and listen.

He stood and stretched, and Scout did the same. Ginger had told him that she and her husband once used this cottage as an office. He could just imagine Bertrand Delavie at one desk—maybe even the one he sat at—penning his books, while Ginger sat at another desk, poring over ciphers. In the smaller bedroom closet was a sturdy, standing safe with a date painted on it: 1940. How long had it been since it had been opened? He imagined that was where Bertrand and Ginger might have kept confidential papers.

What was in there?

Ginger was a fascinating subject, but then, so was her granddaughter. Watching Marina transform her life and conjure a new career was inspiring. As he teetered on the edge of a life transformation, he needed all the inspiration he could find.

What he felt for Marina was beyond what he'd ever experienced before. And yet, he couldn't waver in his commitment to Leo. Vanessa's health wasn't improving.

Every time Jack saw Leo, he longed to take the boy in his arms and tell him the truth. But Vanessa wasn't ready. He had to respect her wishes.

As Jack stretched, he spied a high window above a ledge. A few old books stood on the shelf. If he could open the window, that would help to ventilate the small room. On a whim, he climbed on top of the desk. Reaching toward the window, he spied a binder in a far corner. He slid open the window, then reached for the old book.

Just then, through the window he saw Marina walking

toward his door. She'd seen him. He scrambled off the desk and opened the door.

"Hi," she said brightly. "I've made some test dishes and thought you might like to join me for lunch on the deck."

"What a treat, thanks." He smiled. Spending time with her was always a treat.

"What are you doing with that?" Marina asked, pointing at the dusty binder he held in his hands. It had a brass, zippered closure.

"I just found it on that ledge up there."

"If it's Ginger's, I'd like to see it."

"Come on in." Jack opened the door, and Marina walked inside. After brushing a thick coat of dust from the cover, he unfastened the temperamental zipper. The binder was a relic from another time. As he opened the cover, a black-and-white photograph stared up at him.

Marina reached across him, her arm brushing his as she traced her finger along the edge of the photo. "This is one of Ginger's old photo albums, but I've never seen it. Look how young my grandparents are. And the styles. Skinny ties, beehive hairdos. Judging from that, this was taken sometime in the 1960s." She turned the page and ran her finger under each photo where someone had made notes. "Paris, April 1961. Boston, May 1962. Look, there she is with Julia Child in the kitchen."

Marina turned another page. Early color photographs had faded to muted shades of red, green, and yellow. "Some of these are from holidays, and I recognize others taken with dignitaries."

"Your grandmother was a pioneer in her field," Jack ventured, recalling the research he'd uncovered. It was a risk, but maybe Marina could help him. He needed to be as prepared as possible for his meeting with Ginger in the morning.

Marina grinned. "You mean as a small-town math teacher, statistician, or a Cold War cryptologist? She's a chameleon."

At least Marina wasn't upset with him this time. "Your grandmother might have called herself a statistician, but when I was writing a story on another person, I found evidence that indicates she did far more than that." Since he'd come to know Ginger, he'd found her to be self-effacing. "Ginger seems naturally curious about everything around her, but I haven't heard her talk much about herself or her accomplishments."

"No, she never has." Marina tapped a photo. "Look at that hulking computer behind her. They took up entire rooms and floors back then. Kai and I found some old photos online of Ginger with a prominent woman in the field."

Jack eased into the conversation he wanted to have with her. "In the course of my research for that article," he began, "I discovered that Ginger was a brilliant mathematician and cryptologist. She was one of the most valued code-breakers of the Cold War era. Ginger was also responsible for creating methods of encoding confidential transmissions from diplomats around the world."

Marina was quiet. "And you know this how?"

"Not much has been written about Ginger specifically, but I've found her mentioned in other articles. It seems she was the force behind many men who took credit for her work. Or perhaps she preferred to remain low-key. Has she told you anything about this?"

Running a hand across her brow, Marina shook her head. "I know what she said the other day, but Cold War codes? Sounds like something out of a movie, and I still find that hard to believe. But then...I don't." She stood up. "I want to show you something in the main cottage. And I want to look at this album with Ginger." She picked up the album and opened the door.

"Stay," Jack said to Scout, then hastily shut the door and

followed Marina, who'd already started toward the house. He jogged to catch up.

Marina led him into her bedroom, which held an antique armoire and a fluffy white duvet thrown over the bed. It also smelled deliciously feminine of powders and lotions and other soft scents that he'd detected on Marina. He tried to stay focused.

"Look up there." Near the top of the ceiling was a wallpaper border that ran around the room.

"The border?"

"It was a plain border that Ginger painted by hand. She challenged us to figure it out."

"It just looks like designs." Squiggles and curls and shapes in shades of ocean blue, aquamarine, and seafoam green formed a fanciful border.

"Look closer," Marina said. "See the spaces between some characters—and they *are* characters. That's a cipher."

"You mean a code?"

"No, that is different," Marina said, turning back to him, her eyes lit with intelligence. "I know this is a little academic, but think of a cipher as Morse Code, which is misnamed. It's actually a cipher because it operates with symbols, or syntax. The dots and dashes stand for letters and can be transmitted by sound, light, or simply writing. A code affects the word itself, whereas a cipher transposes each individual letter."

"Wait, I don't understand." Jack pushed a hand through his hair, confused not by what Marina said, but by Ginger's intent behind it all. "Your grandmother taught you this but never told you she was a cryptologist?"

"Merely semantics, I suppose." Marina gazed up at the border and smiled. "She taught my sisters and me codes and ciphers when we were young. As games. The same way she taught us mathematics and foreign languages, although Kai is better than I am at languages."

Jack processed these details. "What she introduced was

mental flexibility, an understanding that the same concept could be presented in different ways. Through language, code, or mathematical expression."

"That's right, though she went even farther, using sound and light, as with Morse Code."

Jack followed her gaze. "I suppose you can read that?"

"It's a phrase she used to tell us how much she loves us." Marina pointed to the symbols above. "As deep as the seas, as wide as the sky, forever through time, my love for you." Marina quirked her lips. "Although we didn't figure that out for a long time. I remember one day I was sick and confined to bed. As I stared at the ceiling, it began to make sense. I figured it out on a piece of paper. And do you know what? I felt better right away. That's the power of love—and being loved. Of course, she was delighted that I figured it out. She loves games."

Jack nodded slowly. "Are there other examples around the house?"

"I've seen some on pottery and needlepoint pillows she made years ago. That was a little game between her and Grandpa, I gathered. Kind of sweet when you think about it."

"What exactly did they say?"

"They had private ways of telling each other of their love without others knowing," Marina said. "Symbols and signs, sort of like that comedian Carol Burnett, who used to tug on her ear at the end of her television show to tell her grandmother that she loved her. That probably came in handy during boring diplomatic parties. If you ever saw them together, you'd have no doubt of their mutual love and admiration."

They spoke a little more, and then Marina suggested they eat on the deck. She served a spinach salad with strawberries and feta cheese, topped with a creamy lemon balsamic dressing she had made, along with baked parmesan crisps. But to Jack, the best part of the meal was simply being with Marina.

He could sure get used to that.

At one point, Marina asked how Leo was doing, and Jack told her that he was taking him fishing in a couple of days.

"You're going to be a great father," she said, her voice full of certainty.

Jack appreciated her confidence in him, but he'd spent many sleepless nights thinking about Leo and their future. He'd never experienced that twisty feeling in his gut that left him wondering if he was doing this parenthood gig right. Except that right now, he had only friend-status in Leo's eyes.

"I'm trying," he said. "I worry about what Leo will do when we tell him about me. As a kid, I probably would've thrown a fit, jumped on my bike, and ridden until I collapsed. I have no idea how Leo will take this news."

Marina gripped his hands, and her empathy was reassuring. "I know you'll do just fine."

Although their conversation centered on Marina's plans and Ginger's accomplishments, Jack, unsure of how Marina would react, didn't tell her that he was pitching a book based on her grandmother.

There would be time for that later, he assumed, if his final proposal was accepted. And if it weren't, he'd have to find another topic to write about anyway.

They were cleaning up when Scout bounded onto the deck.

"Hey, you," Marina said. Scout placed a paw in her lap and turned his face up to her with a playful expression.

"I forgot to lock the door." Jack shook his head. "Guess Scout's ready for another walk. If I left it up to him, we'd spend the entire day on the beach." He leaned toward her and touched her hand. "But I want to help you with the dishes."

She laughed and patted his arm. "Go on. I've got this. But I'll take a raincheck on that offer."

Jack left with Scout, regretting that he couldn't stay longer with Marina. He consoled himself with the thought that he had the rest of the summer to get to know her better. Although, given the challenges before him, he might be deluding himself with that thought.

LATER THAT AFTERNOON, Jack headed to the beach house that Vanessa and Denise and John were renting. Vanessa had called him after his lunch with Marina.

It's an emergency, Vanessa told him. She asked that he come prepared to talk to Leo.

Jack knew what that meant.

Mentally preparing himself, he stood on the porch and knocked on the door.

"It's open," Vanessa answered.

Jack walked in to find Vanessa sitting outside on a chaise lounge overlooking a flower garden. A fountain bubbled to one side, and jasmine and roses perfumed the air. Her eyes were rimmed with redness as if she'd been crying. She clutched a crocheted poncho around her.

Vanessa pointed toward the loft. "Leo is up there."

"What happened?" Jack asked, kneeling beside her and taking her hand.

"He overheard Denise and John talking in their bedroom. I don't blame them because their bedroom is just below the loft, and somehow the sound carried up there. These old houses at the beach aren't that well insulated, and with all the windows open..." She stopped, looking weary.

"It's time he knew anyway," Jack said, easing into a chair next to her. "He looks a lot like me."

"I've heard the comments, too," Vanessa said softly. "Are you ready?"

Jack's insides churned with anxiety, though he tried not to let it show. Would Leo be upset, angry, or pleased? He didn't know that much about ten-year-old boys, and it had been a long time since he'd been that age. Nor did he know what it was like to have a mother who was gravely ill.

"I'm ready," Jack replied. "I think it might be helpful if Leo had someone else he could talk to about all this. A professional."

"That's a good idea. We had a child psychologist in L.A. that he visited a few times when I got sick." She lifted a hand and let it fall. "Would you ask him to come down here?"

"Sure." Jack left her and climbed the stairs to the loft, where Leo was racing miniature cars on a track he'd created on the floor. Jack had done the same thing at his age. "Hey, Leo. How's it going?"

"Okay," he said, not looking up.

"Your mom wants to talk to you. Can you come downstairs?"

Leo sat back on his heels. "I know what she wants to talk to me about."

"You do, huh?"

Leo nodded, looking miserable. He picked up a little car, opening and closing its doors. "I heard Samantha's parents talking. I didn't mean to listen in on them." He rocked back and forth a little. "I asked mom about it."

"Well, she wants to talk to you about that." Jack swallowed hard. It was time to man up for this little boy. "And so do I."

Leo looked up at Jack with pure, bright eyes. His lips quivered as he spoke. "Samantha's parents know who my dad is. They said that my mom should tell me now and not wait."

Jack knelt beside Leo and picked up a little car. Spinning its wheels, he asked, "Do you have any idea who your dad might be?"

Fighting tears, Leo shook his head. "I'm afraid," he whispered.

"What are you afraid of, bud?" Jack's heart went out to

this little boy, who was already dealing with so much in his young life.

Leo dropped the car and wrapped his arms around Jack. His tears came fast, wetting Jack's neck as his little body shook with fear and grief. Jack put his arms around the child and rubbed his back. "That's okay. Just let it out."

Sobbing, Leo blurted out, "I'm afraid...that whoever it is...won't be nice to me. That they won't be anything like you."

Jack's eyes misted, and he nuzzled his head against Leo's. "What if I could be your dad?"

Leo hesitated, then nodded and cried even harder.

"Hey, hey," Jack said, rocking the boy. "It's going to be okay."

"But you're not, you can't be," Leo said through muffled cries.

Jack wrapped his arms around Leo tightly, just as his father had done when he was a boy. "I've got a surprise for you that I think you'll like. I know I do."

Sniffing, Leo pulled back and looked up at Jack.

"I'm going to be your dad from now on. There's no one else, Leo. I *am* your dad."

Clutching Jack, Leo broke down with tears of joy, and Jack hugged his son to his chest, his heart so full of love for this young boy—a love fuller and more complete than he had ever imagined it could be.

Looking over Leo's shoulder toward the stairs, Jack saw Vanessa sitting on the first stair, with tears of joy streaming down her face as well.

Later, Jack figured Leo would want details, but for now, this was enough.

Chapter 23

*L*eaning against the counter in the kitchen, Marina consulted her menu and recipes for her first pop-up dinner. Denise and John had scheduled this evening and included Vanessa and Jack, along with two other couples in technology and entertainment from Los Angeles.

Marina was just beginning her prep work for another recipe when a familiar voice rang out.

"Mom, are you around?" The screen door banged shut.

When Ethan rounded the corner, Marina met him with a hug. "Darling, I'm so happy you're here. What a surprise, though I wish I'd known you were coming."

Marina was thrilled to see her son. Ethan had grown taller since she'd last seen him over the holidays. Though slender, he'd filled out with more muscles and looked more like Stan every day. But to her, he was still an overgrown boy on the inside.

"Sorry I didn't call," Ethan said. "I got a last-minute flight." Then, waggling his eyebrows, he added, "Smells good. Anything to eat?"

Marina hugged him again. "This is for my first dinner

reservation tonight, but I've got a leftover quiche in the fridge or fresh oatmeal raisin cookies in the cookie jar."

"Heard about that." Ethan grabbed a couple of cookies. "Wow, that's an amazing deck out there," he said, peering outside. "I saw Aunt Kai's social media posts about that. Pretty cool." He eased his lanky figure into a chair. "How're you doing, Mom?"

"Much better," she said, rushing to put on her mitts to take her loaves of bread from the oven. "I'm hosting my first dinner here tonight."

"Oh, yeah? Your website is pretty cool, by the way."

"Glad you think so. Kai designed it." Marina thought of her conversation with Heather. "Have you spoke to your sister lately?"

Ethan looked miserable. "Heather won't take my calls, and she ignores my texts. She acts like I abandoned her in North Carolina."

"Do you think you did?"

"Mom, come on. I have a life to live, too. And college just isn't my thing."

Marina placed the hot pans on a cooling rack. "But it's important to Heather. She followed you there."

"She didn't have to," Ethan said, looking slightly guilty. "Hey, could I have a glass of milk?"

"It's in the fridge," Marina said lightly. He was old enough to take care of himself. "Heather thought you would need help with your studies. She spent a lot of time helping you, didn't she? More than you'd probably like to admit. Which kept her from making many friends."

With a heavy sigh, Ethan got up and poured a glass of milk for himself. "You have no idea how bad I felt about leaving her there, but she'll ace her final exams. I couldn't do that, Mom. Everything gets scrambled up in my brain when I'm staring at a book or an exam. But when I'm on the golf course, all that falls away. Out on the greens, I'm like anyone else." He grinned. "Only better than most. I told you that some of the top golfers have dyslexia, too."

"I understand that," Marina said, trying to keep her patience in check. "You have my support to give a pro career a chance. But I'd also like to see you apologize to your sister. She'd always got your back, more than you can imagine."

Ethan studied a cookie. "I try to support her, too."

Marina shut the oven and took off her mitts. "It's mutual, honey. Try to reach out to her another way. But wait until her last exam is over. She's pretty focused right now."

"Yeah, I know how she gets during final exams." Ethan dipped a cookie in his milk and took a big bite. "I think she'd like to come back to California to go to school with her friends. She was talking about that."

Marina nodded. "We'll go over that this summer."

Ethan wolfed down the last cookie and drained his milk. "I'm on my way to see friends in San Diego and might have a job there. But could I crash here a few days?"

"Brooke's old room is available. Be sure to check with Ginger."

"I'll get my stuff and throw it in there."

"I said, ask Ginger first," Marina called out as he left the room. *Boys.* Were they all like that? Ethan was a good kid overall, but she was concerned about his infatuation with golf. She hoped it would offer him the satisfaction he craved.

Marina was thrilled to have Ethan here for a few days, and if he found work in San Diego, he'd be close enough to visit often. She went back to her prep work for the appetizers, which included her luau spareribs and pear pancetta crisps with goat cheese and honey. A mixed green salad with spring vegetables was chilling in the refrigerator. And Denise and John were bringing wine.

Consulting her menu for the evening, she moved on to prep the next course. *Limoncello langostinos*—sort of a cross between lobsters and shrimp—with vegetables over brown and wild rice. And for dessert she'd baked *palmiers*, French puff pastries sprinkled with coarse sugar, topped with homemade vanilla bean ice cream and poached berries, with a warm strawberry sauce drizzled over everything.

Hearing footsteps across the deck, Marina looked up. Jack was making his way toward the kitchen with an armload of citrus she'd asked him to pick from Ginger's orchard. She would slice the lemons to use as garnishes and squeeze the sweet blood oranges for the coolers.

"Am I too late with these?" Jack asked.

"Just in time. Could you wash them for me?"

Moving to the deep sink, he washed the fruit and put it aside to dry. "You should have a chef jacket to wear," he said, teasing her. "And a tall, *toque blanche*."

"No chef hats for me," she said, laughing. "And T-shirts suit me just fine." However, that was a fun thought. "Maybe someday I'll have the *Coral Cafe* emblazoned on a chef's jacket." She held up a sliced, sweet yellow pepper. "Want a taste?"

"Sure do," he said, leaning over as she lifted it to his mouth. "Hmm, crunchy." He brushed his lips across her cheek in a swift motion, surprising her with a little kiss.

Marina giggled, enjoying the attention. They hadn't talked about that kiss at the beach.

Ethan's voice rang out. "Who's this?"

Whirling around, Marina felt her face flush with embarrassment. "This is Jack. He's a writer, and he's staying in the guest cottage."

Jack extended his hand. "A pleasure to meet you."

"Yeah. Likewise." Ethan tilted his chin. "You guys dating?"

"What? No, Ethan, it's not like that," Marina said. "We're just friends."

"I saw him kiss you, Mom. Geez, be honest. And you just got rid of that creep Grady. Are you that desperate for attention since Heather and I left?"

"Ethan William Moore, I'm ashamed of your manners."

"Whatever." Shaking his head, Ethan bounded out the door.

Raising his brow, Jack rubbed a hand across his neck. "I'm sorry. I didn't even see him."

"Ethan just arrived. Surprise visit." Marina glanced out the window at a car that was pulling up to the cottage. She recognized the kid behind the wheel. "Looks like Ethan called one of his summer buddies he knows here, so he was going out anyway." Still, Marina felt uncomfortable that her son had seen that little kiss and inferred a lot more from it.

"Guess that wasn't the best way to start meeting your children," Jack said, sounding apologetic.

Marina stared at him, not quite grasping what he meant by that, so she let it go. She still had a lot of work to do, and she was feeling anxious about the dinner. "He'll be here a few days, so maybe you two can start over." She put her hands on her hips. "And you're distracting me, so get out of here."

"Is Kai going to help you?"

Marina washed her hands and picked up a hand towel. "She's going to meet and greet, serve the welcome Coral Cottage Coolers, open the wine, and serve the courses. And the kids?"

"Leo and Samantha are going to hang out in the guest cottage," Jack said. "Denise is giving them an early dinner, and I'm providing unlimited games on the computer and streaming movies. They'll be close enough to check on during dinner. I'll make sure they lock the door, so Scout won't go out gallivanting across the beach with the kids in hot pursuit."

During a walk on the beach, Jack had told her that Leo knew he was his father now. Marina was glad that had worked out and that the two of them were growing closer. Maybe Vanessa's health would improve, too, although she knew the woman was having a difficult time. For tonight, Marina had also prepared a beef broth with julienned vegetables that Vanessa could sip.

"Guess I'd better go finish my work," Jack said. "And figure out what to wear for dinner to this fancy restaurant."

Marina smiled. "I'm sure your finest T-shirt and best flip-flops will suffice."

"Are you feeling nervous about tonight?"

Since Marina knew half of the party, the pressure wasn't too bad, although she knew that Denise and John had excellent taste. "Only a little. The dishes are coming together, and the weather looks clear. What could go wrong?"

"Don't tempt the gods." Jack stepped forward and squeezed her shoulder. "You've got this. I can't wait to see you in action."

Just after Jack left, a text message from Denise floated across Marina's phone as she was squeezing the blood oranges for the Champagne coolers. *Is there enough for one more hungry diner? A Summer Beach VIP. Happy to pay extra!* A string of happy-face emojis followed.

Marina froze. She had the precise number of *langoustines* and not enough time to buy more—even if the market had any. She'd placed a special order for them several days ago.

Just one more person. She didn't know how, but somehow, she would make it work. She texted back. *That's fine, looking forward to serving you all.*

Because of the children, Denise had planned an early dinner. Marina expected the party about five-thirty, with wine and appetizers first. By nine o'clock, they would probably be on their way home with the children. The other two couples were staying at the Seabreeze Inn.

A little while later, Kai sauntered in dressed in a blush-pink sundress and espadrilles. Her hair was brushed back in a ponytail with loose tendrils around her face. She had a little pink lip gloss and blush on, but she didn't need any more makeup.

Marina looked up and smiled. "You look especially nice, Kai."

"Do you think? I just didn't have the energy to go to very much trouble."

Ever since Axe's lack of response, Kai had been moping around, humming wistful tunes like "Memory" from *Cats*.

Marina opened the refrigerator to take out her chilled ingredients. "Any word from Dmitri?"

"He's giving me the silent treatment again. But before that happened, he was talking about coming here for a visit."

"Better to know what you're dealing with now," Marina said, arching an eyebrow. While she was supportive of Kai, she didn't think this relationship had much of a chance. "Still, it would be good for him to meet everyone."

"He'd have to pass the Ginger test," Kai said, frowning. "But for tonight, I'm not going to think about Dmitri or Axe. This is your night, your debut, and we're going to have a good time." She hummed a sad little tune.

"Just one request. Can you change the soundtrack? 'Send in the Clowns' is a little downbeat."

Kai lifted a corner of her mouth. "I'll put on jazz in the background." Axe had left wires so they could have music on the deck, and Chip had hung speakers for them.

When Kai returned, she said, "Smells wonderful in here. You might have to teach me how to do some of this."

Marina glanced up and grinned. "I'd be happy to."

Easing onto a stool, Kai swept a finger through the air, indicating Marina's outfit. "You still need to change, though."

"I'm fine. This is the beach." Marina brushed stray hairs back from her face and glanced at the clock. As she did, she saw two cars pull in front of the house. Tamping down the anxiety that welled in her chest, she said, "They're here."

"And we're ready to rock." Kai slid off the stool.

As Kai hurried to greet them, Ginger entered the kitchen carrying an open bottle of wine and two antique wine glasses she'd found at a Paris flea market decades ago. She stored wine in an alcove near the dining room outfitted with racks, a special refrigerator, and all the accoutrements.

"For the chef," Ginger said, putting down the glasses. "It's an old tradition to sip a little while you cook." She poured a generous splash of rich, golden wine into the glasses and slid one toward Marina.

"Oh, I don't think I can." Marina had to stay sharp this evening.

"Nonsense. Julia Child often had a glass of wine while she cooked." Ginger smiled at her memories. "And this was one of her favorite wines—the first one she introduced me to. A white Burgundy. I remember that Julia used to sip wine on the show while she cooked."

Ginger held up her glass in a toast to her beloved friend, motioning to her well-used copy of Julia Child's *Mastering the Art of French Cooking* on a kitchen bookshelf in a place of honor. "Always marvelous, my dear. And her Bouillabaisse, superb." She swirled her glass, aerating the wine. "Julia once said, 'I enjoy cooking with wine. Sometimes, I even put it in the food.'" She touched her glass to Marina's. "A few sips will make you less anxious."

"How could you tell?"

"You're running the risk of a permanent frown between your eyebrows." Ginger ran her thumb over Marina's forehead, smoothing her frown. "Break a leg, dear."

"That's my line," Kai said as she came into the kitchen. "And where's my wine?"

Marina raised her glass. "This is on chef's orders. Is everyone here?"

Kai nodded. "Almost. I seated them, and Jack is taking the kids to his cottage. Still one more guest coming. I'll save my wine until later." Kai lifted a carafe of Coral Cottage Coolers and whisked outside.

Marina took a sip and fluttered her eyelids. "Exquisite."

Ginger pulled an apron from a hook. "I'm ready to back you up, my dear. Consider me your *sous chef* for the evening."

"Where were you a few hours ago?" Marina asked, only half-kidding.

"In a lovely lavender bath listening to Tchaikovsky. Had to do something to drown out Kai's sad songs."

Marina laughed, but she was relieved to know that Ginger was here with her. Not that she couldn't manage this by herself, but having Ginger here was more fun. Like old times, when her grandmother had taught her how to cook.

Marina borrowed a clean apron from Ginger's stash and went outside onto the deck to greet the guests. The new outdoor space looked sunny and cheerful, with lush green plants and colorful cushions in a coral-and-turquoise floral print. A light breeze, just enough to cool the deck, wafted across, carrying the fresh, salty scent of the sea, which she loved. Jazz played softly in the background, and everyone looked relaxed. Marina couldn't have been happier with the effect on the deck. The Coral Cottage was officially open for business.

"Welcome to the inaugural dinner at the Coral Cottage," Marina said as Kai stood by beaming. She glanced around the table. Denise and John, Vanessa and Jack, the two new couples. "Do we still have one missing?"

John leaned back in his chair and waved at a guy in a truck who was just pulling in. "Here's Axe now. We met with him and an architect today about building a new home here. We made the decision today, so we're celebrating tonight."

Axe walked along the new brick path, admiring it. "You did a nice job finishing the deck and firepit area," he said to Marina as he greeted everyone.

"Couldn't have done it without my family," Marina said. Then she noticed Kai had shifted behind her. "And Kai, of course," she added, stepping to one side.

Axe's face registered pleasant surprise. "Kai, it's good to

see you again."

"Hi," Kai said with a little wave. "Let's pour the wine." She pressed a corkscrew into Marina's hand and whispered, "Can you do this?"

With a hint of disappointment on his face, Axe watched Kai leave. "I'll open the wine bottles."

"Thanks," Marina said, passing the corkscrew to him. With his large hands and muscular build, Axe made opening the wine bottles look effortless.

"That's not all we have to celebrate," Vanessa said, glancing at Jack with a sweet smile. She reached for Jack's hand. "Jack got a call today. He has a special announcement."

Marina's hand flew to her throat, and she tried to hide her trepidation. Were Jack and Vanessa...? She couldn't bear to finish the thought, although it wasn't as if Marina and Jack were dating. And then she thought of Leo, and immediately chastised herself. This wasn't any of her business. Kai wasn't the only one who needed to go to the kitchen.

"I really can't talk about it yet," Jack said, shaking his head.

Denise laughed. "You told Vanessa. Now tell us."

Vanessa was certainly proud of Jack, but Marina couldn't help but wonder what kind of secret he would share with Vanessa, but not others.

"Jack got a book deal," Vanessa blurted out. "And tell them who you're going to write about." Her eyes sparkled. "Marina, I think you're going to like this."

Marina nodded as she poured the wine, striving to remain calm.

"Vanessa, I can't say." Jack looked uncomfortable.

"Ginger Delavie," Vanessa said. "Isn't that wonderful?"

Shocked, Marina splashed a little wine onto the table cloth. Hurriedly, she wiped it up with the edge of her apron.

Since everyone was staring at her, Marina asked, "How did you decide on that?" *And have you asked Ginger, and what are you writing about?* She had so many questions, but most of all, she was dismayed that she was finding out this way. He could have had the decency to tell her. She couldn't fault Vanessa though, who probably didn't realize Jack had overstepped the boundary of family.

Shifting in his chair, Jack said, "Ginger is a remarkable woman, isn't she?"

Marina was so angry she didn't trust herself to answer that. Instead, she explained the menu as calmly as she could, and then returned to look for Kai, who was in the kitchen nearly hyperventilating with Ginger.

Now wasn't the time to tell Ginger about Jack's intention to write a book. Marina was sure that Ginger would have been the first to mention it. Trying not to let her anger overwhelm her, Marina took a deep breath. Besides, Kai was in extreme distress.

"Why didn't you tell me Axe was going to be here?" Kai wailed, covering her face with her hands. "And me, looking like this. I'm so horribly plain."

"Shh," Marina said, admonishing her. "What are you, Fancy Nancy or something? You're fine, and Axe is glad to see you. Now pull yourself together and get back out there. We're professionals."

Kai rolled her eyes. "I'm so dead." She slid off the stool and opened the door.

"Don't forget the pear and crispy prosciutto appetizer," Marina called out, motioning to a platter. Kai picked it up, forced a smile, and carried on. She was, after all, a very good actress.

Ginger shrugged. "Kai is beautiful. What's the problem?"

"I think she's been wearing stage makeup so long that she forgot how to see herself without it." Marina threw up a hand. "I think this reaction should also give her a fresh perspective on Dmitri. If she's still swooning over Axe, how committed can she be to Dmitri?"

"A woman's heart is a miracle of complexity," Ginger said. "What's next on the menu?"

"Luau spareribs." Her grandmother had a point. Marina thought of her mixed feelings over Jack. He'd shown his true colors tonight, and that was something she could hardly ignore. *Red flags waving in the breeze out there.* She took an extra sip of wine and turned her attention to the next appetizer.

The night progressed with no further incidents until the *limoncello langostinos.*

Marina rested her hands on the counter. "We're short a langoustine due to the extra guest. But I have an idea. I was going to serve these butterflied, but let's cut them in half. Instead of plating these, Kai can serve them and offer guests a choice of one or two. I'll bet that a couple of the women— probably Vanessa—will only take one. And I think another one of those women from L.A. is on a diet. She hasn't eaten much either."

"Brilliant solution," Ginger said, hefting a large chef's knife. She sliced through the langoustines, and soon, the dish was complete.

Marina explained the change to Kai and sent her out. Watching the guests, Marina breathed a sigh of relief. "Exactly what I thought," she said.

After that, it was time for dessert. Ginger helped put it together by scooping ice cream while Marina plated, added berries, and drizzled a sauce.

While Kai was serving dessert, Marina turned to Ginger. "Jack just announced that he's writing a book about you. Are you aware of this?"

Ginger shook her head. "That's not correct at all."

"No, it's not," Marina said. "Jack has behaved most incorrectly, and I'm going to have a word with him."

Just then, Kai burst through the door. "Final round, cognac by the firepit. Do we have the right glasses?"

"I'll help you." Marina gathered the glasses while guests

moved to the firepit. As she and Kai passed glasses around, everyone was deep in conversation. Marina returned to the kitchen while Kai lingered, chatting with Axe and Denise.

Marina was relieved. So far, the dinner had been a success. When Kai returned to the kitchen, Marina gave Kai and Ginger high-fives, and they bumped hips. "We did it."

"You did it," Kai said. "That was so professional. Our guests have also asked that the chef join them by the firepit for cognac. But first, how about that wine I was promised?"

As Ginger was pouring wine for Kai, a gust of wind whipped up, knocking over the new palm trees on the terrace.

"Wow, that was sudden," Kai said, racing outside. "I'll get them."

Staring out the kitchen window, Marina sucked in her breath. Just off the coast, barely visible in the clouded moonlight, a dark funnel spiraled from the sea to a leaden sky. Dread coiled within her as she tried to assess the threat. Hadn't it been a calm evening? Rain hadn't even been in the forecast, and yet, there was no mistaking what lurked offshore.

"Ginger, there's something you should see."

Her grandmother peered out beside her. "It's a waterspout, and it's moving inland." She grabbed a yellow rain slicker from a hook by the door.

Another gust ripped across the patio, dislodging the lights they'd carefully hung. One of the women from Los Angeles, her hair swirling around her face, whooped with laughter at the sudden wind.

"We have to get those guests in the house right now." Ginger jerked open the door.

Marina watched in terror as the funnel neared and shifted, hurling its growing intensity directly toward the guest cottage where the children were.

Racing outside into the eerie wind, Marina pounded toward the cottage with a prayer on her lips.

Chapter 24

The wind from the ocean raged across the yard. However, engrossed in conversation, the dinner guests hadn't noticed noticed the rogue waterspout over the ocean that had made landfall and was now a tornado churning toward the guest cottage with increasing ferocity.

Her heart pounding, Marina tore across the yard, ignoring the rain stinging her face and palm fronds hurtling past. Scout's desperate yelps of warning erupted from the cottage. Glancing back, she was stunned to see the funnel's leading edge ripping across the beach, lifting sand into its whirling vortex.

Marina tripped over a branch blown in her path. She tumbled and struggled to her feet again, her shins bruised, but she kept running. *Closer, closer.*

The twister lurched forward again. Instantly, she knew it was too late to get the children out of harm's way. The edges of her vision blurred as she focused on reaching the small cottage.

Suddenly, the door burst open, and Scout frantically plunged into the night with Leo and Samantha grasping after him.

"Get back in, stay in," Marina screamed as the wind whipped her words into the void. Reaching out, she tried to snag Scout, but the dog was too fast, too powerful for her.

The children.

Her words seemed to echo behind her. "Get inside," roared a deep voice.

Jack. She gasped for breath, but she couldn't look back.

Swirling leaves slapped her face, and a spiky palm frond sliced her forearm. "Inside," she screamed, gesturing at the children. As Marina reached the patio, Samantha tumbled backward into Leo in fright.

"Shelter in the tub," she yelled, hoisting them by the arms to their feet and half-dragging them to the bathroom between the two bedrooms.

A deafening noise roared around the cottage as Marina pushed the children into the tub and threw herself on top of them. Sobbing with fright, Leo and Samantha huddled together.

"Hang on to the spigot and knobs," she cried, panting. With prayers on her lips, she wrapped their trembling hands in place.

As the cottage shook from the fury, the bathroom door banged open. Jack dove inside, dragging John behind him by his shirt collar. Sprawling protectively over all of them, Jack yelled, "Hold on!"

A moment later, the ceiling peeled back, and rain pelted down on them.

"Daddy!" Samantha cried while Leo clutched Jack with all his might. In a thunderous roar, roof tiles clattered into the wind like deadly dominoes.

"Cover your heads," Jack yelled.

Clinging together, they rode out the chaotic twister, which blew through as quickly as it had come upon them, leaving them soaked and exhausted. After a few minutes, they eased up. Glass from a broken window littered the bathroom and crunched underfoot.

Marina's heart pounded, and she fought to catch her breath. "We made it. Oh, thank goodness."

"Careful not to cut yourself," Jack said, picking shards from the children's hair and backs.

Samantha sobbed against her father's shoulder, and John cradled his daughter in his arms, rocking her on the floor. Tears squeezed from his eyes as he clutched Marina's hand in gratitude. Blood dripped from a cut on his head.

"You're hurt," Marina said.

John grimaced. "Almost got knocked out, but nothing keeps me from my baby girl." He kissed his daughter's cheek.

"Where's Mom?" Leo asked, shivering in shock.

"She's in the big house," Jack said, wrapping his arms around Leo and smoothing his son's hair back. "They're all okay; the funnel missed them."

Trying to catch her breath, Marina peeked out the doorway. Shards of broken pottery littered the room like confetti exactly where the children had been. The heavy iron chandelier Ginger had brought back from Mexico lay on the couch in front of the television, where the children had probably been sitting when Scout scrambled to escape.

The magnitude of what the children had narrowly escaped hit Marina, and she drew back, her teeth chattering, horrified at the thought of what they might have found had she arrived a few seconds later.

Poor Scout. Marina pressed a hand to Jack's shoulder, wondering if Scout had made it. She wished she could have saved Scout, too, but she had only a split second to choose between grabbing the dog or getting the children to safety.

Seeing the destruction in the cottage, Jack put his arm around Marina and hugged her tightly. "You made it just in time, thank you. John and I weren't far behind, but I don't think we could have..." Jack choked up, unable to finish.

Marina buried her face against Jack's shoulder. His shirt was soaked and torn, and beneath it, his skin was scratched and bleeding.

As they pulled themselves up, desperate calls erupted from outside. Denise and Kai picked their way through the rubble of the cottage to reach them.

Sobbing with relief, Denise fell to her knees to hug Samantha.

"They're okay," Kai called out. She held out her hands, steadying Marina. "Thank heavens you reached them."

Marina felt limp in Kai's arms. "We're going to need some first aid here. John's got a bad gash on his head."

"That iron chandelier took me out," John said, gingerly touching a growing welt on his head.

"Did you see Scout?" Marina asked.

"He's not here?" Kai asked. Looking between Marina and Jack, she added, "Poor little fellow. Maybe he's hiding somewhere."

Their small party emerged from the shelter of the bathroom, picking their way through the littered rooms. Ginger had brought Vanessa, who sank into a chair and held out her arms for her son. Leo stumbled into her embrace, and she closed her thin arms around him, enveloping him with her love. Jack touched her shoulder, and she looked up at him with gratitude.

"Jack kept me safe," Leo said to Vanessa. "I mean, my *dad* did." He hesitated, twisting the edge of his T-shirt. "Can I call him Dad?" A mixture of happiness and pride filled the young boy's face.

"If you would like," Vanessa said.

A wave of gratitude overtook Jack as he knelt and embraced his son. "That would mean a lot to me, son," he said, his voice catching on the last word.

Leo flung his arms around Jack, and Marina watched them through misted eyes. Although they had their disagreements, watching Jack filled her with a new respect for him. She met Vanessa's gaze and smiled. Marina knew how challenging it was to raise a child alone. Even though Heather and Ethan hadn't known their father, they still missed his presence in their lives. Jack and Leo were so fortunate to have found each other.

In the distance, sirens wailed through the night, and the flashing light of emergency vehicles split the darkness. Somewhere, others might not have been as fortunate as they were, Marina thought, biting her lip. They needed to check on their neighbors, too.

Ginger handed Marina and Kai flashlights and beach towels she'd brought. "Let's get these folks back to the house where they can get checked out. The power is off, so be careful. There's a lot of debris in the yard."

The parents bundled their children in beach towels, and Marina draped one over Vanessa's thin shoulders. Vanessa raised her head and clutched Marina's hand. "Jack said you saved Leo. How can I ever thank you?"

"I'm just glad I got here in time," Marina said, smoothing her hand over Vanessa's parchment skin. "I have children, too." She thought about Ethan, praying that he wasn't in harm's way. She patted her pocket but realized she'd left her phone in the kitchen.

Spotting Kai outside, Marina carefully stepped onto what remained of the tiled porch. The awning was gone, and the bistro set lay across the yard.

Staring at the damage, Marina felt weak. They had made it, but only barely.

"Kai, do you have your phone?" Marina asked. "I have to check on Ethan." A sickening feeling gathered within her. What if he and his friend hadn't seen the tornado coming?

"I'm sorry, I don't." Kai's eyes grew wide. "I hope he wasn't in the path of that."

"What's his number?" Jack asked, stepping outside.

Marina told him, and he dialed the number for her. Her hands were trembling so, she could hardly hold the phone still. The phone rang several times, and Marina closed her eyes, willing him to answer.

Finally, Ethan picked up. "Who's this?"

When she heard his voice, relief flooded her. "It's Mom. I'm calling from Jack's phone. Did you see that waterspout over the ocean? It hit land. Did the twister come anywhere near you guys?"

"We're okay, but it hit pretty close to us. Are you okay?"

Marina heard shakiness in his voice. This was the first time he'd seen nature's wrath up close. "It hit the guest cottage, but we all survived."

"Oh, wow," he said, sounding stunned. "We're helping some people dig out of their house. I'll be there as soon as I can."

"Stay and help. We're a little banged up, but nothing too serious." However, she was concerned that John be examined. Nearly knocked out, his head wound was still bleeding.

Ginger set off for the house, leading the way with a lantern. The wind had died down though it was still raining. After the tornado had roared through with force, the area seemed eerily quiet.

Marina stepped over wet kelp, splintered driftwood, and cracked roof tiles that had been strewn across the chopped up yard. As she neared the main cottage, a howl went up, which set off other frightened dogs in the neighborhood.

Marina's heart leapt with hope. "Scout?" She called for him, and Jack joined in. After a few moments, Scout slunk toward them, visibly shaken. When he saw Jack, he whimpered and flipped his tail back and forth. "He made it," Marina cried gleefully.

Kneeling, Jack took Scout into his arms and hugged him. "Outran that nasty storm, did you? That's one way to do it."

"I think he was trying to warn us," Marina said, kneeling

to scratch Scout's neck. This time, she welcomed the scent of *Eau de Wet Dog*. Scout leaned against her, wagging his head as if in agreement with her assessment. "He was barking and charging toward the big cottage."

"Good boy, Scout." Jack clasped Marina's hand and looked down at her bruised legs. "You're hurt. Can you still walk okay?"

Numbly, she nodded. "Maybe the wine I had is taking the edge of pain off." Or perhaps it was the adrenaline rushing through her system.

The dinner she'd been so worried about now seemed trivial compared to how the evening had turned out. While she was still irritated over Jack's determination to write about Ginger, rendering aid to neighbors was critical.

"Ethan is helping some people nearby, and we need to check on our neighbors. I know some of the older ones who've lived here for a long time. Will you come with me?"

"You didn't have to ask," Jack replied.

"Ginger and Kai can take care of everyone here." Marina could just imagine the clean-up they'd have tomorrow. "I imagine our dinner guests will be on their way soon. But can you make sure John gets his wound examined?"

"I'm sure Denise will see to that," Jack said with a reassuring nod.

Once everyone was safely ensconced in the large cottage, Ginger lit candles and brewed tea and coffee on Myrtle, the dependable old gas stove. Kai cleaned and applied bandages to cuts and scrapes while Marina quickly changed into dry clothes and rain boots. Bits of glass tinkled the floor when she took off her jeans. Again, she thought of how lucky they'd been.

Marina brought out one of Ethan's T-shirts and a pair of sweatpants for Jack. "He won't mind," she said. After Jack changed, Marina met him in the kitchen.

"Ready?" she asked.

"You bet." Jack snapped his fingers for Scout. "This pup has a good nose. Might be helpful."

Outside, Marina and Jack picked their way through scattered debris. They went from one house to another, knocking doors to make sure everyone was okay. A few other homes had also lost roofs. Marina was shocked at the clearly delineated path the funnel had taken and the damage inflicted.

Marina saw Bennett and Chief Clarkson standing in front of one home that had collapsed. They were both wearing gloves and boots and looked like they'd been assisting in the clean-up. Firefighters on the scene were calling out and removing debris as quickly as they could. Marina recalled that Ivy had told her that Bennett was a volunteer firefighter. She and Jack hurried in their direction, with Scout staying close to Jack.

Bennett waved them down. "Marina, your son and his friend have been a big help to folks tonight."

"Ethan is a good kid." She glanced at Jack. "Once you get to know him."

Jack nodded. "And he's very protective of his mother, as he should be."

The police chief gestured toward the house. "Ethan is around back. He heard someone in there and called for help. We've been digging for a while now, but this house was the hardest hit."

"Maybe we can help," Marina said.

"That structure isn't stable," Chief Clarkson said, frowning. "Our emergency personnel are trained in search and rescue." He took a swig of water and angled his chin toward Bennett. "Time we go back in and help."

Suddenly, Scout perked up his ears and barked.

Bennett stopped and turned around. "Does he hear something?"

"What's wrong, boy?" Jack rubbed the dog's neck, but he couldn't console Scout.

Marina's heart raced. "Scout thinks someone is in there."

"We're concerned about the Petrovs, a young married couple who live here," Bennett said. "No one has seen them. They could be away, but the car is here."

Scout paced in front of the house, barking and whining.

"Have to try," Jack said.

Bennett gestured to them. "Let's go."

They picked their way to the rear of the house, where Marina saw Ethan working alongside the firefighters.

Ethan looked up and acknowledged her with a nod, then continued working. "That's about where I heard a call," Ethan said, pointing where a firefighter swept a flashlight. "I think it was there. It was pretty dark."

Scout broke free and raced toward another spot. He planted his paws and barked at the rubble.

Jack ran after him. "Scout found something."

"Let's go," Chief Clarkson called out. Everyone began digging in that spot. Marina and Ethan worked side by side with Jack and Bennett.

Once the area was clear, Scout jumped forward, pawing at a spot.

"Right here," Bennett said, hefting a door and pushing it aside. "Can you get in there, Jack?"

Marina spoke up. "I'm smaller," she said, glancing at Jack. He nodded, and she squirmed in on her stomach. She wriggled through a small opening. "Anyone in there?"

Silence.

Marina poked her hand through a smaller opening and waved. "Hello? Can you hear me?" She waited a moment, and then, miraculously, another hand touched hers. Marina's pulse quickened. "Someone is here," she cried out.

A woman's faint cry sounded. "Help us," she said in a strangled voice.

Several firefighters pushed aside a dresser while Marina

reached under the remains of a bed, and clasped the hands of a young woman.

"My husband is here, too. We got as far as the bedroom and dove under the bed."

Everyone worked together to help them out. Thankfully, though shaken, the couple didn't seem to be seriously injured. Even so, after consulting with the couple, emergency personnel took over and helped them into an ambulance to the hospital.

Marina put her arm around Ethan. "I'm so glad you heard them. I'm proud of you."

"You, too, Mom." Even though Ethan seemed pleased, he shrugged off her compliment. "Austin and I were just doing what we could. What you always taught me to do." He lifted his chin toward Jack. "You got right in there, too."

"Had to be done," Jack said. "You did a good thing tonight." Scout nudged his way among them and leaned on Ethan, wagging his tail and angling for attention from the new kid. And Scout seemed to have the largest grin of all.

Ethan bent down and rubbed the dog's ear. "Couldn't have done it that fast without this furry guy."

"Are you coming back to the cottage now?" Marina asked Ethan.

"Mind if I crash at Austin's house?" He nodded toward his friend.

"Go ahead," she said. "We'll put Jack in Brooke's old room. The guest cottage is a mess, and he can't stay there."

"I've got my van," Jack said. "My sidekick and I can sleep there."

Ethan gave Jack a half-grin. "Take the room. Nice outfit, too, by the way."

The two shook hands, and Ethan left with his friend.

Marina and Jack talked with Bennett and Chief Clarkson a little more, and after determining that there was nothing else they could do tonight, they made their way back to the main cottage. Scout loped along beside them with his funny gait.

As they walked, Marina looked around. Tomorrow there would be plenty of work, but tonight, all she wanted to do was ease into a hot bath and a warm bed. And then she thought about Jack and his dilemma.

As if reading her mind, Jack said, "Staying in the main cottage will be a little awkward, don't you think?"

A note in his voice made Marina feel small for thinking that after the night they'd been through. Grudgingly, she said, "But you have to have a place to stay. And your clothes and computer…"

Jack shrugged off her concerns. "I didn't have much with me. I'll dig through the mess in the morning to see what I can salvage. As for the computer, I learned to guard my work against accidents a long time ago. I'll make some calls for other accommodations in the morning."

As he said that, Marina realized she would miss him, even though they didn't always agree. "Are you planning to stay in Summer Beach?"

Jack hesitated before reaching for Marina's hand. "I have several compelling reasons."

Although the touch of his hand rippled through her, Marina yanked her hand back. "We still need to have that talk about the book you're writing about my grandmother."

Jack looked slightly hurt. "You should talk to Ginger about that."

Marina quickened her step toward the cottage. "If she's worked in sensitive areas as you say, revealing confidential details about her and her work—and Bertrand's—could bring unwelcome scrutiny and endanger her. Don't think I'm letting that go."

"Marina, I'm sorry. But I can't—"

"*Won't*, not can't." Marina stalked off ahead of him. For a man to betray her was one thing, but to betray those she loved was much worse.

Chapter 25

"*F*ound a computer," Marina called out against the blare of classic Beach Boys music that Kai decided was the perfect soundtrack for their beach cleanup. Though still on edge, Marina had to admit the music lightened the workload and brought back childhood memories on the beach.

Gritting her teeth, Marina tugged a padded case from the debris in the living room of the guest cottage. She hadn't slept much thinking about Vanessa's announcement about Jack's book last night. Even though she was barely talking to him, the guest cottage was her grandmother's property. With Ginger in charge, they were all working together.

The entire household had been up since dawn when Scout decided it was time for a walk, though it hadn't been a restful night. Jack slept in Brooke's old room next to Kai's bedroom, and that was enough to disturb Marina, though she hated to admit it. During the night, the electricity was restored. Lights flickered on, and the jazz they'd been playing at the party last night blasted through the house. As the sun rose, Marina staggered into jeans and a T-shirt, guzzled Ginger's bracing coffee, and went to work.

Marina stepped over piles of debris into the kitchen, where Kai was sweeping as Jack scooped the soggy mess into trash bags.

"Do you want to check your laptop?" Marina dangled the case in the air. Tension sizzled between them. He might have helped protect the children during that sea-monster twister, but that didn't absolve him from going ahead with Ginger's biography—without her involvement. Her grandparents had dealt with classified information, and Marina worried that Jack's audacity could endanger Ginger—as well as others. At the very least, his work could bring unwelcome scrutiny in Ginger's golden years.

Jack straightened. "That should be a waterproof case." He unzipped it on the counter. "Perfectly dry. I'd put it away when Leo and Samantha came over."

He pressed the on-button, and the laptop blinked to life. "In my line of work, I never knew where a story would take me or what I might encounter. I took all kinds of precautions."

Marina snapped one of the thick yellow gloves she was wearing. "Like when you write unauthorized biographies about older women?"

"You've got that all wrong." Jack turned off the laptop and set the case to one side.

"Why don't you explain it so my lady-brain can understand it?" Marina picked up a pile of soggy papers.

"Hey, careful with those," Jack said, taking the papers from her. "That's my work."

Kai swept aside jagged remains of broken pottery. "This is getting interesting. Shall I bring out the boxing gloves?"

Marina shot a pointed look at her sister. "Don't you have an opinion? She's your grandmother, too."

Wearing work clothes and duck boots, Ginger walked through the open door. "All of you need to calm down. There is nothing to argue about." She stepped through the chaos toward the smaller bedroom.

Marina followed, her ire escalating. She couldn't understand why Ginger wasn't as upset with Jack as she was.

Ginger knocked on the old standing safe in the closet of the smaller bedroom. "Nothing gets past this fortress." She spun the dial.

"What do you need from there?" Marina asked.

Ginger swung open the door of the safe. Inside were stacks of papers. She pulled out an old notebook.

"These are the stories I began writing years ago," Ginger said. "I'm not a professional writer or an illustrator. But everywhere Bertrand and I traveled generated a wealth of ideas, so I wrote them down." She secured the safe door and made her way back into the living room.

Marina trailed her grandmother, her curiosity growing.

Ginger flipped through the pages of her old notebook and looked up. "When I saw Jack's sketches of Scout and Leo and Samantha, I thought we could work together. I gave him the idea I had for the first book, and he developed the concept and sent it to his agent."

"That's the book the agent accepted," Jack said pointedly as he picked up shards of broken glass.

Skeptical, Marina crossed her arms. "A children's book? That's not what Vanessa said."

"At one time, I mentioned to Vanessa that Ginger would make a fascinating subject for a book," Jack said. "But that's not the book I pitched. I couldn't clarify that without giving away Ginger's surprise."

Finally, it dawned on Marina what they were talking about. "These are your stories," she cried. Ginger might not consider herself a writer, but she was the consummate storyteller.

"That's right," Ginger said. "All the stories I used to tell you girls. Jack and I are partners now. Imagine that."

"That's so cool," Kai said.

Another complication, Marina thought, glancing at Jack. But she was thrilled that Ginger would be bringing her stories to life—this time in book form. "Which story are you working on?"

Ginger's eyes sparkled with excitement. "The first one will be about a boy and girl, rather like Leo and Samantha, who solve mysteries using ciphers and codes."

Marina recalled the fun she and her sisters had with Ginger's games. These would be fun for children.

"Other books might draw on mathematics, science, and technology," Jack said. "We'll start with illustrated books, but I think we could expand into chapter books for elementary ages."

Marina was surprised that Ginger had been planning this with Jack, but now it made sense. She turned to Jack. "What about your career in journalism? Are you giving that up?"

Jack swept glass from a littered counter into a trash bag. "Now that I'm going to be more responsible for Leo, I can't go tearing around after hot stories like I used to. I have to make changes, and this is a chance to do what I enjoy. Like you're doing."

"Don't forget about that position with the local paper," Ginger said. "We need good reporting in Summer Beach, too."

Kai laughed. "I can't imagine that there are many deep secrets in Summer Beach to investigate."

"One never knows," Ginger said, arching an eyebrow. "You must ask Ivy about the priceless artifacts discovered at the Seabreeze Inn."

Summer Beach was proving more fascinating every day, Marina decided, casting a small smile of apology toward Jack. Maybe she'd been tough on him, but when it came to family, no one threatened them and got away with it. In her former position on the morning news, she put up with a lot to provide for her children.

Not anymore.

Kai tapped her music. She lowered the volume and switched to a song called "In My Room." She flicked a teasing look at Marina before turning to Jack. "Will you be staying on in the main cottage, Jack?"

"I told him he's welcome," Ginger said. "We can put Ethan on the Murphy bed in the den. Or vice versa."

Marina wasn't sure how she felt about that. Given the range of emotions that Jack brought out in her, two doors down the hallway was a little too close, and yet, a persistent feeling inside told her it wasn't close enough. She raised her gaze to him.

Jack caught Marina's look and held it for a few seconds longer than necessary. "Thanks, but I checked in with Ivy, and there's a room in the back with a grassy area for Scout."

Kai leaned on her broom. "Are you saying you'd find it hard to work in a household with three women? Can't imagine why."

Just then, a truck pulled up in front of the house, and Axe stepped out.

Kai quickly removed her gloves and brushed her hair from her face. "Terrible timing again," she muttered.

"This should be exciting," Marina said. It was easy to see that an attraction was developing between Kai and Axe. Yet, just this morning, Dmitri had called to tell Kai that he'd booked a trip to Summer Beach. Kai would soon have to make a choice. Beach town contractor versus Broadway producer. Marina slung her arm around Kai. "Just kidding. I've got your back, sis. Follow your heart."

"Thanks," Kai whispered, her eyes lighting.

Axe stepped inside, bending slightly so as not to hit his head in the low doorway. "Getting cleaned up, I see. How's this temporary roof holding up?"

"Fairly well," Ginger said. "Jack is moving into the Seabreeze Inn until the guest cottage is habitable again. How soon can you replace the roof?"

"Since you were the first to call, you're first in line," Axe said. "I'll have a proposal for you this afternoon." He tapped the brim of his cap. "If there's nothing else, I'll be on my way."

Kai leaned her broom against the counter. "Axe, I've been meaning to ask you about summer stock theater around here."

A smile spread across Axe's face. "Walk with me to the truck, and I'll tell you all about it."

Watching them strolling toward the truck, Marina said, "It's going to be an interesting summer around here."

"Kind of sorry I'll miss it," Jack said.

Ginger tucked her notebook under her arm. "You're not going far. I have a feeling you'll be able to see the fireworks from where you are. Now, since the cottage is nearly clean, I'll take my leave." She tapped her old notes. "I want to refresh my memory."

Marina finished sweeping while Jack packed his belongings. "Let's leave all the windows open to let the interior dry." Together, they slid the window sashes.

After carrying the last of the trash bags out, Jack hoisted his backpack, computer case, and duffle bag over his shoulders. "Guess I'll be off."

"Guess so," Marina said, at a loss for words. Scout was waiting for Jack in front of the cottage.

At the door, Jack hesitated. "I probably don't have any right to ask this, but would you like to join me at the inn for a swim later? Might feel good after all this messy work. The sunset is amazing, and I'm sure I can arrange a couple of Sea Breezes."

Marina shook her head. "Jack, I don't know what to say. All that business with Ginger…" Frankly, she was a little embarrassed now. More than that, was she up for another relationship? She still had Ethan and Heather to think about, and a business to get off the ground. Or was that even what Jack was offering? Maybe she was leaping to another conclusion.

Jack waited. Finally, he said, "Ginger wanted to be the one to tell you. I think she wanted to have a little celebration to share the news. I'm sorry the way it came out at dinner."

That sounded like something Ginger would have done. As Marina considered this, she figured forgiveness was in order. Just then, Scout trotted in, rubbing against her leg and whining to reinforce Jack's request.

Marina laughed. "That's quite a wingman you have there."

"Then you'll come?" His voice kicked up a notch. "I'll be waiting at the pool."

How could she resist two sets of plaintive eyes?

SLINGING a straw beach bag over her shoulder, Marina strolled through the tropical grounds of the Seabreeze Inn, past Shelly's sunny yellow hibiscus and fragrant white pikake flowers. Marina wore a sleek blue-and silver swimsuit she had bought for vacation but was unable to take due to one of Hal's last-minute decisions. It still fit, though she spilled over the top a little now. Kai had assured her it was fine. But then, Kai would.

Still, this was all Marina had on such short notice. Not that this was a date, exactly. She'd also bought the matching swimsuit coverup with silvery threads running through the gossamer fabric—the kind of item she used to buy because of its sheer beauty, though she seldom had a chance to wear it. It helped cover her bruised shins from last night. She'd also borrowed one of Ginger's large floppy hats, which Kai had wrapped a silver scarf around.

Marina strolled into the pool area, feeling a little theatrical in her outfit and dark sunglasses. Yet, the pool, with statues surrounding it, was a stage unto itself.

True to his word, Jack was waiting on a chaise lounge under a marine-blue umbrella. A fluffy white towel covered the chaise next to him, and two chilled pink cocktails sat on a table between them. He'd cleaned up and now wore swim trunks and a white shirt.

Nice legs, she thought, admiring his thigh muscles. *Who said the forties were over-the-hill?*

"Welcome to paradise," he said, rising to greet her. "You look amazing."

"Not too much?"

"Too much is not even enough," Jack said, taking her hand.

"And this from a man who was going to sleep in a VW van." Marina laughed lightly. "Are you quoting de Beaumarchais?" That was the French author of the *Figaro* plays. *Where love is concerned, too much is not even enough.*

"Ah, but it's a fully renovated van." As Jack handed her a cocktail, a smile played on his lips, though he didn't answer her question. "This is where we met, and since we got off to a rocky beginning, I thought we could start over. Shall we try this again?"

Marina sipped in thought. "No sprained ankles, no wet dogs, no waterspouts. I don't know. It could be a little boring."

"I have a feeling the Delavie-Moore clan is never boring."

They had the pool area to themselves this evening. While talking about the aftermath of the twister, Jack shared that Chief Clarkson had stopped by earlier to see Imani, who was still living at the inn.

"The chief said the young couple that you pulled from the wreckage of their home is fine," Jack said. "She's four months pregnant, so they were pretty concerned. Except for a few bruises, they'll be okay."

"I wonder where they'll go?"

"They just checked in here." Jack nodded toward the main house. "Seems this is the fashionable place for the displaced. Especially for reformed news jockeys like us. Ready for that swim?"

"Sure." Marina slipped off her coverup and followed Jack into the pool. When he took off his shirt, she saw the scratches he'd sustained yesterday in the twister. The saltwater pool was refreshing yet warm, and she swirled her hands around. The relaxing effect of the cocktail was taking the edge off her stress.

Jack brought in a plastic floatie shaped like a life-preserver, and they each took a side, paddling around and watching the sun sinking toward the horizon. The sound of the ocean, steps from the property, created a mesmerizing accompaniment to the sunset. As they floated, they talked about their plans.

"How are plans for the Taste of Summer Beach event going?" Jack asked.

"Since the deck survived the storm, it's still a go," Marina said, lazily fluttering her legs beneath the water. "I've contacted a lot of local restaurant owners, and Bennett has shared a few dates on the Summer Beach calendar that are open. I'll confirm with everyone, and then all we have to do is promote it and put on a great event. I thought we could accept donations for those who need assistance after the storm."

"That's a good idea," Jack said thoughtfully. "You seem to have thought of everything."

Marina appreciated his confidence in her. "The chefs are the real stars, so I don't have to do very much. Seems fairly easy. Really, what could go wrong?"

Jack chuckled. "What did I tell you about tempting the gods? Last time you said that we practically had a reenactment of *Sharknado*."

"There wasn't a single shark in that twister," Marina said,

pressing a finger to his lips. "And don't talk about sharks so close to the beach."

Jack began humming the tune from *Jaws*, and Marina swatted him. "Stop that," she said, laughing. "I want to hear more about the illustrations you have planned for Ginger's books. This is quite a career departure for you, isn't it?"

"I never thought I could make a living with my artwork. This book is a start. I'll have the summer to finish it and see if it sells." His expression turned serious. "When you're young, you embark on a path, hardly knowing where it might take you. Then, one day, you wake up to a sharp left turn."

Marina enjoyed listening to him talk. "I know how that is."

Jack reached across the floatie and stroked her hand. This time, Marina didn't draw back. On impulse, she twined her fingers with his.

Maybe she was ready to take a chance.

"You've inspired me," Jack said. "You handled all the muck thrown at you, yet you held your head high. That kept me going, too."

Marina could tell Jack's words were genuine. His voice had a husky, emotional edge to it, so different from Grady's. With surprise, she realized Jack reminded her of Stan. The two men shared a core of decency and commitment that Grady lacked.

"I've thought the same about you," Marina said softly. "When I see you with Leo, I can see the love growing between you."

Jack's eyes glazed with emotion, and he brought Marina's hand to his lips, grazing her skin with a kiss. "Knowing what lies ahead for him makes me care for him even more. I want to protect him from the inevitable with his mother, but I can't. That's what hurts the most. When you love someone, you want to spare them anguish and heartbreak."

"Being there for him is what counts." Marina understood

that Jack's first commitment was to Leo, just as her primary responsibility was to Heather and Ethan. Even after her children graduated and had careers and families, they would always be her life. And yet, seeing how Ginger had balanced her responsibilities with living the life she wanted inspired Marina.

"Someday, I'd like you to share your single-parent superhero manual with me," Jack said.

"Leo seems like a wonderful boy, and I'm sure you'll figure it out. New bikes and frisbees are a good start, but warm hugs will seal the deal. And having Scout around is bound to help."

Marina smiled, recalling the enjoyable and challenging times she'd had with her children. A vision of a future with Jack grew in her mind, but that seemed so premature, so distant, that she cast it aside. Yet, being close to Jack was even better than Marina had imagined in her dreams.

Oh yes, she had dreamed, even though she hadn't dared admit it.

Jack chuckled. "A year ago, if someone had told me I'd be right here, in this new life, with a dog and a son, I wouldn't have believed them."

"Any regrets?"

Jack held her in a steady gaze. "Not one. Especially now."

The setting sun cast a burnished glow across the pool, enveloping them in a magical light. As they talked, they floated together until they were side by side on the edge of the raft, their heads bent toward each other, the warm water lapping gently around them.

Golden rays illuminated Jack's vivid blue eyes, which seemed endless as the ocean stretched out beyond them. As the sun kissed the horizon, he folded her hand in his and pressed them to his heart.

A current swept Marina to him, and she ached to feel his arms around her. Taking a chance, she slid her hands along his shoulders. The touch of his skin sent thrills through her, but more than that, she felt a closeness that she hadn't experienced in many years.

Without hesitation, Jack wrapped his arms around her. "Do you think that with all the challenges before us, we might occasionally carve out time for us?"

"Like this?"

"Just like this. And more." His lips curved into a smile, and he cupped her face with his hand. "I believe our future can be what we make it."

As the sun slipped beneath the skyline, filling the heavens with brilliant hues of shimmering rose gold, Marina lifted her face to his. When their lips met, she felt as if she were entering a paradise of the heart. Neither of them could know what the future held, but Marina sensed that their lives might entwine for a long time.

When Jack pulled away, his eyes glowed with the hint of love that Marina had known only once. In his eyes, she saw a reflection of hers, bright with passion. This spring, despite upheavals, they'd sown critical seeds. She wondered what the summer harvest would bring.

As Marina brushed her lips against Jack's, she sensed that this was the beginning of an unforgettable summer.

The End

NOTE FROM JAN MORAN

THANK YOU FOR READING *Coral Cottage*, and I hope you enjoyed it. Find out what happens next in the *Coral Cafe* as Marina pursues her dream of a beachside cafe, Kai finds a new artistic passion to pursue in Summer Beach, and Ginger reveals more stories. If you're in the mood for holiday cheer, see what Ginger Delavie and Ivy Bay have planned in *A Seabreeze Inn Christmas*. And if you haven't already read the *Summer Beach: Seabreeze Inn* series with Ivy and Shelly Bay, start with the *Seabreeze Inn*.

To hear about my new releases, please join my VIP Readers Club. Thank you very much for reading.

MORE TO EXPLORE

If you like historical novels set by the sea, you might like to read *The Chocolatier*. Set the Italian coast of Amalfi, the saga follows a newly widowed chocolatier from San Francisco who discovers her husband's mysterious past. You'll be whisked away into a fascinating world. Between chocolate tastings and fabulous 1950s styles and music, this was one of my favorite books to research.

My next novel is *Hepburn's Necklace,* which is set in beautiful Lake Como, Italy. Discover what happens when a costume designer discovers a necklace that Audrey Hepburn gave her great-aunt—and the long-buried secret its discovery reveals.

And if you like reading contemporary series, you might enjoy my *Love California* collection of linked, standalone books, beginning with *Flawless.* Meet a group of devoted friends and their romantic interests, and join them on their adventures with a trip to Paris, France. My love of travel inspired these stories, so get your literary passport ready.

CORAL COTTAGE COOLER
RECIPE
COMPLIMENTS OF GINGER DELAVIE AND MARINA MOORE

The Coral Cottage serves a refreshing juice tonic tinted in a lovely shade of vibrant coral to match the cottage. Blood orange juice is sweeter than regular orange juice, and the fruit is seedless. Blood oranges originated in Italy and Spain, and varieties include Tarocco, Moro (also Morro), and Sanguinello (also Sanguigno).

This fruit juice blend is delicious without alcohol, too. Adjust the ratios of juice to sparkling wine or club soda for taste as desired.

Coral Cottage Cooler
Blood orange juice
Champagne, Prosecco, Cava—or club soda
Strawberries
Mint garnish

Mix equal parts blood orange juice with Champagne, Prosecco, or any sparkling white wine. For a refreshing non-alcoholic version, substitute club soda for alcohol. Serve in a chilled glass with or without ice. Add a garnish of fresh mint and strawberries.

If you can't find blood orange juice, you may substitute pomegranate juice. Or regular strained orange juice with a dash of red grenadine for color.

Serving suggestions: This juice cocktail is a refreshing pop of color at summer parties. Serve in Champagne flutes, highball glasses, mason jars, or any pretty glassware.

Enjoy!

Of course, always drink responsibly and don't drive and drink.

ABOUT THE AUTHOR

Jan Moran is a *USA Today* bestselling author living in generally sunny southern California. A few of her favorite things include a fine cup of coffee, dark chocolate, fresh flowers, laughter, and music that touches her soul. She loves to travel and her favorite places for inspiration are those rich with history and mystery and set against snowy mountains, palm-treed beaches, or sparkly city lights. Jan is originally from Austin, Texas, although she has lived in California near the beach for years.

Most of her books are available as audiobooks, and her historical fiction is widely translated into German, Italian, Polish, Dutch, Turkish, Russian, Bulgarian, Romanian, Portuguese, and Lithuanian, among other languages.

If you enjoyed this book, please consider leaving a brief review online for your fellow readers where you purchased this book, or on Goodreads. Thank you for sharing!

Made in the USA
Monee, IL
01 October 2020